where the edge is

Gráinne Murphy

Legend Press Ltd, 51 Gower Street, London, WC1E 6HJ
info@legendpress.co.uk | www.legendpress.co.uk

Contents © Gráinne Murphy 2020
The right of the above author to be identified as the author of this work has
been asserted in accordance with the Copyright, Designs and Patents Act
1988. British Library Cataloguing in Publication Data available.

Print ISBN 978-1-78955-9-415
Ebook ISBN 978-1-78955-9-408
Set in Times. Printing managed by Jellyfish Solutions Ltd
Cover design by Steve Marking | www.stevemarking.com

Gráinne Murphy grew up in rural West Cork, Ireland. At university she studied Applied Psychology and Forensic Research. In 2011 she moved with her family to Brussels for 5 years. She has now returned to West Cork, working as a self-employed language editor specialising in human rights and environmental issues.

Follow Gráinne
@GraMurphy

For

Oisín, Ali, Cara

(You're all my favourites)

'Si la vie était plus logique, elle serait encore moins vivable.'
Were life more logical, it would be still less livable.
Christian Dotremont (1922–1979)

Sleepy-eyed half smile
Cartoon hair, morning breath. Sweet
With kept promises.

CONTENTS

PART ONE – DOWN

IDLE SPECULATION

Afterwards, those at a comfortable distance will wonder if something small might have made all the difference. If they hadn't all been sitting at the back of the bus, say, the weight distribution or the force of the impact might have changed just enough. A fool and his theory are hard parted.

It is human nature, maybe, to shiver in the unknown interplay of physics and fate and the delicious horror of being thisclose yet thisfar. There will be much talk of meaningful everyday choices, about destiny and free will, but those comments are twenty-four hours away yet. The talk-radio shows that will draw them out are only in the early stages of their planning. Their schedules contain nothing more urgent than weather, reality programming, the endless cycle of politics.

Nothing can change the fact of the handful of early-morning passengers climbing on and moving towards the back of the bus. Pushed there – shamefully, inadmissibly – by the presence of the muttering woman pacing the aisle.

The driver knows her, it seems, but that is not in itself remarkable: everyone in the small town of Kilbrone knows Crazy May. She haunts the bus yard in the mornings. *Keeping the bins company*, the drivers say among themselves, although they know it is simply because fewer people bother her there. Some of them put the run on her, it's true, but most turn a blind eye, let her ride for free.

Today's driver nods May on as she waves someone else's out-of-date bus pass, dug from a bin or a bag or who knows where. They swing down the hill, just the two of them, and onto the ring road towards the start of the route without bothering one another. She never stays on for more than two or three stops. Just long enough to warm her bones after the night's cold. Never further than the boundaries of her own small world.

At the first stop, several others get on and sidle past her without making eye contact. Afraid of her low growl. Her dirty plait of hair. Haircuts are only a memory for May, part of a normality fallen by the wayside long since. The others know – as rational humans, of course they know – that homelessness, dirt, madness, are not catching. Yet they will not risk her presence, lest her life leak into theirs. One by one they file on and put enough distance between them and her to feel safe. It is biology, this choice they make, not physics at all. That is what the armchair engineers will never be able to account for.

The bus is quieter after May gets off. People catch each other's eye and smile and settle into the stop-start rhythm of the bus as it takes the bends towards the centre of town. The traffic is light, they are a good hour ahead of the morning scramble. The driver keeps the pace steady, reaching each stop right on schedule.

Is there a slight popping sound as the bus leans into the curve of the bend? Or is that simply put there later, imagined into being by well-meaning bystanders?

When the floor of the world disappears, the noise it

makes is surprisingly small. Like nothing so much as the metallic splash of a handful of cutlery, fresh from the dishwasher, into the drawer.

The bus hovers for a blink before it falls. Fast and clumsy, the road melting away to let it pass through to the nothingness below.

Help will be here shortly, they probably think, as they cough dust out or pull it in. Or perhaps it is some other cliché that comes to mind. At such a moment, even clichés are forgivable.

Wait for the dust to settle.

Keep your feet on the ground.

Weigh it up. Suck it up. Sit tight.

A thousand and one ways to say: do nothing; say nothing; pretend. This too shall pass.

Chance knows no such limits.

NINA

Nina woke when the clock radio clicked on. She kept it tuned to a pop-music station, the uniform nasal drone of the DJs a small price to pay for the certainty she won't be caught off guard by anything real.

Dress. Bathroom. Make-up. A morning in five-minute slots. To dress last would be to risk climbing back into bed, a lesson learned once, sharply. Her suit hung on the outside of the wardrobe door and her jewellery was laid out on the dressing table, the last task before going to bed. It helped her to sleep, seeing the shadowy outline of her tomorrow self. A skin all ready to step into, to show her who she was. One less thing to struggle with when the weight of the morning curled her into herself, the shiver of remembering like a comb running along sunburn.

The early news had a breaking item about a bus crash in Kilbrone, some half an hour outside the city. She held her breath, then released it. She didn't know anyone living there. It wouldn't affect her commute too much, either. The studio was on the opposite side of the city.

A final couple of minutes to double-check everything before she left: plugs, doors, windows. The last stop on the tour was Aisling's empty room, the best and worst part of every day.

Put your coat on in her room and close it up tight

against you to keep in the last of her air, her spirit. Taking her with you when you leave the house. Imagining you can smell her on your skin, the sweet and sour of baby shampoo and spit-up milk.

Once she was safely out of the house and in the car, the morning news brought Nina back to life, as it did every morning.

'The road has been closed and emergency services are at the scene. Locals describe seeing the bus crumpled on its side...' They cut to a woman's excited voice, 'like a dog knocked sideways by a car', she said, her voice almost gleeful.

The expression was wonderfully visceral. Everyone listening would be picturing roadkill, Nina thought.

Settled at her desk, she turned her attention to her computer screen. One of the segments for next week's show was due to go to the editing room and the process would go much more smoothly if she was clear about the direction she wanted for the piece.

She had spent a full day interviewing the staff and residents of a geriatric hospital that was universally lauded for its innovative holistic approach to the well-being of its residents. Budget cuts had seen it slated for closure under cost-cutting measures, but with a general election looming early the following year, the hope was that some publicity would prompt a local politician to make it part of his campaign platform.

Such were the pieces Noel assigned to her since she came back from her leave of absence. The kind of human-interest angles that she used to consider fluff pieces, only good for filling time after the main news. But Noel had felt it would suit her, this place of individual stories, and he was right. People told her things now, she had become a magnet for the personal sorrow of others. She understood their preoccupation with the little things, how the boundaries of their damaged worlds were suddenly too narrow to admit scale.

She paused the footage on an elderly couple beaming into the camera, holding hands like newly-weds, then pressed play to hear her own voice.

'So, tell me, Mary, what are you doing today? You look like you are all dressed up for something special.'

'Today is date night, Nina,' Mary said. 'Jim and myself are going to the pictures, like we used to when we were first stepping out.'

'But you're not going out to the movies, Mary, are you?' Her on-screen face settled into its interested pose. It was one of several she had to practise now. Interest, shock, empathy. Reminding her face of what was acceptable.

'No, pet, I wouldn't be able to go out like that any more, not these days, but, sure, I don't need to.'

Her husband, Jim, finished her sentence for her, frowning with the effort of not looking at the camera. 'The movies are coming to us tonight, Nina.'

Here, Ben panned the camera around the room behind the couple. It was all set up like a tiny cinema, with rows of chairs in front of a pull-down projector screen. Beside the door stood an easel with an A4 poster of *Singin' in the Rain*, above which someone had written, Matinee 12.30 p.m. / Evening show 5.30 p.m.

Not so long ago, she would have smirked at the idea that half past five constituted evening. But there were days now when she, too, climbed into bed before eight, unable to fight her way even to the quasi-respectability of the geriatric waterline that was the nine o'clock news.

Nearby, Noel's office door banged shut, breaking her

concentration. She glanced up. Inside the glass cube of the office, her colleague Mark was talking and talking, waving his hands as if channelling the traffic of his thoughts safely through to his mouth. He was pitching for the bus story, no doubt. If there was an angle, Mark would find it. 'Without tears it's worthless,' he told her once. 'You have to get them to cry, whatever it takes.'

On the screen, Mary and Jim were collecting their bags of popcorn from the vending machine, their laughter charming and grateful and guaranteed to horrify the middle-aged voting public. Tears were assured in living rooms up and down the country.

How strange to envy Mary and Jim their old bodies. To see all the years they shared and know that even if she met someone else this very minute, she would still never have what they had. Her mother had lately started making noises to that effect, telling her she needed to 'get out more', to 'find a hobby', to 'meet new people'. All of the standard euphemisms for finding a man. For looking for one. As if it was what she should want. At every turn, it seemed, there was the world with its judgemental pointy finger. '*Never*,' that finger told her. '*You. Will. Never.*'

'Noel?' She was on her feet and at his door without stopping to think. 'Do you have a minute?'

'We're nearly finished here. Can it wait?'

'No… this concerns Mark too, I think. I want the story, Noel. The bus crash. Well, not the crash as such.' She took a breath, jumped. 'The families, I want the families.'

* * *

Less than an hour later, Nina was parking in a makeshift car park and heading into the regional fire station, where

8

a room had been allocated to the media. Looking around the room, she spotted Ben and slipped into the seat behind him, nodding hello to the familiar faces she passed.

'Apparently the driver and a woman got out,' he told her. 'There are more on board, but I don't know how many. People are saying anything from two to twenty. Statement is due any minute now.'

'The driver got out?'

'The first-response team pulled him out, along with a woman. Rumour has it that that might have been a mistake, destabilised the road or something.'

But Nina hardly heard him. She was looking instead at the man who introduced himself to the room as the Senior Executive Fire Officer. A new title to match his new role, she thought. When she knew him, he was simply 'the Chief'. His voice hadn't changed, it was as calm and reassuring as ever. 'Don't mind the one-day-at-a-time crap,' he had whispered to her in the hum and hush of the funeral-home receiving line. 'Take it one breath at a time.'

'Public safety is our priority at this moment in time. We don't yet know the underlying cause of the road collapse, so we need to evacuate the immediate vicinity before we can do anything else. The main population vulnerabilities are the community hospital on the far side of the junction and the primary school three hundred yards to the south.'

'How many people are we talking about?' a voice called from the crowd.

'Some four hundred in the school, give or take. It's harder to say with the hospital. The HSE lead is evaluating whether to evacuate the whole hospital or just the wing closest to the site. So somewhere between thirty and one hundred and twenty, depending on that decision.'

'How long for the evac?' another voice called.

'An hour. Ninety minutes, tops,' the Chief said.

'What about the people on board the bus?'

'We believe there are six people on board. Two are already safely out, as I outlined earlier, and we are working to get the others out as soon as we can. In the meantime, there are hundreds of vulnerable children and elderly people that need to be moved out of harm's way.'

'Out of harm's way?'

'If there is an issue with the stability of the road—'

'Was it a bomb?' someone called out and the room erupted in questions.

The Chief shook his head and gestured for silence. 'No. We're working on the assumption that there is an issue with the road surface. The county engineers are here with us, assessing the necessary risk factors—'

The greater good was what it boiled down to, Nina knew. Policies, procedures, all designed with numbers in mind.

'Let's not get ahead of ourselves,' the Chief finished. 'Step by step is the best way to help everybody.'

Fuck the greater good, with their big lungfuls of air. Nina was on her feet, 'What about the families?'

The Chief nodded, the only sign that he recognised her. 'We have four Gardaí responding to all phone queries to identify the families in question—'

She imagined the people sitting at home shaking their heads at the news, then slowly putting it together with the phone call that hadn't come.

'We heard that at least one has been identified,' she pressed. If the few were to be sacrificed for the many, they should not remain nameless underground.

'No names can be confirmed yet, but some of the

families have indeed been informed and are on their way. I trust they will be accorded the decency their situation demands.'

It was hard to blame him for fearing false identification. Relief was often quick to turn to anger at the wasted worry. Not so lucky are the real families, the victims of the small ways that conspire to put the wrong person in the wrong place.

When the Chief left, the room buzzed with questions and people turned to their neighbours, trading impressions and rumours. At the start of her career – or even a few years ago – she would have dived into the chatter with the rest, clutching her high ideals of truth and justice. But journalism had changed. She herself had changed. So many things were easy to say. What wouldn't be easy, she knew, was the awkwardness of her colleagues, who still lived by the mantra that today was all that mattered. If it wasn't news, it was nothing.

'I need to make a phone call,' she told Ben. 'Text me if anything happens.'

'Sure.'

The hallway was quiet, people dotted here and there on their phones. In her late teens and early twenties, moody distance was signified by standing alone with a cigarette. She took out her phone, holding it at a believable screen-reading distance. Was it really about being alone back then or was it more about giving the impression that aloneness was desirable? Perhaps it was the impression itself that was desirable. Now, as then, her sister came to her rescue, the phone vibrating in her hand even as she looked at it.

'I can't talk right now.'

'Then why bother answering?' Irene said.

They had always been the wrong way round. Although Nina was the elder of the two, exasperation had been Irene's default position for as long as either of them could remember. They laughed about it during a daquiri-fuelled conversation on their first night out after Aisling was born.

'You've always acted like you're older than me,' Nina pointed out, slurring the tiniest bit after two drinks. 'Dónal Óg will always be older than Aisling, so I'll never have as much experience as you.'

'You'll catch up and pass me,' Irene assured her. 'I never obsessed over things the way you do.'

She was right. By the time Aisling was six months old, Nina was reading ahead to the toddler years. Carelessly counting her chickens.

'Hello?' Irene said. 'Are you still there?'

Her annoyance was welcome. Her refusal to tiptoe around Nina the way others did. 'I can only talk for a minute. I'm at work.'

'What are you working on?'

'The bus crash,' Nina said, after a moment's hesitation. Irene would find out anyway and she worried enough, even when Nina was truthful.

'I thought Noel wasn't going to—'

'I asked for it.' She could feel her sister waiting for more. 'I felt ready. I am ready.'

'I'm glad to hear it. Especially since I was phoning to ask you about taking Dónal Óg out for an afternoon.'

At the mention of his name, her heart burned. She loved that little boy from the minute he arrived, red and roaring, in her sister's arms. Three years older, he was fascinated by Aisling, then puzzled by her sudden disappearance. 'I had a cousin but she died,' he would tell people randomly, in lifts and restaurants and airports, the places of excitement in his small life. 'That's why everyone is so sad all the time,' he might add, swinging off the nearest railing while Irene tried to shush him.

His honesty comforted Nina, housed as it was in the warm weight of his small body. She clung to him in the days after Aisling's death. She and Irene took him to a water park outside the city one dull Saturday morning. He begged her to take him on the water slide and she wanted, with sudden intensity, to be the one to make him smile and shriek with joy.

'You're the coolest, Auntie Neen,' he assured her as they climbed the steps.

Sitting at the top, one hand on the bar, the other around the knitting needles of his ribs, she was startled by a gang of teenagers racing towards them and flinging themselves down as if the plastic surface was no more than the hollow fibre of her pillows at home. Her head blew back with shock and she let go without planning to. She entered the pool horizontally, dragging Dónal Óg down under the water with her instead of keeping him above it. It lasted seconds only, but long enough to teach her that one tragedy did not grant lifelong immunity. Aisling's death did not grant a protective force-field.

'You did it wrong,' he accused her, in tears at the side of the pool. 'It was supposed to be fun!'

'Want to try again?' Irene had asked, oblivious of those underwater seconds, only anxious that their day together not be spoiled.

'Once was enough,' Nina said. Her legs shook all the way to the burger stand. *You could no longer tickle him until he fell to the ground in a happy ball. The curve of him brought back the hospital. Holding your girl in a tight C-shape while they ripped into her back with needles. You standing quietly by, as if doing nothing more taxing than watching a stiff-lipped waiter fillet a sea bass in a restaurant.*

'Well?' Irene cut across her thoughts. 'You could take him this weekend?'

'No!' She cleared her throat. 'I can't promise anything – work is going to be crazy for the next while. Speaking of which, Ben's calling me, I have to go back in.'

She stayed where she was after hanging up. The heat of the room, the airlessness and greed would kick awake her demons and today she needed them napping. The anxiety came and went. It was a fickle foe, waking her in the night to tell her the baby monitor was humming gently, or freezing her in cafes with the certain knowledge she had forgotten Aisling somewhere. Even now, when she could never again be left anywhere but the ground in which she rested.

Nina breathed in and counted to thirty in her head, the number of steps from the graveyard gate to the foot of her baby's forever bed. Irene told her, with the black humour of sisters, that she now had something on which to pin her anxiety, and it was true that she sometimes felt relieved that the worst had already happened. The world could still hurt her, she knew, but it could only ever be hurt of a different order.

She needed fresh air. No, she needed to be in the water with her head submerged, just her and her thoughts. A lie, clearly, when it wasn't her thoughts she wanted but her memories. She dragged herself away from the edge of the rabbit hole and texted Ben to meet her outside. If the families were here, that was where they would want to be. To watch and hope.

Outside, a small crowd had gathered behind the police cordon. Everyone wanted to be the first to spot something: a family member, a limb, the hand of God. Nina watched the police move lines of children, delivering them from one section to the next in an eerily quiet crocodile. True terror was calm, she knew. She had seen it at the hospital, the quieter the ward, the bigger the fear. On the street in front of her, the smallest children cried, while the older ones' faces were tight with worry. The ones in between, whose ages gave them the perfect ratio of bravado to ignorance, waved at the cameras, gurning and giggling, all defiance and joy.

'Where do you want me?' Ben asked.

'I'm going to roam around for a bit and see who wants to talk,' she said. She held up her recorder. 'I'm fine with just this.'

Let Ben have the footage of smoke and tears, she wanted the faceless voice cracking, the blank space that others could put their own bodies into.

'Okay. I'll film the scene, get some context stuff,' Ben said easily.

Joe and Joan Public were all anxious to talk. They lined up to tell her where they were when they saw, when they heard, taking interminable minutes to describe the shallowness of their feelings. *Empty vessels make the most noise.* All old wives' tales held a kernel of truth.

'My cameraman, Ben – see him over there? – he may want to take some footage, if that's all right with you all?' She left them to their useless delight and twittering.

She rounded a corner and leaned against the wall, fighting the instinct to return to the safety of her office. If she did, it would be a long time before Noel trusted her judgement again. The therapist had told her – in her first and only session – that she needed to confront her pain instead of looking for ways to deflect it.

'If you feel your thoughts spiralling,' she said, leaning in as if they were friends, 'let them. It might take you somewhere you need to go.'

As if real life worked like that. Instead, Nina catalogued the sources of her distraction and trained her thoughts not to settle. Her distractions allowed her to slide into the stuff of minutes, the stuff of nothing: the weather, an ad for kitchen towel, a list for her grocery shopping. Individual minutes easing her through the day.

The universe didn't have a plan. Good things happened. Bad things happened. Work with it, against it, around it. There were only events and the people to whom they happened. That was all it amounted to in the end.

She nodded once and walked back to the site. The children and office workers had disappeared from the road and reappeared on lists, transformed by bureaucracy from 3D into 2D, reality sucked out of them like air out of a plastic bag.

A single figure paced the perimeter, a woman with a long grey plait. From the way she was talking to herself and smacking at the air, Nina guessed she was one of the poor souls released to the community when the old psychiatric hospital in the city closed down. They were given six months' warning before being sent out into the world with neither skills nor motivation for anything but the rhythm of walking. For putting their lives down one step at a time.

Nina watched the woman as she approached, muttering curses or prayers.

'Shocking,' Nina said, when the woman got close enough. She nodded towards the hole.

The woman crossed herself in response. 'He always lets me on, Richie does. *Two little dickie birds sitting on a wall*,' she sang, her voice cracking.

'*One named Peter, one named Paul.*' Nina finished the nursery rhyme.

The woman smiled at her. 'The dickie birds are the good ones.'

'Aren't they just?' Nina held out her hand. 'I'm Nina.'

The woman put her hand out too, but not quite far enough, their almost handshake a disembodied thing belonging to neither. 'We're all going to hell,' she said, conversationally.

'Can't argue with you there,' Nina agreed.

'They're gone already,' the woman said. 'God between us and all harm.' She began to cross herself over and over, as if the words had loosened some strap that held her fingers still. On she went, intoning the blessing, the sharp edges of her sign softening until she was simply waving her hand in figure of eights between her face and chest.

'Do you want to tell me anything?' Nina asked the woman. It was a technique she found useful when interviewing psychiatric patients – the broader the question, the better the answer. Minds that swept the edges struggled with the limits of normal questions.

'They took them,' she said.

'I know,' Nina touched her own arm, proxy comfort for the skittish woman. 'But they've gone to the hospital to be looked after.'

'They're better off dead,' the woman said, suddenly firm. 'Better off dead,' she repeated, backing away. Her laceless sneakers slapped as she walked, barely equal to the task of keeping them on her feet.

Nina watched her walk away on ankles of almost Parisian thinness. Here was no country girl. She took the two sides of the footpath and Nina could imagine others giving her a wide berth as she walked down the street.

You used to think people steered clear of you, too, leaving a person's width either side. As if your grief skipped alongside you, holding your hand.

Better off dead, the woman said. The ungrateful bitch. Taking up space in a life she didn't want when you and others like you would have given all you had to grab even the beaten-down dirty shell of that body if you could shove your daughter down into it. A day, an hour, you'd take whatever you could get.

You spent all your time swallowing these thoughts – was it any wonder you had no appetite?

* * *

'All I'm seeing is that those kids are just fine.' The man's voice was loud, his accent a harsh twang.

Nina and Ben stood in the lobby of the fire station, waiting for the lift to take them back up to the temporary media centre upstairs. The station was a bare few hundred yards from the accident site, a cruel joke for any believer in some almighty theatre director. She kept her eyes on the floor, fingering her press pass, waiting to hear more.

'What I want to know is what's happening with Paul,' the man said, louder.

Several others stood with him, among them the Chief and a weeping woman. They formed a loose group. Casual, almost, were it not for the fact that they were subtly trying to move him along.

'While you're out there fussing around with people that are already fine, what are you doing about my boy?'

Ben lifted an eyebrow towards his camera, but Nina shook her head. The last thing they needed was to be asked to leave.

'We are doing everything we can to help your son.' The Chief's calm voice trying to defuse the situation. 'We can't complete our assessment of the site until after the evacuation,' he continued.

'Just stop,' shouted the man. 'I don't care about that. Just tell me what's happening with Paul!'

The Chief tried again, 'For now, what we know is—'

'I'm not asking what you know. I don't care what you know. You know nothing. I'm asking about Paul. Do you not understand the question?'

'Sir, once the evacuation is complete, we'll be able to get a better image read of the area around the hole. Then we can decide which of our rescue plans—'

'You're not listening. You're not listening to me. What's happening with Paul? What are you doing to get my son out of that hole? What kind of operation are you running here? Why won't you answer me? Do you not understand English? What's. Happening. With. Paul.'

'I understand you're upset, but this isn't helping your son,' a new voice said.

Nina froze at his voice. Tim's voice. *I understand you're upset, Nina. I understand this isn't what you want.*

The lift pinged and the group crossed the lobby. Tim nodded at Nina and Ben. 'We'll take this one. You won't mind waiting for the next.'

The lift doors took a long time to close. In another lifetime, she could read his eyes, his every gesture. Now, she could no longer interpret him.

'Who's Mr Straight-talking?' Ben asked, pressing the button to call the lift again.

'That's Tim,' she said, simply. 'My husband. Ex-husband.'

TIM

Tim escorted the man and his wife into the lift, asking their names and giving every appearance of listening to the answers. Nina. For a moment he thought he had imagined her. That his brain had overlaid one crisis on another.

'Elmarie, Jason, I'm taking you up to the canteen, which we are using as a family centre.' He had to raise his voice a little over the sound of the woman's weeping.

When they got to the door, the couple standing by the window turned to look at the commotion.

'Fix it, Jason,' she kept saying. 'Tell them it's a mistake.'

'Stop crying.' His voice was as sharp with her as everyone else. 'It's not helping anyone. What was he even doing here, Elmarie? Why was he even on that bus? That wasn't his bus.'

Why was anyone anywhere? Tim gave himself a little mental shake. He needed to focus on the here and now, but the sight of Nina had unsettled him. It wasn't that he didn't want to see her, exactly, it was just the unexpectedness of it. The way she appeared out of the blue, like the pedestrian behind his car the time he failed his driving test. The woman he swore must have dropped out of a tree.

'So this is your grand plan? To shut us away in here?' Jason pronounced each word loudly in Tim's face. 'You pretend to be a great little country, but you're nothing. There's no morality here, it's all who you know. What's a man supposed to do who knows nobody? It's a lie—'

'Enough.' The father from the other family – Denis, Tim remembered – turned from his vantage point at the window. 'You're upsetting my wife. We all have family in there. These people are doing the best they can, so we would all appreciate if you would let them get on with it instead of shouting the odds and wasting their time. Have a bit of common decency, can't you, for the love of God.' He turned back to his wife at the window, his shoulders shaking.

'We're doing everything we can. Now that the area is evacuated, we have greater freedom to move, to put a rescue plan in place. Again, my name is Tim. I'm the Information Liaison and it's my job to make sure everyone knows what they need to know. I'll be updating you regularly with the facts.'

'We'd better see some results soon or there'll be hell to pay.' Jason glared at him before sitting down at the nearest table, his hands gripping the edge as if he might flip it over.

In the window's reflection, the scene outside was overlaid with the worried faces of Denis and his wife. Tragedy was like that, Tim wanted to tell them. Life felt like something you were watching through a window, everyone else moving but you.

'Denis, Vera – you said earlier that this is Orla's usual bus. Is there any chance she might have done something different today?'

Vera shook her head. 'Not our Orla. She's like clockwork.'

'What happens next?' Denis asked.

'During the evacuation, the team here started to examine the best – and safest – way to access the bus. That means knowing what the ground is like so that they can avoid any further disturbance. Think of it like a frozen lake – we'll check the edges first, then slowly move towards the centre.'

Tim knew by their faces that they weren't taking in a word of it. How could they?

'What do you do, Vera?'

'I'm a primary school teacher.'

'Okay. Then think of it like teaching someone to read. We're making sure we know our alphabet before we start on phonics.' He was rewarded with a watery smile.

'They'll have them out soon, won't they? Orla—' Vera's voice broke on her daughter's name. 'Orla doesn't like the dark.'

'Building blocks, that's all it is. I know it might feel slow, but it's steady and safe. Focus on that.'

'Steady and safe,' she repeated.

Tim didn't add that time could outrun optimism. That sometimes all the waiting and wishing in the world couldn't stop the axe from falling.

He felt rather than saw Nina waiting for him outside the door. She created a faint crackle of impatience in the air, the sense of things getting done.

'Seems like your man doesn't like the way we do things,' she said.

We. The offhand way she said it. As if she was still part of it.

It was true that he was the one who had moved on. He had kissed Deb goodbye not three hours ago, tiptoeing around and dressing on the landing so as not to wake her.

He and Nina stood awkwardly for a moment, before speaking at the same time.

'I didn't expect—'

'I didn't know you were—'

'I'm not on active duty any more,' he explained. 'I'm the information guy at HQ these days. The Chief called me down here as a favour.'

'This is my first live story since... I told Noel I wanted it.'

'Do you?' Her careful make-up didn't quite conceal the dark circles under her eyes.

She scratched gently at her arm. 'I was thinking about the families and... well, they'll need someone who...' She shrugged.

'Someone who isn't Mark?' he finished for her, giving them both an out.

She smiled. 'Imagine you with a desk job! You finally gave in.'

Impossible to tell her why. To explain that leaving the house that morning, he stopped outside the children's rooms, unsure if he had yet earned the right to kiss them goodbye. They would be teenagers shortly, more robust with each day. He settled for pressing a kiss to each of their door frames and sending up a quick prayer for their safety.

'It's new,' he told her. 'I thought... well, I thought it would open up different opportunities.'

'Here you are, though, in the thick of it still,' she said.

Her tone was pleasant. A casual observer would have

called her polite. But that casual observer wouldn't have heard the echo of late-night arguments about his insistence that his job wasn't an issue, that their baby's impending arrival shouldn't change anything. Nina would raise her great bulk off the couch and accuse him of putting other people's families first.

But if he expected an argument, he wasn't getting one today. Instead, she changed tack. 'Is it too weird for you to have me here?'

'Would you go back to the office if I asked you to?' Though he intended the question to be teasing, his tone didn't carry it off.

'Would you ask me to?'

The same old stalemate. He shrugged. 'The Chief will be doing most of the media stuff. We probably won't even see each other.'

Her smile didn't reach her eyes. 'That works for me.'

'Fine.'

'Fine.'

He took the stairs two at a time, resisting the urge to look back over his shoulder at her.

The meeting room was already badly overheated and struggling to contain everyone. Tim tried not to think of the air-conditioned cool of the city fire station. The Chief was in a huddle with the county engineers, taking turns around the maps, like penguins keeping the colony warm. Beside him was the Assistant Chief, Leo. He seemed solid, but it stung Tim to see someone in the job that used to be his.

All eyes were on the computer monitor as the little remote-controlled jeep edged into the hole and disappeared from sight. If it wasn't for the state-of-the-art camera mounted on top, it could have been mistaken for something Santa left behind on Christmas Eve. Tim didn't draw breath – he would bet nobody did – until a faint glow brightened into infrared and, all of a sudden, they were underground.

It reminded him of the science fiction of the gastro-oesophageal camera descending his throat into his stomach, the time of that first ulcer, the month after Aisling died. The picture on this screen, though, would not be fixed by any magic tablets.

The gap between the rocks was narrower than he expected, although had he been asked, he would have answered that he didn't have any expectations at all and would have believed himself honest in saying so.

The jeep moved forward as far as it could, bumping up and over obstacles to inch its way along. When it finally stopped, the gap was no wider than the top of a teacup. The technician fiddled with the zoom and the side of the bus flickered into what seemed like touching distance. Turned on its side, the panelling was twisted and buckled, with one small patch of cheery advertising still visible. 'Be better', it told them, sternly.

'Subsidence, I'd say, if I had to call it,' one of the engineers said. He rubbed his hand over his face, already tired from this day that was barely halfway to lunchtime. 'Too early to say for sure, but it looks like the ground has eroded in the area all around. Probably started years ago. The road was basically just surface and the weight of the bus was too much.'

'Give it one last 360 and then pull it up and out,' Leo instructed. As the camera swivelled to retrace its steps, they all saw it: a patch of condensation on the bus window.

'Someone's breathing in there.'

Tim tried not to let the knowledge carry him away. Around him, plans were sketched out and phone calls made. His hands were calm as they moved across the whiteboard, tracking the details needed, the information received. His mind, all the while, skittering around the edges of a hole he couldn't afford to fall into.

Aisling's breathing. She's still breathing.

The hope, the fucking starburst of it. As if breath was all it took. When it still seemed as if there was a way to make it right. If they waited in the right way, maybe, or believed hard enough, or hit on just the magic combination of words to find God's ears.

When he stood up, he was nearly dizzy with wanting.

'I'll take a quick walk down the site,' he said. 'Gather up any of the family members who have gone down there so we can let them all know together.'

He was out the door and running for the stairs. Outside, it was easier not to think about it. To focus on sky and air and today.

The police cordon was nearly within spitting distance of the fire station gate. Practically on its own doorstep. Jesus, fuck. The irony could kill a person. Or maybe it wasn't irony at all, he often struggled to tell.

The site was busy – in a small town, anything out of the ordinary excited disproportionate interest. The news had found them all, it seemed: the rubberneckers; the school-run mothers; the pensioners on their slow way to the shops for the single chicken breast that gave them a reason to leave the house; the ones with nowhere else to be. Accident sites had a smell, and although his brain knew that it was simply the plastic of the tape, his heart insisted it was hopelessness.

He needed to pull it together. The site wasn't his business, not any more. His territory was inside, marking the plan into bite-sized pieces that the media could understand. Keeping both sides looking competent and pissing off neither. Diplomacy was what he needed today, not selfish spiralling into his own story.

He kept to the side of the footpath until he could see the hole in front of him. A dust cloud hung in the air, making it difficult to see anything beyond the edges. Underfoot, there was the odd scuffling noise, the road still moving, shifting around to get comfortable in itself again. Two already out, six still trapped. A miracle and a disaster, one buried within the other.

The sound of muttering floated behind him and he turned to see a woman in the side street beyond the cordon, drawing pictures in the air with a broken umbrella. May, the Chief had told him. She was often around, he had said, engaged in her daily work of pacing the streets. But whatever she might know, she was likely to keep close.

Tim walked a wide, careful arc along the edge of the cordon and over to the lip of the street, not wanting to spook either the road or the woman.

'Hello there. May, isn't it? I'm Tim.'

Her eyes cut over to him for a brief, suspicious second.

'Did you see what happened here?' he asked.

'They were called,' she said. Her laugh rose dry and rusty and her umbrella flicked towards the hole.

He tried again. 'Did you see what happened? I know you're often around these parts.'

'I'm here since God was a boy,' she nodded. 'And before that and every day since.'

She moved over, close to him, her skin giving off the sweet, tarry smell of rotting fruit.

'The aliens came,' she whispered.

'Aliens?'

She nodded, her eyes doll-wide. She didn't have anything to tell him. In real life, no truths hid within the ravings of the disturbed, waiting to be picked out like jewels from glass.

'Little ones and big ones and black tubes for their faces and their arms turned yellow as piss on a winter morning from the air down here.'

It wasn't the first time he'd heard the team called aliens, although it was more common from small children.

'They took two of them for testing,' she said.

'Thanks for your help.'

'They didn't get me though.' She danced one hand around her head, the sudden and shocking length of her wrist poking out of her sleeve, dainty and stained as used china.

'That's good fortune.'

'When they call you, you have to go,' May said, turning away. 'Goodnight and God bless and no right of reply.'

She was a pity, Tim thought, watching her go. Her and plenty others like her. He hoped her parents, if they were still alive, were spared the knowledge of what their dreams had come to.

The day Aisling was born he wrote to Nina. Awed by what she had achieved, what she had endured to give them this gift. It rendered him speechless, drove him to paper.

'Today our family was born,' he wrote. 'The world

is both big enough and small enough for us. The world is finally the perfect fit.'

Emotions were running high enough that he gave it to her without a shred of self-consciousness, with kisses and promises to add to it every year on Aisling's birthday.

'By the time she's eighteen,' he said, reckless with ignorant joy, 'we'll have a record of our journey.'

When he unpacked his boxes in the one-bedroom flat and found it tucked into the side pocket of his washbag, he drank until he hardly remembered his own name.

On the way back to the station, he passed a group of volunteers, waiting for their six-hour shift to begin, he guessed, or maybe just finishing up. One of them had his back to Tim as he whistled long and low. 'It was just lying there on its side,' he said. 'There'll be nobody come out of it alive.'

Tim grabbed the younger man's arm and dragged him aside. 'What did you say?'

'Whaaaaat?'

'You're standing out here where everyone can see you and everyone can hear you making thoughtless comments.'

'Relax, man, nobody heard me.' He tried to shrug it off. 'It's not that big a deal.'

'It is a big deal,' Tim said. 'It's a very fucking big deal to the families who might have to hear your ignorance.'

The young man turned pink, most likely embarrassed in front of his colleagues.

'You don't know me, but I know the Chief and now I know you, too. I strongly suggest you keep out of my way and pray you didn't flap your mouth where anyone heard you or there'll be a disciplinary when this is over.'

Tim let him go. If he had a genie and one wish, he'd have the little prick fired.

He took the stairs up to the meeting room, stopping in the stairwell on each of the floors to do a breathing exercise his counsellor gave him. Breathe into the big box of his lungs, fill the box, push the edges to make it bigger. By the time he got to the top, the anger was gone and he let his breathing return to normal before pushing open the door.

'Get the last of those cars moved and get the ambulance loading point in there.' The Chief indicated the line of cars parked in a little bay on the street just outside the police cordon.

'They're nearly finished,' Tim said.

'They better not want paying,' the Chief said. 'Outsourced service, my hole. What was wrong with the council doing it?' He didn't wait for an answer. 'Nothing, that's what. Only it didn't suit someone whose brother or uncle or child wasn't making enough as a private contractor.' He took a packet of cigarettes out of his pocket. 'I was down to three a day. Now lookit,' he waved the pack, 'my willpower is shot to fuck.'

Less than half an hour later, however, the Chief looked calm and assured, speaking Tim's words to the cameras in a smooth and confident flow. It was a simple reiteration of the facts as they knew them. Almost all of the facts. Vastly different to the briefing for the families shortly before, in which that patch of condensation was the only subject of any importance. They held onto it, it lit them up. They hugged each other, not yet competitive about who among them might have a legitimate claim on that flickering hope.

The Chief was light on their rapid-response time,

sidestepping questions of what might have been done differently. The media were already on them like vultures. 'Thirty seconds to get ready, even less to think about what they were doing,' screamed banners across the tops of web pages and ticker tapes along the bottoms of screens. Tim wouldn't want to be in the shoes of the man that made that initial decision. The poor fucker would never trust his own judgement again. If Tim was a betting man, he would give him until the end of the year. No doubt there was a pool going already. At least the media didn't have his name.

He and Nina used to argue about that media shift from objective observer to something more insidiously directive. During his own media training last year, he was told his baseline tolerance for spin was low. Too low. He often found himself amped up for a fight after the mildest comment. It incensed him, the amount of power casually handed over to the media, their censure often the prevailing concern. Yet people continued to let them. Laziness, that was all it was. Everyone happy to let others fight their battles for them.

Tim tracked the statement, glad when it neared its end. Hearing his own words from someone else was an unsettling ventriloquism. The title of Chief gave Tim's words more authority, a slurry of optimism spread over the bare facts as if hoping solutions would grow there.

* * *

'Nina's asking for an interview,' the Chief told Tim afterwards. 'I told her she can have five minutes. You okay with that?'

'Sure,' Tim said, although he was annoyed at her

cheek. The least she could have done was ask him directly. 'We spoke briefly earlier on. It's fine with me.'

'In my office in five.'

* * *

Deb answered on the second ring. 'I got your note. I hope things aren't too bad there. It's all over the news.'

Her gentleness was soothing. Her lack of interest in the gory details.

'Hard to say yet. They're in a tough spot.'

'God love them, the poor things. And the families.' She paused. 'They must be tormented with reporters.'

He liked it, when they first met, that she had no time for the media. There was something refreshing about her dismissal of anything that smacked of posturing. Today, however, it seemed cold and he felt disloyal, somehow, at the thought of telling her Nina was there. It hardly mattered, he told himself. The events of the morning were bigger than who was where.

* * *

'I can give you a couple of minutes, that's all,' the Chief warned, sitting down on the corner of the desk as if everything was under control. 'Ask away.'

'I got the basics from the statement, but that's not really my angle. I'm building a longer piece. The victims, their families, the personal face of things.'

She was careful, Tim noticed, not to call it a tragedy. Not yet. Another legacy, that awareness of individual words, their power to bruise.

'Can you talk me through the identification of the

people involved?' she asked. 'Just to round out the scene and get a sense of where it started for the families?'

The Chief's phone buzzed and he checked it, frowning slightly. 'Tim? Can I leave this with you? I'm needed upstairs.'

'What do you need to know?' Tim asked, after he left.

'Phone lines, staffing, elimination of people…' She shrugged. 'Anything. Everything.'

She took notes as he talked, the side of her hand dragging lightly on the paper and gathering ink as it went. He could picture the mark she would leave on the tablecloth at dinner time. If she remembered to eat.

'Still suffering with the rashes?' He pointed to where her left hand was scratching gently at the underside of her right forearm. They came from nowhere, sudden flares of pain, resisting all efforts at easement.

She closed her notebook and looked up at him. 'It's hardly suffering. What's the Assistant like? Leo, right?'

'He's very capable.' He fidgeted with the paper-clip holder. 'How are the family?'

'They're all well, thank you.'

Still trying to get her to talk about it, no doubt. They were always so anxious to pick through the broken pieces, while Nina kept insisting that everything was fine. They used to go to her parents' house, the odd Sunday after Aisling. Big roast dinner with all the trimmings, both red and white wine open on the table, heated debate about the issues of the day. And all the while their daughter like a ghost that only he could see. Some days, out of frustration or hurt, Nina's mother or Irene would drop Aisling's name like a bomb into the conversation. Whenever that happened, Nina would have them in the car within ten minutes. They need to grieve too, Tim reminded her, but she only shook her head. They could leave her out of their grief, she said. She had enough of her own to be getting on with.

'The evacuation must have been frustrating for you all,' Nina was saying. 'Having to wait, I mean.'

'It had to be done,' he said. 'The first rule is always to—'

'Secure the site.' She finished it with him.

He smiled despite himself. 'Besides, there were sick people and children to consider.' He sounded like a mealy-mouthed Rose of Tralee contestant, with his stiff answers. Careful to stay within the bounds of what was acceptable. *All I want is world peace, Dáithí.*

At the door, she turned. 'Do you think people are still alive in there?' she asked.

He could see the weight of it on her, the question and the answer. 'I do,' he said, and the words grew until they filled the space between them.

RICHIE

'In your own words, Mr Murray, can you take us through the events of the morning?'

The guard was only doing his job, Richie knew. It was hardly his fault that the morning had gone to shite. Yet Richie couldn't pull his thoughts together. If they wanted feelings, fine, he had feelings to burn. Thoughts… thoughts were a different ballgame altogether.

'People say it helps to close your eyes,' the guard said kindly. 'When you're trying to remember, I mean.'

'Everything was grand. The same as normal. No bother, like,' Richie began.

He closed his eyes and hoped for the best.

From the driver's seat of the bus, Richie could see the skyline through a narrow hole of light. Only the tops of the houses were visible, making him feel like a peeping Tom. Like the time he was out searching for Buddy and got caught looking in the Widow Quinn's bedroom window. The seat belt was tight, pressing his piss dangerously close to bursting. Shouldn't have had that second coffee, Richie-boy. After a few seconds of panic, he managed to open the buckle and breathed a little more easily. His toes wiggled at his command, his fingers too. He had seen enough of TV hospital dramas to know that this was a good sign – his spinal column was in one piece, or at least connected enough to talk to his brain. Sandra spent years telling him it was a waste of time. 'Not that depressing shite again,' she used to say. 'Haven't we enough misery ourselves without borrowing more?' She'd have to eat her words now, wouldn't she? It would give him an excuse to phone her, in any case. A reason less flimsy than whether or not she wanted the dog basket out of the shed. 'What are you still hanging onto that for?' she asked him. 'Buddy was put down years ago.'

Behind him, somewhere in the darkness of the bus, he heard whimpering and laboured breathing. He didn't look over his shoulder. He was afraid of what he might see without the protective glass of the TV screen.

First things first.

He nudged himself along the seat, careful as a full pint glass. The windscreen was partly gone and he could feel glass in his hair, but that could be dealt with later. Future Richie's problem, you might say. For some perky nurse with a crisp uniform and manicured nails, if he was lucky. But, then, when had he ever been lucky? Look at him now, for fuck's sake, almost buried alive. He needed to get himself up on the seat and into the tunnel of light just above him, up where life was still going on.

The movement of his belly against the steering wheel rocked the bus and he held his breath, sucking in as hard as he could while every takeaway dinner of the last few months paraded along in his mind's eye. Heaving himself up was out of the question. Instead, he held still, like he used to as a child, frozen with fear that if he moved, something terrible would happen.

If he just kept his eyes on the light ahead of him. That

was the thing. That would get him through. As long as the light was there, so was he. Hold tough, Richie-boy. Wait it out.

Sirens woke him, screaming into his dreams, leaving no room for anything else.

'Hello?' A helmet filled the hole, shining a torch into Richie's face.

'Hello,' he shouted, through a thick throatful of tears.

'Hang in there, we'll get you out,' the helmet said. 'How many of you are there?'

'Eight, I'd say, but I couldn't swear to it.' He lay back against the seat, limp with relief.

Above him, he heard shouts and the distracting sounds of machinery. His father had always had a bit of a soft spot for farm equipment and what he didn't know about them wasn't worth talking about, or so it seemed to small Richie. He wasn't a man for games, his father, but sometimes, if the Sunday sermon was dragging on, he would tip his head to listen to a tractor passing outside, then put his lips to Richie's ear. 'TE20', he might whisper, or, if his eyes were bloodshot, simply 'Massey Ferguson', and it would feel like the two of them against the world. The rare contact of his father's lips on his skin made it memorable, even if that skin was only his ear. His lughole, his father called it when he had drink taken and swung at Richie. But, on Sunday mornings, Saturday night's threats of clatters round the lughole were a whole week away again and it was easy to forget the shouting and be on his father's side again.

'Hey!' he shouted into the gap, then, 'Hey! Hey! Hey!' until the man in the helmet reappeared. 'I can smell petrol,' he said. Hearing his own voice say it loosened the knot inside him and his bladder, renowned in the Tap Tavern for its manly record of four pints had and held, let go of its burden.

The helmet disappeared, the machinery stopped. In the endless silence, he strained so hard, he was afraid he would hear the priest of those long-ago Sundays. Years it was since he'd been to Mass, but hadn't he the years put in before he quit? If the Almighty was picking names to fill out some of the cheap seats above in heaven, Richie's name might well be on it. Somewhere down the bottom, granted, but still there.

'Sir? Sir?'

How long had they been calling him? 'Yes.'

'Do you think you can climb out?'

'I don't know. I can try.' It was the decision of a split second, not to tell them about the rocking when he tried earlier. Survival instinct or deliberate oversight? Try as he might, later on, to parse his thoughts, there was no pinning it down.

'Try now, please. We need to get you out before we can get our team in past you to the others. If you can get out onto the front of the bus, then we should be able to pull you up.'

Such words to hear! Words to lighten his legs, and up he got.

He wobbled his way out of the seat and looked at the small gap in the shattered glass of the windscreen. With one hand, he pushed in his belly and squeezed through. It was a difficult ask, like trying to get a sausage back into its skin. Behind him, he heard the sound of crying again and, this time, knowing freedom was only an arm's length away, he risked a glance over his shoulder.

A young woman was crawling slowly up the aisle of the bus, her hand held out to him.

'Please,' she said. 'Please.'

In front of him, two arms waved him forward.

'Please.'

He looked from her face to the arms above him. The last move he made rocked the bus; if she climbed up here with him, it could upset the apple cart entirely. But she couldn't weigh more than seven or eight stone. He lost half that much the last time he and Sandra tried to make a real go of things. When he gave up the Guinness and the full-fat butter and the two of them went walking together in the evenings with Buddy.

He took her hand and helped her through the glass and out onto the bonnet with him. The bus shifted slightly, but it was no more than a kind of gentle grumbling.

'Thank you. Thank you.'

He nodded, his head at an awkward angle, his chin raised to clear the top of her head as he shuffled her past him towards the waiting arms. They were so close, he could feel her shaking through her clothes, heat coming off her in waves. It might have aroused him, if circumstances were different, if he couldn't feel the coldness of the piss seeping through his trousers. She slipped through easily enough – another wobble – then two sets of arms reached down for him.

* * *

Richie opened his eyes to find the two guards looking at him. He cleared his throat. 'That was about the size of it,' he said. He shifted around on the hospital trolley to get more comfortable. 'The men above pulled and I pushed. Then they brought me straight to the hospital here.' No need to mention that it took three men to haul him out.

The guards nodded and closed their notebooks. One glanced at the other and cleared his throat. 'You're absolutely sure there was nothing unusual about any of the passengers getting on?'

'Unusual how?'

'Perhaps someone had a large gear bag? Or seemed unduly agitated...?'

Shit, Richie thought. They knew he let Crazy May on for free. But she hadn't been on the bus when it crashed, he realised with relief. 'No. Nothing like that,' he said, with confidence.

'That's all for the moment, Mr Murray. If we need anything else—'

'You'll find me in the Bahamas.' He made a grand gesture around him at the walls of Accident & Emergency, but the joke fell flat. What in the name of God was wrong with him that he had to make stupid jokes at a time like this? No wonder some people didn't give him the time of day, they could smell the try-hard on him.

They left the door slightly ajar and he could hear the busy sounds of the ward. It was very quiet earlier on when he was whisked past the waiting room, still strewn with the debris of the night before. Crumpled cans of Red Bull, blood-stained tissues, torn magazines and, inexplicably, a single shoe. They'd settled him on a narrow trolley in what they called the 'treatment room'. Good job he wasn't a man for panic, or the name alone would have drawn out worse than piss.

'The doctor will be with you shortly,' the paramedics had told him and left before he remembered to thank them. His mother, God love her, would kill him, if she could recognise him.

40

He wondered where they had taken the woman. She weighed next to nothing in his arms. He took off his trousers, stiff and stale, and looked around for something to put over his greying boxer shorts. He was peering into the boxes on the shelved wall when the door opened.

'Are you all right there?' asked the doctor.

'I… ah… my boxers were wet, so I was looking for something to put over me,' he said.

The doctor stuck his head out the door, 'Can I get a towel in here, please? And some clean scrubs?' He came back in again, 'Right, let's get you checked out. Can you tell me what happened?'

Richie went through it all again while the doctor listened. The disappearance of the road under the bus. The falling. The dust and the coughing. Trying to move and not to move. The smell of petrol. The winch and the woman.

'You're quite the hero, Richie,' the doctor said, as he pressed and pushed, seemingly at random. 'Big breath now, please.'

'Ah no, sure she was only a little thingeen,' Richie said, pleased.

While the doctor went about his business, turning and twisting him up and down like a pig on a spit, he rolled the word around in his mind. A hero, he said, Richie-boy, and who wouldn't warm to that?

Wouldn't it be the price of Sandra to see him hailed on the TV after telling him he was smothering her, that she would rather die than spend another night under his roof. She needn't think that she could just swan back in either. She walked out on him and he wouldn't forget it. In the middle of all that mess at work, what's more. When he could have done with her standing by him. His mam would know no better, God help us, she hardly knew her own name any more. The lads over in the Tap, they would get a kick out of it all right. 'Richie, the hero.' He'd get some doing from them, mind you, but there would be a few pints stood and a bit of respect at the back of it all.

The woman herself, and why not? He remembered again the feel of her in his arms, a fragile little bird, she might like the idea of a strong man. A few less of those victory pints with the lads – switch to the vodka maybe, it was better for the waistline – and walk the mile home after. Sure, in a few weeks he'd be slim, trim, and brimful of energy, as his old mam used to say. He had a little wink with himself at how he might use up some of that extra energy.

'Is the woman all right, do you know?' he asked the doctor. Maybe she had internal injuries or was dead already. Jesus, how sick would that make him, lying here thinking about her and half-wishing he was on his own.

'We're not allowed to give out information except to family,' the doctor said, snapping the file back onto the end of the bed. 'We'll get you down for a chest X-ray shortly.'

Shortly turned into an hour and eventually a vacant young lad pushed a wheelchair in the door of the treatment room. He had the jerky movement of the cartoon puppets Richie used to watch on Saturday mornings growing up, while his mam cooked his dad's special weekend breakfast as soundlessly as she could.

'X-ray?' the orderly asked and waited while Richie climbed in.

Out on the ward, people were walking and talking

and pagers bleeped. Somewhere, a woman screamed in fits and starts and Richie wished she would stop. The TV in the waiting area was tuned to a news programme and he recognised the square in Kilbrone. They were showing the bus crash.

'A rescue team at the scene is meeting with county engineers to plan how best to evacuate the remaining passengers. No numbers have been confirmed yet,' the news anchor said. She leaned forward to let the camera peek down her blouse into the dip of her tits, in such a way that it might be a hundred people or none at all, for all the notice anyone would take of her words. 'The bus driver and one passenger were winched to safety early this morning after claims of a petrol leak led to fears of fire. A spokesman for the fire service says there is no immediate risk of fire but refused to comment on whether that initial rescue was, in fact, a mistake.'

From hero to mistake inside one hour. Good man, Richie-boy. Why did he think it could ever be different?

On the way back to his room, they queued for the lift with another orderly. An older man, the very spit of that comedian his mam used to love, especially at Christmastime. What was his name, again?

'Awful about the crash, isn't it?' the man said. 'Terrible. Them poor creatures.'

The man's voice was enough to jog Richie's memory: Niall Tóibín, that was the comedian's name. Richie wished he had a tape recorder.

'This was the driver.' Richie's own orderly finally stirred himself to speak.

Richie was surprised he had picked up on that much, he seemed like the type to have trouble remembering which direction gravity went.

'Would you go on out of that! Jaysus, how are you, lad?'

Niall – as he would be evermore in Richie's head – peppered Richie with questions. He was the kind that would repeat the story in the locker room and again over the dinner table with his wife. He had the slim physique of a man who had someone at home making sure he had his five-a-day. Richie could nearly picture the pair of them, reading the obituaries out loud to each other over their granola and shaking their heads in morbid glee, treating the In Memoriams with the reverence that Sandra's friends held for royal wedding spreads in *Hello* magazine.

'You must have got an awful shock, all the same. I don't know how you did it, climbing out like that, and dragging that poor woman with you,' Niall Tóibín continued. He eyed Richie for confirmation he had his facts right.

'It was nothing really.'

The light dimmed a bit in Niall's eyes, so Richie added, 'In the heat of the moment, I mean. Sure, you do what you have to do.'

'Say no more. A man does what he has to, all right, but—' he leaned in towards Richie, ''Tisn't every man would do it.'

Richie ignored the apparent contradiction in the man's logic and settled instead for a kind of reluctant-hero grimace, the kind he imagined Peter Parker might wear.

'I believe herself is doing fine. Hardly a scratch on her,' confided Niall. 'Although they're keeping her in for a few hours' observation, same as yourself.'

Do you hear that, Richie-boy? She was here. Surely

44

he would meet her, after everything that happened. He couldn't assume he was owed anything, mind you.

'Thank God!' he said.

'Where are you taking him?' Niall demanded as the lift pinged its arrival.

'The treatment room in A&E for now,' shrugged the young lad, who either didn't notice or didn't care that he was party to what must surely be a major breach of patient confidentiality. But then he didn't seem like the sharpest knife in the drawer. One wave short of a shipwreck, wasn't that how the song went? Great karaoke number, that one. The finest he was, Freddie. God love the poor fucker.

'I'll pop in later and let you know how she's doing,' promised Niall. 'You saved her life; you've a right to know.'

Richie took his new smile for another spin as the lift doors closed. Niall had a touch of romance in him, it seemed. A love of black-and-white movies, maybe, or a bit of ballroom dancing with Mrs Niall of a Wednesday night.

His mood lifted further when he got back to his room to find a nice plate of corned beef and cabbage waiting for him, with sponge cake for dessert. No matter that it was cold, the white sauce congealing on the side of the plate – everything tasted better when he hadn't made it himself.

* * *

'I've someone here wants to see you,' Niall's voice announced from outside the door.

The tea trolley had come and gone and time was starting to hang heavy again. The television was no good. It was all footage of the crash, interspersed with the front of the fire station and – inexplicably – the untouched town square, and he was afraid to hear what they were saying about him.

'Here he is, the man of the hour.' Niall pushed open the door with a theatrical flourish. There was definitely a touch of the community theatre about him. Richie could see him playing the barman or the landlord in some little annual play. Then, there she was. In a wheelchair of her own, her neck in some kind of brace and the hair still sticking up on top of her head where the dust thickened and raised it up. He wondered if he should tell her but, mercifully, thought better of it.

He didn't know whether to get off the trolley or shake her hand or what, but she was up and out of the chair and over to him – oh-ho, Richie-boy! – with her eyes shining and her arms around him. He went with it, closing his eyes against the unfamiliar sweetness of being on the receiving end of a hug. Soft git that he was.

'I thought we should say thank you together,' she said.

'Thank you for what?' he said, still doing his reluctant-hero bit. Would his cheeks produce some kind of endearing modest flush, he wondered, or would it be hidden behind the broken veins? 'Anyone would have done the same.'

'Not thank each other,' she said, her tone a soft disapproval. 'We should *give* thanks.'

Richie looked at Niall, who was busy lifting up the seat of the empty wheelchair and patting it back down again. 'Excuse me?'

'To Allah. For saving us,' she said and suddenly the shiny eyes looked a bit mental and she was standing far too close. Easy does it, Richie-boy, you've been down this road before, hit the crazy pothole more than once in your life. Humour her, that was the only thing for it.

'We were lucky to be at the front of the bus, all right,' was the best he could manage.

'There is no luck.'

Richie nodded dumbly. He had no words for this kind of situation. In the doorway, Niall had moved onto polishing his ID card, clipping it in and out of the plastic sleeve with all the intensity of his mam when she was waiting on the last bingo number for a full house.

'What is your name?' she asked.

'Richie. Murray. Richie Murray.'

'I'm Alina O'Reilly.'

The mother must be Middle Eastern. The father wouldn't be the first Irishman to like his women exotic.

'I suppose a quick prayer would do no harm,' he said helplessly.

'Give me your hand,' she said. She took his hand between the two of her own and began some kind of sing-song racket. He was startled to hear his name coming out of her mouth among the garbled words, like a spell was being cast, or a curse.

Her eyes were closed and all he could remember was the way she held up her two arms to him like a little child. He closed his own eyes: Lord, let her finish and be gone before the tears came.

She quietened and he took his hand away. He hadn't the wherewithal to muster a public prayer himself, if that was what she expected.

Niall abandoned his fidgeting to step into the breach with a mumbled Hail Mary.

'I'll see you again,' she promised and Richie felt a lift in his spirits at the prettiness of her smile. Just his spirits, thank God. The scrubs they lent him wouldn't have with-stood much, especially not with him going commando.

Shock could do funny things to a person. It was no wonder she was a bit emotional after it all, she was only a young little thing, in her twenties still. An O'Reilly to boot. Sure, there couldn't be any harm in her.

'When my husband comes, I'm sure he will want to thank you too.' She was gone before Richie could process the idea of a husband, much less the prospect of another joint prayer session.

'Christ on a bike,' he muttered, then flushed.

What did that even mean, Richie-boy, other than being a swear mild enough for his old mam to tolerate?

* * *

To pass the time, he braved the television, waiting for the news bulletin with his heart pounding the way it hadn't since the disciplinary hearing at work last year. He didn't catch the start of the news properly – he was too busy looking out for people holding placards blaming him – but once the report switched to the technical aspects of the rescue, he relaxed enough to listen. The fire service was using special equipment, some sort of radar for finding people after earthquakes and the like. It was all very dramatic. The reporter made it sound like something out of a sci-fi film. The same lad was a bit weak for himself, Richie could tell. The way he made sure to use the technical term for everything, as if he hadn't just had it explained to him off camera.

The others weren't out of the bus, that was the gist of it, but all was not lost. Hopes were not yet fading.

Richie wished he had his mobile phone. It must have

been lost or smashed in the crash and he had nothing to do with his hands. He wasn't a great man for texting, his thumbs were too big and he spent as much time deleting as he did typing, but he missed the feeling of having something to keep him company. Would it be too much, he wondered, to phone Sandra, and decided it would.

When one of the nurses passed the door – one of the foreign ones, not the pretty kind with liquidy eyes and shiny hair, but the other kind, with skin the colour of dirty potato jackets – he called out to her. 'Is there a phone around I could use?'

In fairness, she went and got a landline from somewhere, bending down at the side of the bed to plug the jack into the wall. Her face mightn't have been much to look at, but she had a nice little arse on her.

Sully answered on the third or fourth ring. 'You're a bit of a hero now, Richie, is it?'

'Go on out of that, Sully,' Richie said, delighted.

'You're all over the radio.'

'Is that right?'

'Yer man, your aul' buddy that does the morning show,' Sully laughed, allowing for Richie's hatred of that particular broadcaster, 'He was onto the boss-man this morning about you and all.'

'What did he say?'

'Himself was all praise for you,' Sully was confident. 'It was all, "Richie Murray is a solid man, the best of them" and that type of aul' shite.'

Richie relaxed.

'Everything that happened last year was only a misunderstanding, like.'

The pit of Richie's stomach fell for the second time that day.

'What? What did…? How did last year come up?'

'Didn't I just tell you? The boss-man had your back. He explained that yourself and Emmanuel had a bit of argy-bargy, punches thrown, drink taken and whatnot. Things said on both sides and you being laid off for the couple of months while they looked into the racism complaint. A thing of nothing, Rich.'

At the time, he had reassured himself it would pass. That once his twelve months' probation was up, it would be ancient history.

He should have remembered that once thrown, shit stuck. That was the holy all of it.

Sometime last year – he couldn't swear exactly when, but he was wearing his heavy green jacket, so it must have been winter – he was walking down to the Tap, when he passed a man and a woman arguing. As he came near them, the woman walked away. There was something in the way she moved, it had a two-fingers to it.

'You fucking… you fucking bitch!' the man called after her.

She only smiled and shook her head. 'You are ridiculous,' she said, barely loud enough for the man to hear.

At the time, Richie thought the man came off worst, the woman was so clearly in control of it all. But then, a couple of weeks later, he passed her in the street and, without even really recognising her, his brain told him, *There's the fucking bitch*. So who was the loser there, when it came right down to it?

With effort, he dragged himself back to Sully's voice.

'But you're all right and everything, like?' Sully asked.

'Grand. I'm grand. A bit shook is all.'

'Do you want me to tell your mam?'

'No. It would only frighten her. I'll go over and see her later on.'

It was the habit of a lifetime, keeping things from his mam. He went to great lengths to hide his suspension from work, even though she was starting to get confused by then and didn't leave the house much. She was still sharp enough that he had to watch the little details. Make sure she wasn't left on her own with any of the neighbours. A thing like that, it had made its way around Kilbrone faster than any vomiting bug. He told everyone he wasn't allowed to talk about it, but Sully let slip one or two careful details. A matter of honour. Self-defence, nearly. His mam wouldn't see it like that though. So it was two long months of getting up in the morning as if he was going to work and driving up to the restless anonymity of the city. Two months of coming home and making up stories about what happened that day and who he saw. When the hearing was all over and he went back to work, he had to guard against relief loosening his tongue. But since she moved to the nursing home, she just sat all day and watched whatever was put in front of her, her beloved daytime talk-radio gone and forgotten.

She was a hard woman to please, that much was sure and certain. She used to get this look – 'the face', he always called it in his mind: Mam's making the face, don't let her make the face. Do anything to avoid the face. Her lips pulling slowly sideways, taking her whole face over with them. Words were never kind from that sideways mouth.

She was placid most of the time now. There was little need for censure in the beige world she inhabited. The odd time she got excited, her opinions were those from long ago, suddenly remembered, and as soon forgotten: their neighbour Margaret, with her clean house and her dirty morals; de Valera; and, of course, his father 'that bastard, God forgive me'. Mostly, her opinions were those of the nurse of the day. Nine times out of ten, when he turned up for his evening visit, she only parroted the last thing she heard.

The staff told him she could still have good days, there was no way of knowing how much she took in or remembered, even if it came out all skew-ways.

Jesus, Richie-boy, it would finish her if he was blamed for making the crash worse.

It would finish him.

Hero, his hole. If the boss was after telling the whole world that he was suspended on racism charges last year, he'd be Richie the racist evermore, no matter that Alina was as near as dammit to black. Racism was a better story than equality to those radio bastards. He could imagine Pitch Flynn sidling up to him in the pub, slapping down a pint with a wink of conspiracy like they were right-thinking men together. And Fran the barman, wasn't he some kind of Indian or Mexican or something? Not Fran himself, like, he was born here all right, but not too long ago either. His father or mother, maybe. Holy fuck, Richie-boy, he wouldn't even be able to go down the Tap to while away the time of an evening.

When the matron came with his discharge letter, he was lying there, trying to think and not think about Sully's words at the same time.

'RTE want to interview you before you go,' she said. 'What do you say? Did you ever think you'd see the day?'

He could just imagine what they wanted to talk about. 'You hardly allow that kind of thing here in the hospital?' he said.

'Don't we have a little interview room and everything? It's all about being accessible, you know, part of our "programme of transparency".' She made little air quotes, beaming at her own reflected modernity. 'Gone are the days of hospitals hiding behind ministers. You deserve a bit of thanks anyway,' she added. 'After the heroic rescue and everything.'

Heroes didn't have those two months in their file, a file that would be dug out and waved around. Those two months were him, not the two minutes this morning. He knew it, and now everyone else might too.

What if his mam had one of her clear-thinking moments and heard them bad-mouthing him on television? What if that was the Richie she took with her when she sank back below the surface of her face, the son who was only ever a source of shame?

Easy now, easy. Think through the odds: how long was it since she had a clear day? Since she knew him after being prompted? Four months or more.

Don't go borrowing trouble, that was another of her staples. Hold onto the good parts. He rescued that woman, didn't he? They couldn't take that away from him. Don't forget that the investigation found him innocent of a racist attack – guilty of throwing a punch all right, but he never argued the toss on that one – and reinstated him in his old job. The file would have to say that as well, surely be to God?

Sometimes a flicker of light was just a flicker of light, Richie-boy. It didn't always have to be dragging a train behind it.

ALINA

Alina looked at the meal the kitchen lady had put down in front of her. She tried to be friendly, to ask her name, this woman with the skin like hers. Skin like golden syrup, Seán called it, when they first met.

The woman heard her, her eyes flickered over for a moment, but she didn't answer. Not rudeness, Alina guessed, but self-consciousness about her accent, her choice of words. Her mother sometimes pretended that same deafness.

She poked at the items on the plate, causing the chicken to slip in its own grease. What she would give for some mujadara, with its sweet crunch of onion, or even kibbeh, despite her recent distaste for red meat. She sighed and picked up her knife and fork.

'Always cut up what you haven't eaten,' Margo never tired of saying. 'That way, the bastards can't reuse it.'

Alina would nod along, unsure why the waste of perfectly good food was something to be desired, but anxious not to annoy Margo, who had a habit of turning on people and who was, in any case, her only real work friend. The others were polite, they asked about her husband, her holidays, her plans for the weekend, but she could never shake the feeling that they were always nicest to her just at the moment of her leaving.

She liked her job, she reminded herself every day on the way home, and she had plenty of other friends, even if seeing them now required careful effort. Her move to the countryside, their growing families, everyone's life at breakneck speed. Their casual Saturdays in coffee shops, restaurants and bars were all the more prized because they were rare.

'Be nice to people and they will like you,' her mother had advised her before she started school, speaking quietly so that Alina's father would not overhear and worry. Despite being six when they moved to Ireland, she joined the junior infants class, a full year older than the others. Her English was not good enough for senior infants, they said. Juniors would be better. They were right, it was. Right up until secondary school, when her classmates seemed to look around and realise that she looked different. After eight years of history, alliances made and broken and remade, she found herself, at thirteen, subject to stares. Her fragrant lunch box suddenly an object of sniggers. It made little difference that she, too, mourned Diana, the People's Princess. That she listened to Mary Robinson calling on mná na hÉireann and felt a pull of pride, of possibility.

'It's a difficult age,' her father soothed her mother when she worried about Alina's sudden moodiness. 'Teenagers take time to get used to one another. I am sure there is no malice.'

To Alina he repeated the words of Khalil Gibran, 'To belittle you have to be little. Be bigger, that is who we are.'

He had known such delight as a young student in the West to discover his beloved Gibran held in such esteem, his works quoted and studied by others. A

Lebanese poet with words for the world! How alive with possibility everything must be! His habit of peppering his speech with favourite quotes dated from that day, as did his sense that he belonged there, in that world far from home.

'Gibran!' her mother said, out of her father's earshot. 'A man who lived in America, where everything must be printed on T-shirts.'

When she was older, she came to understand that Gibran had left his homeland as a child. That in his displacement, her father saw the seeds of his success and drew strength from it. All she knew then was that once his mind was made up, her father was softened steel. His fondness for the south coast of Ireland was unshakeable after a two-year stint there as a young doctor. It was a place to find the warmth lacking in London, he said. A place with first-hand knowledge of the sadness of leaving, coupled with a charming arrogance that applauded the good sense of foreigners choosing to settle there.

'They know, as we do, what it means to leave family behind for family's sake,' he said, on the night he told them that with Lebanon entering a new peace, it was time for them to find a better life. He believed that the presence of Irish peacekeeping troops in Lebanon had forged a bond between the two nations and, for him, perhaps it did. Perhaps nobody looked at him with the hateful eyes of a teenager whose father, brother, uncle, was fighting the battles of a stranger.

She was startled out of her thoughts by the appearance of a nurse, catlike on rubber shoes.

'Just taking your blood pressure,' the nurse told her. She pulled the door closed when she was finished, telling Alina to get some rest. Alina nodded obediently and lay down, then sat up almost immediately when the tea trolley arrived. They told her that her dizziness was from a possible blow to the head in the crash, but she knew it was from wanting to do the right thing.

Seán came in when the tea was taken away and she was once again lying down with her eyes closed and her mind bursting open.

'Alina. Sweetheart. My phone was turned off while I was in class. But when I saw it on the news, I dropped everything and ran.' He held her hands in his, kissing first one and then the other. 'Are you all right?'

'My clavicle is broken,' she gestured to the collar around her neck. 'My head hurts, but there's no sign of concussion.'

'Thank God,' Seán said, attempting to gather her into his arms.

She let him hold her, breathing in through her mouth and out through her nose, willing the pain down to a manageable size.

'How did you get out?'

She told him the story, explained about Richie. 'He's okay too. They took me to see him earlier, to give thanks.'

'To say thanks,' Seán corrected her automatically.

She let it pass. 'Is everyone else safe now?'

'Not yet. They evacuated the area and then did some radar survey to see if they could be sure where to dig, I think.'

'Those poor people, still in there. Jesus,' he hugged her again. 'You were so lucky.'

He saw no contradiction in his words. It was the way of Irish people, she noticed it often. Their faith was superstitious, about avoiding, not doing. Their god was an everyday token, often in their mouths. He did not live in their secret souls, guiding their actions, but out in the world, in the things the neighbours could see and talk about. It made her smile, this thing they did. It was charming, an extra piece of being Irish. Until you noticed what it took away.

Seán draped his coat over the back of the chair and turned the TV on before coming to sit beside her, his long legs stretching almost to the end of the bed. He stroked her hand and waited for the next news bulletin, careful to keep his boots from touching the quilt. She closed her eyes to rest.

Remembering instead the day she first put on the hijab. The memory that she held onto, a talisman from another life. She asked for her mother's help and saw the pride in her eyes as she took her into her own room, that space of adults, and talked to her of modesty.

Her father did not approve. 'People will think you are a poor refugee,' he said. It was his harshest criticism. 'They will think you come from the direct provision centre.' Alina looked at him, her gentle father, so ready to lock the gates behind them, then stepped carefully past him out the front door.

With the stares came a feeling of power. She heard – duller now – the voices of her classmates giggling in the rows behind her. Let them keep the silliness of girls, she thought. She alone knew the secrets and mysteries of being a woman.

The excitement wore off quickly and she was an oddity only at sporting events and the visits of other schools. 'Did you ever kill anyone?' those new eyes would demand, raised on television stories of child soldiers. Her classmates rolled their eyes and told them to get a grip. That she grew up in the same city they did.

She began to feel pity for those other girls, their skirts rising shorter and shorter to be noticed. She could have told them – as her mother told her – that boys are quick to discover that there is little more to find out. With the barrier of clothing already half-lifted, where could a girl go but onto her back?

She wore what she should wear, her own uniform of hijab and jeans. With clothing came mystery, that was the truth they did not understand. But at university, her own understanding grew shaky. When she met Seán, for the first time she began to worry that what she protected under her clothes might not be worth the journey. What if his excitement came solely from the idea of unwrapping her like his Christmas present? What if the excitement lasted just once and then left, leaving behind the mothball smell of disappointment?

It was gradual, the change her fear brought. By the time she met his mother, she wore the hijab only for prayer, telling herself it was sufficient. When the ring came, she folded her scarves into a drawer, protected by the solidity of her finger. Her father said nothing, only laid his hand on her hair and nodded. When her mother cried, Alina told her that she was crying only for what was on the outside. That the happiness of her heart needed no tears.

'You should believe what I do,' Alina said, firmly. 'That Allah can see the modesty of my soul.'

A modesty that did not last until her wedding night. But he loved her so much, her Seán, and she felt guilty for the discomfort of his longing. She listened to the hitch of his breath and told herself that her love was true.

Mothers did not know everything. That, too, was true.

Seán stroked the inside of her wrist, his eyes glued to the screen on the wall, where, it seemed, those trapped were about to be named. She watched their hands move together on the blanket, her wedding ring bright against the beigeness of everything around it.

Time, the years alone, taught her to let her silence breathe, to wait for a path to become clear. This hospital room was caught between two moments, a quiet space before everything could be known. This time, this silence, was a gift she must not squander.

PART TWO – IN

FROM THE RIGHT ANGLE

If this were a film, the camera would pan silently across the empty schoolyard, resting for a moment on the lunch box dropped and forgotten by the emergency-exit door, tinfoil-wrapped sandwiches visible through the clear plastic of the lid, jaunty juice-box unaware of its abandonment.

Slowly, slowly, the camera would come to rest on the lone woman inside the cordon, the end of her long plait swinging, buffeted by the shouts of the police to get her out of there.

But it is no movie.

On Twitter, the volume rises to a roar as she skip-walks across and ducks under the barrier. A two-fingers to the world, some call it. And isn't it admirable, all the same, how fearless she is? Someone whose sense of social justice outstrips their sense of timing posts solemn commentary on the greater tragedy she represents.

Meanwhile, the lost lunch box becomes the symbol of the crisis. Images of lidless Tupperware are added to profile pictures and messages of support. Well-meaning and useless.

#corkbuscrash #pray

Any two things can be edited to belong together.

LUCY

Lucy woke up coughing, with a burn in her chest that was hard to identify. Was she smoking last night? It was a late night, that much was clear. Her head was pounding and she seemed to have more bones than she had the previous day, each one aching. She tried to roll over in the bed, but her leg caught on something hard.

When she opened her eyes, there was nothing there and she closed them again in fright. Panic, thick and choking, finally caught up. The bus. She was on the early bus. Some kind of crash, a drunk driver or a tyre blowout, spinning them onto their sides and back again. She must have hit her head when they fell. But why would they fall?

Stay calm, she told herself. This was Ireland, and even if she no longer lived in city civilisation, nor was this some chicken bus out in the back arse of Ecuador or somewhere. She was probably only out for a few seconds. If it was longer than that, so much the better. Help would be that bit closer.

She opened her eyes again and waited, counting as she breathed slowly in and out, all she could remember from a couple of terms of yoga classes back when she was seeing Rainfall. Eoin, really. Jesus, to think it seemed attractive that he had renounced the name his parents gave him.

Focus, Lucy!

The bus appeared around her, spooky as an old Polaroid, everything in shades of ghostly green from the low light thrown by the emergency-exit signs. They were tilted at an angle, her shoulder hard against the metal of the window frame. The seat in front of her had buckled inwards, trapping her ankle in the bend. A couple of experimental wiggles confirmed that she wasn't going anywhere. Hikers in the Amazon or wherever might chew off their own limbs, but that wasn't something quite-nice girls from West Cork were brought up to do. She would give herself sepsis and die, no doubt, and her mother would perish of shame just so she could follow Lucy to hell and spend all eternity tutting her disappointment. Satan would have it put up to him to find a worse torment.

In front of her, she could make out the dark shape of someone slumped in their seat. The boy. The teenager that got on the bus at the same stop as her. At the time, she thought he might try to sit in beside her, but instead he had swung into the seat just in front.

'Excuse me?' Her voice came out small and she cleared her throat and tried again. She tried to cough but couldn't draw a full breath, the burn in her lungs as bright as a New Year's Eve sparkler. 'Hello?'

He didn't move. He mightn't have heard her. He still had his headphones in, although she couldn't hear any music. What was he listening to? He wore the teenage uniform of skinny jeans and hoodie. Something indie, she would bet. Not rap anyway, she couldn't hear any telltale bass thump.

She was so cold, it hurt her skin to move, a cheese grater stroking under the thin layers of her clothes, catching in the creases of knees and elbows. Why was it the survival instinct said to hold still in order to stay warm, even though the opposite was true? Conservation of energy, prolonging life, of course. Was that something she should wish for or not? Silly to panic, to send her heart rate into overdrive when her body had suffered God knew what damage already. Obviously, they – whoever they were – would get her out, there was no other option. People like her didn't die in situations like this.

Had it been long enough for someone to have contacted her mother? If not, she might not even have heard about it. She rarely listened to the radio, preferring the television in the background while she sat at her dressing table and put on her outside face. Lucy loved to sit on the bed and watch the tired lady in the nightgown turn into her mother.

'You look lovely, Mam,' she would say and her mother would hug her close if she wasn't too tired and show Lucy how to hold a tissue under her eyelashes to apply the coats of mascara.

Her eyes prickled, then settled. Everything was too dry for tears.

She used to sit in her mother's bedroom before school, watching the parade of teenage mothers, abusive boyfriends, addict parents, that graced the sofas of the chat shows that were her mother's obsession. The people changed, there was a different story every day. The sofas, though, were always shades of red, as if blood itself held the whole thing together. It was a revelation. Irish television chat show sets had neutral tones. No fear the emotions expressed might get out of hand on a brown or navy sofa.

How much time had passed? She should have kept the stupid watch Kieran gave her, instead of leaving it beside the bed in the hope that it would be reason enough for him to contact her. A reluctant meeting – at his suggestion – wouldn't raise his suspicions. She pushed the thought away. She had the same sense of vague fear she felt each time she lifted the lid of a public toilet, holding her breath before it, afraid of what she might see there. A syringe. A rat. A foetus. In reality, all she ever found was other people's shit.

If she knew what time it was, she could tell where in her morning beauty routine her mother might be. Would she pause in the act of smoothing on her base coat to answer the phone ringing in the hall?

She would look back on this and laugh, she told herself firmly, in the hopes she might believe it. She would feel foolish when she saw how very far from real danger she was. They might want to interview her for the six o'clock news. Would she do it? Not the news, no. A chat show, maybe. Herself in a bright dress, defiant in the face of adversity (and brown sofas). An emerald green shift, say, or deep purple. Something that made her look strong but fragile. Not blue. Too capable. Too many associations with politicians and newsreaders and women who had their shit together and needed no one.

Lost in outfit planning, she became slowly aware of noise far above her head. Machinery noise. If she closed her eyes, it was summer afternoons at her aunt's house in the middle of nowhere, denim shorts and vests in the days before bras, hearing cars turn the corner at the crossroads a clear mile from the house. How clean everything seemed, how logical. A car noise meant a car was coming.

Her mother presented her with a car when she got her

Leaving Cert results and they knew she would be going to university after all. Her friends were speechless with jealousy. They saw only the car, not the conditions it was wrapped in.

'You'll be able to commute,' her mother said. She gestured at the multicoloured study plans that still papered Lucy's desk. 'God knows, you're organised enough.'

She was, too. She already had a neat list of things to buy to furnish her new room, each item printed neatly in one of three columns: 'Personal', 'Communal', 'Optional'.

'I'd be lost without you, you know that,' her mother said and leaned in for a tight hug.

This machinery, whatever it was, stopped and started. Should she shout? They would never hear her. She felt around her for something she might throw but nothing shook loose.

When she was interviewed, the host would be unsympathetic, she was suddenly certain. People were funny about prettiness, they took it personally. For years she told herself it was the childishness of teenagers, of college students. But the offices of Lucy's life were staffed by unhappy women whose day was lifted by the inflicting of small pains. Fat clerks lost her applications and misfiled her claims. Their eyes, when they looked her up and down, showed no remorse. She already had enough going for her, they seemed to say.

'I don't have all day to wait so make it quick!' her friend Caroline told her when she went to renew her driver's licence, a luxury she kept as proof of her adulthood despite having sold the car. 'Here, undo another button and make sure you lean down on the counter when you're filling out the form.' Caroline was so sure it would work. With her ordinary face, no doubt it would have.

For a female interviewer, she could play up the strong woman line. 'I knew that as long as I could picture my life after I got out that I was in no danger of dying,' she could say. 'To be honest, I was wondering in my head what I might wear if I was interviewed on television.' And they would laugh together, co-conspirators in the everyday efforts of women.

For a man, she could show a bit more fragility. 'There was so much I knew I still wanted to do.' Her eyes wide and her hands palm-up to show openness and vulnerability, the way Oprah did when she talked – again – about her weight loss journey.

If she didn't make it out... a fantasy too irresistible to ignore.

She could see the camera crew at her mother's house. Her mother letting them in, standing in the doorway as they panned around the room of Lucy's girlhood, the dust generously ascribed to sentimentality rather than laziness. 'I want to keep everything just exactly as it is,' Pat would say in her most sincere voice. A few months later, she would change her mind and decide to turn the room into something else, telling herself that Lucy would want her to move on. The reverse was true, Lucy should tell her. Keep my room as a shrine, thank you very much.

During the clear-out, her mother would find things she had no business finding. The small tin of tobacco and rolling papers. The postgrad course catalogue with telltale pages folded down. The letters from past boyfriends – weirdos mostly, who else wrote letters any more, for the love of God, and more fool her for keeping them – listing the things they loved about her, which, of course, were really about themselves. Pat would sell the letters to the cheap-paper magazines. Lucy as just another pretty girl with poor judgement. Another sad anecdote to be skimmed while waiting for the hair dye to take. Her mother would stack them neatly under the coffee table, intent on making a scrapbook, a goal forgotten during the winter-sun break in the Canaries, paid for with her only daughter's dignity.

There were no diaries. Not since the time her mother found one. She read it aloud, following Lucy from room to room until it was done. Then she slapped her with the flat of her hairbrush and didn't speak a single word for six days, until she needed someone to help her with a French manicure on her toes for a night out. No diaries. That slap, it turned out, a small and prescient mercy.

There were emails, that was true. Would her mother guess her password and read what she had written? The final indignity, small-scale publication of her mortifying sentiments, her slang and typos? There was something, wasn't there, that allowed people to organise and direct their information after their death? An app of some kind. That was one for the to-do list. Once they got her out.

How much time had passed? It was first light when she got on the bus. Was that an hour ago, or two, or ten?

'Me and you together, pet. Me and you,' her mother used to say, squeezing her so tight their giggles came out in fart-sharp bursts.

This time, the dust and dryness didn't stop the tears.

* * *

'I'm Lucy,' the voice said, over and over. 'I'm Lucy. There's been an accident. Someone will be here soon to help us.'

It reminded him of something and Paul struggled to

69

remember what that might be. That old TV show, *Lost*. The pre-recorded message that played in case anybody came.

He coughed and the voice stopped. A sudden break in regularly scheduled programming.

'Don't try to move, you're all tangled up,' the voice said. 'Wait.'

He felt rather than saw her hand pulling the earbuds out of his ears.

'There. Can you hear me? I'm Lucy. There's been—'

'Paul,' he said. The effort made him pant.

'Hi, Paul. You must like music. Anytime I see you on the bus you have headphones on.'

He thought a smile but couldn't make it happen. She noticed him.

She was right, he wanted to tell her, he did always wear headphones. His mother didn't like him wearing his hood up, so headphones were the next best thing. Since Gemma, he turned the sound up louder, trying to frighten away the memory of it.

'Do your family know where you are?' Lucy asked.

His eyes closed without his say-so, but it didn't seem worth the effort to argue the point with them.

His mother knew he had taken the early bus the last couple of weeks. Ever since he and Gemma had finally done *it* and he couldn't look at her any more. The sight of her waiting at the bus stop or sitting a few seats in front of him made him dizzier than Friday nights drinking WKD. He wasn't even sure how it had happened, how sex had gone from a sweaty blurry fantasy in his own bed and shower (and sometimes in the living room late at night on his own) to mortifying reality with a girl he fancied too much to be practising on. Everyone pretended previous experience, he told himself. He'd seen pornos at Dec's parties, yeah? The lying was expected, it just had to sound a bit real. He made up a story about a girl at camp and a habit of scratching her face in time to his thrusts.

'If she's scratching while you're banging her, mate, you're doing it wrong,' Dec jeered. Better to be bad at it than not in the game at all.

Sex, he called it in the privacy of his own head. The word fuck reminded him of rappers and he had enough people in his head already, between the porn cast and Dec and Gemma herself, without Drake or Kanye in there too.

He had wanted Gemma, he really had, not just to be done with his embarrassing virginity. It hadn't even been a thing until the summer before Transition Year, when the posturing about who had done what to whom and in what position was all anyone wanted to talk about. He had little to add, beyond shifting in the cinema, a bit of tit-rubbing and frantic dry-riding in the laneway outside afterwards. He wanted to be a real person, not just all talk.

'Pass Maths,' he said, but the words didn't come out properly.

'What's that?' Lucy leaned in closer. 'You're looking for your hat, is it?'

Bastards told him he had to drop down to lower-level maths for the Leaving. The honours class was, they said, some way beyond his ability. He didn't need to tell his father to know what he would say. The thought of it gave him a sudden savage need to do something to mark the event, to be a man of action. Once you took away the talk, it turned out to be surprisingly easy to get into Gemma's pants. To get her out of them.

The constant music blocked out the memory of his

own stupid voice afterwards. Telling her he was sorry, he meant to pull out, really. She kept her back to him and he could see the scatter of pimples on her arse. It made him feel close to her to know that about her.

He winced.

'Try not to move around so much,' Lucy said.

She must be watching him. Wouldn't Dec just love that? An older woman, no less.

In his head, when he reran it, things went differently; he was manly, prepared, sliding smoothly into coupledom. His mother's voice in his head rather than his father's. In reality, he sat on the bus, staring miserably at her back, his own scumminess exponentially increased by Dec beside him, whistling and making V-gestures behind her back, expecting him to laugh along. It gave every morning the feeling of a wet Tuesday morning with double maths. He didn't mind Mondays. That was the kind of thing he could have told Gemma, if he wasn't such a dick. Instead, he started getting the early bus, hating himself for telling Dec that Gemma was pestering him to ask her out.

He wanted to die of shame, seeing the crack of her backside disappearing into her jeans, the set of her small shoulders against him as she struggled into her top, anger or shame making her fingers clumsy. He hadn't even bothered to take off her bra. The image was fuck-all use to him when he half-heartedly had a go at himself in the shower; his langer practically crawled back up inside him with humiliation.

'Bet you're sorry you were in such a rush to get to school today,' Lucy said.

Damn right.

* * *

72

Lucy wished Paul would wake up again. Although, asleep, his breathing deepened to almost normal. She could count his breaths now that the machinery noises above her had stopped.

'I just had to keep talking,' she told her imaginary interviewer. 'It sounds silly, I know, but when Paul was asleep, even the sound of my own voice was comforting.' She could add a brave smile here as well.

As a child, when her mother went out at night, she used to sing to herself. When she ran out of songs or tired of those she knew, she moved on to reciting the alphabet or counting up as high as she could go. The beauty of numbers was that they kept on going. Even a little kid could add one. She was exhausted in school the following day, going around with the hollow eyes of the food-bank kids. It gave her an air of mystery. That and never inviting anyone home.

Then her mother bought her the clock radio and it was a whole new world.

To the sound of the late-night oldies, she watched the digital display for her numbers, the magic ones – 22.22 first, then 23.32 and 23.45. At first, they were signs that her mother would be home soon on the last bus. Then they were proof that she was getting bigger, she was able to stay awake longer. Then they took on another kind of power: if she saw them all, without missing a single one, then the following day would bring good news. She had to catch the numbers unawares though. Watching the clock was against the rules, it cancelled out the spell.

Her love of numbers didn't fade. Looking out bus windows on normal journeys, it was the numbers going past that she watched, enjoying their certainty. The opposite was also true, travelling backwards through the numbers on a street made her anxious, especially when she was between boyfriends. She worried that the street would run out of numbers, that they would reach Number 1 with still more buildings ahead of them. The idea of those poor people living their lives in the negative made her want to weep.

'There was a kid in my class once,' she told Paul in the darkness, 'from South Africa. He seemed so exotic to us. We had no idea how he came to be in a little country school.'

She used to imagine he had been on his way somewhere else and instead became trapped in Ireland, his feet freezing to the Irish surface water like the poor cursed swan-children in the Children of Lir story. His exoticism, though, bleached a little further with every shower of rain, and then a little further still.

'He told us one day in religion class that a tribe in his country believed that every person got seven lives to live, each one better than the last because each time you got to repair the mistakes you had made the last time...'

She remembered it clearly, his use of that un-childlike word, 'repair'. As if children had any business taking apart and mending their own lives.

'Anyway, you kept going until your seventh life when you had fixed all your mistakes and then you lived forever in the perfect life that you created for yourself.'

A comforting idea, those seven lives. Sealing the application for her second postgrad, she had wondered if that was what she was trying to do, relive her college experience over and again. Her psychology degree, so glamorous and uplifting for the first two years, revealed itself in her final year to be a thing of nothing, its uselessness not improved by its kind intentions. 'The preying fingers of hope hooking into the malformed of spirit,' her then-boyfriend – himself an art-college dropout – told her, shaking his head at her naïveté. 'Codology, the lot of it.' His advice sent her to the departmental office with tears and an incomplete thesis and the prospect of repeating the year. He cost her a year of her life, to say nothing of the price of the particular shame he made her feel. The things he suggested she do to atone for the sheer *bourgeois* of her thinking.

If the seven-lives theory was true, no doubt she would be the one who left the biggest mistake until her last life and then had to live with it for always. She shook her head, jarring her ankle. Her mother had no time for self-pity. Even the merest hint of it met her sharp words. 'To the homeless, Lucy, every meal is a picnic.'

The chance to live life over might be wonderful, yet how tiring the prospect of her mother in every lifetime.

* * *

Thirty-seven of the ninety-nine bottles were left on Lucy's wall when Paul next woke. His voice seemed stronger, she told herself, although every sentence was followed by a raspy cough that Lucy found hard to listen to. She worked a summer in an old folks' home, where there had been much talk of the final rattle. This wasn't that. It couldn't be.

It was the creepiest thing in the world to be caught in the dark by something she couldn't see. Every now and then she tried to move her leg, but the fierce barks of pain given out by her ankle convinced her to abandon her efforts. She could move it, that was good. And the pain meant she wasn't paralysed. Also good.

Her back ached and she shifted slightly against the seat.

'Looks like we're sitting tight another while, Paul,' she said, but he was gone again. Kieran used to do that, doze off in the middle of a conversation or while they were watching TV. She didn't mind, it was better than having him stare at her while she tried to concentrate on the storyline.

'I prefer to watch your face,' he said, when she asked crossly how he could follow anything at all. God help her, she found it attractive at the start. Beginnings were always the same, she walked in the rain with a smile, danced in queues.

'You're a pure fool,' her mother told her more than once. 'Any man could take you and you'd let him.'

She didn't lick that off the stones, Mam, now did she?

She would do that newspaper interview, a whole series of them, perhaps. That would show her mother. It would show them all. Her so-called girlfriends, sitting in their couple-y judgement, telling her she needed direction in her life. The old classmates who never managed to make it out of the hole of Kilbrone but instead slung out interchangeable babies and sat at home in their tracksuits, night after night, with a baby on one nipple and a thickening ex-rugby-player husband demanding the other. With her face on the covers of magazines, who would be laughing then?

She reached out and stroked Paul's hair. It was wet and matted, so she shifted to the dry side.

'I always wanted a younger brother,' she imagined saying. 'My mother told me that she risked her figure once having me and who would be daft enough to chance it a second time.' In the darkness, she tried on several smiles, eventually settling for wry. Or what felt like wry. It was hard to tell without a mirror.

James had a son doing his Leaving Cert next year. He didn't talk about him much. A guilt gag, she had seen it before. Once he started paying the rent on her little flat, he could choose the conversations he didn't want to have.

'My family is none of your business,' he told her.

It was hardly a crime to ask how his son was doing. It wasn't like she ever mentioned his wife, although sometimes, when he came home with a little gift for her, she wondered if there was an identical package tucked away in the boot of his car. In a different colour maybe. James was blessed with neither conscience nor imagination.

It was hypocritical to snigger at those particular shortcomings when so many of her own decisions were driven by the desire to make herself into the very opposite of his wife.

'She spends four hours in the hairdresser's every two weeks and goes on about it like it's a job,' James told her the night they met. In Lucy's experience, once the gloves came off, the clothes were not long behind them.

'How boring!' Lucy laughed, almost innocent. 'I cut my own hair.'

'It's so sexy that you don't care what you look like,' he said, in the cubicle of the ladies' toilets, pulling the neckline of her T-shirt roughly enough to ruin it. She pretended insouciance, turning the T-shirt back to front and leaving him panting after her.

She got her hair cut every six weeks, making sure he noticed when it got a little bit shaggy. Tina in the hairdresser's was a friend and gave her the bag of hair clippings without asking any questions. That Tuesday evening she would wait in the bathroom for his key in the door, the hair carefully scattered into the sink and around the tops of her shoulders. Bare skin peeping out the top of her towel, the scissors in her hand.

'I needed a trim,' she would say, arching her neck this way and that as if making sure the sides were even. Men only ever saw what was directly in front of them.

Two weeks ago, in a burst of resolve, she gave up the lease on her flat and moved back to her mother's house. Her independence only lasted as far as packing boxes, not heaving them down four flights of stairs. She phoned Kieran to help her to move and, sure enough, he was there nearly as soon as she hung up the phone. Since then it had been two weeks of casual coffees and other pretend-friend behaviour without any sign of interest from him. He had hardly moved on and, besides, there was no mention of anyone else. Incredible as it seemed, he was exercising restraint. Fucking typical of him to do the exact opposite of what she needed. Last night, she gave in and sought him out. He was unrecognisable from the back, his long hair all shorn away, and she had a moment's hesitation.

'You look like an egg with ears,' she told him, with three-vodka cruelty, but she slept with him anyway, rubbing her hands over the fascination of his skull. She fell asleep afterwards, a dull and heavy sleep, before waking in the hot smother of his arms and creeping out to catch the early bus home.

A small cough broke her train of thought. 'Paul?' Her voice cracked. 'Paul? Can you hear me?'

'I don't think he can hear you,' a voice said from behind her.

Lucy screamed and nearly jumped herself free, cursing as her ankle roared stars across her eyes.

'Sorry,' she said when the pain subsided. 'You gave me a fright. I didn't know anyone else was... awake.'

'I'm sorry.'

'No, it's okay. It's great. Are you all right? Can you move?'

'My seat belt is stuck.'

Jesus, wonderful. Only about ten people in the whole country ever used the damn things on public buses and this girl had to be one of them.

She craned around to look over her shoulder. The girl was on the opposite side, at a lopsided angle, like a home-made Christmas decoration. Around her, metal twisted into long-armed shapes that might, in a different setting, be called modern art. Lucy opened her mouth to share her observation but closed it again. The artistic elements of their situation wouldn't be something most people would appreciate.

'I'm Lucy,' she said, instead.

'My name is Orla.'

Lucy had to concentrate to understand the girl, her voice was low and hoarse with a slight lisp, her s's bouncing off the side of her tongue and sliding out the sides of her mouth, saliva pooling.

'Where were you going on the bus?' Lucy asked. The sound of voices – even those engaged in inane small talk – was better than nothing.

'I'm going to meet Janet, my job coach.'

Not any more she wasn't. 'Your what?'

'My job coach, she helps people to find jobs when they might have a hard time finding them themselves. She'll talk to me about the kinds of things I like doing and see if there's a job somewhere that has those things in it and then she'll ask them if it would be okay for me to work there.'

'Cool. Where did you work before?'

Anyone would think they were just two random people, sitting next to each other at the hairdresser's or queueing for a flight.

'I did some practising in Janet's office in Lota,' Orla said. 'It was fun.'

'Cool,' Lucy said again. She couldn't imagine there was much to enjoy about spending day after day in a special school. As a child, her mother threatened her with the place if she misbehaved or broke something or ran downstairs too loudly. 'I'll give you to Lota if you don't behave yourself and you'll have to spend your days there with the feeble-minded.' Once, she drove her as far as the gate of the place and stopped the car. She got out and opened Lucy's door. 'In you go, if they'll have you.' Lucy had cried herself sick, vomiting her breakfast onto the grass verge at the side of the road.

'I like organising things,' Orla was still talking. 'I'm good at it. Any office would be lucky to have me, Janet says.'

'I'm sure they would.'

'My sister said any office would be lucky to have me because they won't have to pay me, but I think she was just joking. She says things sometimes that might sound mean but really they're just jokes. My parents used to tell her not to, but then they decided it was okay for her to tease me as long as I know she doesn't really mean it. She winks at me and that's how I know she doesn't think it really.'

'Do you ever get to tease her back?'

'Her hair stands up on her head when she wakes up,' Orla's voice was full of giggles. 'She has to have a shower every morning before anyone sees her and finds out she's a hedgehog.'

Lucy forced a laugh.

Had anyone's life ever been as bizarre as hers? Surely this situation was well beyond the usual kind of strange, the my-first-cousin-took-your-sister-to-the-debs-how-mad-is-that benchmark of Irish stories. This right here was the kind of weird that won prizes.

'I have to be careful who I tease her to. Mam says it's not nice to tease someone in front of anybody who isn't in our family. They might think we meant it. You don't think I meant it, do you?'

Lucy shook her head. 'You were very clear that you were only joking.'

In the silence, she heard the sound of dripping water. Was it getting faster or was that just her imagination? She searched around for words to soak up the fear.

'What do you mean they won't have to pay you? Surely if you're working there they have to pay you?'

'No. The government will pay me.'

Lucy caught the pride in Orla's voice. 'Goodness me! You will be important to them if the government are paying you!' she said, but overdid the cheer and it fell flat and fake.

Orla said nothing. Had she noticed and decided to let it go? Imagine her pitying Lucy! Christ.

'It's great that you can take the bus by yourself,' Lucy tried again.

'I did my transport training three years ago,' Orla said. 'My parents told me that it was safer to sit on the side opposite the driver,' she added.

Lucy laughed, stopping when it became clear that Orla didn't intend it to be ironic.

'Where are you going?' Orla asked.

'Nowhere.'

'Oh.' Orla's voice was small. 'You can say it's private, if you want to.'

'It's private, then.'

Her mean streak had been having a field day lately. To her mother, she had to pretend a casualness she didn't feel, claiming she enjoyed the impermanence of her work, that she could move on if she chose. It took a toll, all that fakery. She couldn't understand how her mother didn't see through it. As if anyone could legitimately believe there was anything to enjoy in running the same mind-numbing short-term memory experiments for students that she herself had done in her own undergrad. She left it too late, spent too long gathering qualifications, only to be overtaken by the recession. The best she could look forward to was being whored out to other departments whose own postgrads or postdocs had bigger plans than the daily grunt work of academia.

'I'm sorry, Orla,' she said. 'I meant I wasn't going anywhere in particular, just back to my mother's house.'

'I want my mam and dad.' Orla's voice started to wobble.

'Me too,' Lucy said, surprising herself.

Her mother looked out for her, there was no denying it. All the sacrifices she made over the years, working two jobs, giving her daughter everything in the expectation that it might lead to a more comfortable life for the two of them. A cleaner in once a week, a fortnight in the sun every summer, it wasn't much to ask.

'Your hair is very short,' Orla said, *à propos* of nothing. 'I thought you might be a boy until you told me your name was Lucy.'

'I don't like it,' Lucy told her, surprising herself

again. 'It used to be very long. I think I'd like it to be very long again.' She would grow it right back down to her backside, she decided.

'Why did you cut it all off?'

Because Kieran's had been long too, almost the same shade as hers, she used to plait their hair together while they were sitting on her couch. That was before things turned creepy. Before he started walking her to work. Before he arrived at her desk every day with lunch, waiting outside the door to walk her home again. Before he started hiding her phone and house keys.

The day she left him, she cut her hair to the scalp, sending him her long plait in the post in a mad fit.

'Take that for closure!' she slurred in the pub, bashing her vodka glass against Caroline's. She wasn't Lucy's first choice of drinking buddy, but she was the only person in between jobs and up for blowing off the day. She regretted sending it, of course, waking the following day to a mental picture of him sitting on the couch in the evenings, stroking her plait with one hand and himself with the other. How had she forgotten that closure was often only spite?

'I suppose I just wanted a change,' she said.

Orla touched the twisted stem of the bar in front of her, 'It's kind of pretty, don't you think? Like in an art show.'

That was it, Lucy was going straight to hell. With only her prejudices for company. And her mother. She looked back at Orla. 'We should rest for a while. Save our strength,' she said.

Obedient as a doll, Orla's eyes closed. Somewhere overhead, the hum of machinery started again.

TIM

'The Dublin team are on their way with a GPR unit,' Tim told the families. 'It should be up and running within the hour.'

'Will it show them... inside the bus, I mean?'

'I'm afraid that GPR – Mrs Phelan, isn't it? Lucy's mother? – isn't quite the same thing as thermal imaging. That's the one that picks up traces of heat, you'll have seen it on television during avalanches and the like. GPR looks for objects underground, cracks, changes in material, all things that will show us exactly where the bus is and the safest way to get to them.'

'Is it dangerous? Is there radiation?' Paul's mother, Elmarie, asked. Her husband, Jason, looked sharply at her.

'Only tiny amounts,' Tim told her. 'Less than one per cent of your mobile phone.'

Words of false comfort were useless, he knew that. Every parent's wish: that their child would never know fear or pain. When it was his turn, he sat by Aisling's bed and prayed for painlessness. Yet towards those at the funeral who pressed his hand and talked about an end to her suffering, he felt a monstrous rage. Pain, after all, meant life.

The engineers were younger than Tim expected, full of excitement about their equipment and what it could do.

'Applied engineering, man,' one guy smiled. 'This is what it's all about. I'm Russell, your walker, and Ferg here will run the monitor.'

'Quite a crowd you've got out there,' Ferg said, while Russell fitted safety equipment.

The crowd had increased since the last statement. The whole idea of GPR was lapped up – any kind of gadgetry seen on TV fired the public imagination.

'You'll need to clear people back,' Russell said. 'Her antenna needs a clear twenty feet.'

'What we really need is Finder,' Ferg said, busy with cables and wires. 'Real top-of-the-line stuff. Uses microwaves to detect people's heartbeats when they are buried under collapsed buildings. Works through nine metres of anything.' He shook his head in admiration.

Tim imagined a bank of monitors set up along the perimeter, one after another fading and flatlining while the team moved in bursts, flaring like rubber-soled lightning, here and there and useless. On Ferg's screen, Russell walked in careful parallel lines inside the barrier while Leo watched from the side of the site.

'Any subsurface variations, both metallic and non-metallic, will bounce a signal back. Could be a length of pipe or something, the GPR won't differentiate. A fancier one would give you a density reading and show the metals in colour. We've been campaigning for a new one, but, you know, budget cuts.' Ferg's voice was glum.

When the walk-through was complete, Russell and Leo joined them in the meeting room, to the evident disappointment of the media, whose shouted questions went unanswered.

'There's a consistent metallic read about twenty-five feet east of the road and that's our best guess for where the bus ended up. You saw the depth reading change significantly on that side? Road surface alone wouldn't account for that density of a read. The county engineers tell me an underground car park was started as part of a development that was abandoned during the recession. That would explain the bus ending up at that depth.'

'How close can we get?' the Chief asked.

'There's a pocket that seems solid enough on this side of the site. That might be our safest bet.'

'If we used an excavator instead?' Tim asked.

'Lighter but far slower,' Leo replied.

There was no decision to make – the balance of safety and speed was what they were trained for.

'Let's start at twice the safe distance and get as close as we can,' the Chief said.

'I'll keep the system on. A change in the read will tell us if the stability changes. Should give you enough time to pull back,' Ferg said.

If. Should. Might. Could. The in-between words.

Tim updated the information board, arrows connecting every step to the next, as if each action could simply assume the success of that which went before. They were certain, the arrows. Complete in themselves.

The media did the same thing, delivering life in black and white. Was that the reason for Nina's intransigence, her insistence on absolutes? Or was the reverse true, that journalism attracted her because of those qualities she possessed? It was unsolvable, she was already emphatically herself when they met. They were at the same birthday party, each connected by a different friend. She refused to be impressed by a firefighter, she told him, it implied a recklessness that she could neither understand nor applaud. It should have been a one-night stand, except they went for breakfast, a walk, an afternoon movie. Less than twenty-four hours in and he knew she was the one.

* * *

A quick scan of Twitter revealed that the media hashtag #corkbuscrash, trending for the past couple of hours, had been overtaken by #staystrong, into which the public poured their support for the families and those at the scene.

One-liners and easy, distant sympathy. Every second person sharing that 'there are no words'. If that were true, then say nothing. Or say what you needed to say, but privately.

The cranks and conspiracy theorists were there, of course, with their ugly theories and apocalyptic speculation, sidelining those really involved. He read an article once on the politics of grief, drawn in by its promise to guide him on how not to say the wrong thing. In any traumatic event, the person to whom it was happening was in the centre, with those next most involved in a slightly wider circle out, and so on. Getting it right was simple, the article said, you just had to remember to protect and support those in smaller circles than your own. It would have helped more if he hadn't realised halfway through that Nina believed herself alone in the innermost circle. Who knew, maybe he believed it a little himself.

* * *

'This isn't public information,' the Chief warned.

Tim had closed the office door and asked him straight out if there was any truth to the suggestion that planning misconduct caused the accident.

'When that area was being developed for apartment blocks, the initial planning refused to allow the underground car parks. The area was already very built up and so close to the river. A report said to leave it alone, it was needed for drainage.'

'But?'

The Chief shrugged. 'A change of personnel later and the car parks were back in the plans.'

The prospect of another corruption scandal was wearying. Church, state, the guards, even charities, one after the other revealing the rot beneath the power. There would be a formal investigation, of course, a careful report that did nothing to shore up fragile faith in the innate goodness of people.

'What effect did the car parks have on the road?' he asked.

'The engineers' theory is that the far side had to take on all the drainage and, over time, the volume of water eroded the foundations of the road.' The Chief sighed and rubbed his hand over his face. 'Look, we don't know anything for sure yet and, to be frank, it's not our concern. That'll be a job for the investigation afterwards.'

Every firefighter would agree the worst cases were those that were preventable. But it wasn't Tim's business to judge. His job was to run the board, monitor the information, pull together statements for every eventuality, put words between the politics of it and the people. Necessary work, if not exactly what small boys dreamed of.

* * *

Instead of returning to the crisis room, he found himself pushing open the door to the media centre. He couldn't – wouldn't – tell Nina anything, of course, but he needed to know how far the story had gone. Inside it was quiet, as a man spoke to the assembled group. Dressed in a natty suit, with a manicured moustache, he was out of place in the disarray. Poirot, if he had been born in Ireland. Tim recognised him from a workshop he attended once upon a time. He was a psychology professor at the university, a grief and trauma specialist.

Tim moved further into the room, settling his shoulder against the wall, watching the watchers. Doreen, the HSE social worker assigned to the families, came and stood beside him.

'Is it not a bit soon for this?' he asked, nodding towards the front.

'Dr O'Caoimh contacted us, wanting to help. Do you know any other trauma specialists willing to step in at a moment's notice at no charge?' she whispered back.

'At times like this it is natural to look for answers,' Dr O'Caoimh said.

Wrong, Tim thought. Answers didn't become an issue until afterwards. It was adrenaline that powered people through catastrophe. It was hope – the ultimate survival instinct – that dragged them to the finish line. It was only later that the quest for meaning started, the picking apart, the if-onlys that drove people to despair, to a frantic search for meaning, to drink.

'What advice can you give the families to help them through these difficult hours?' asked one of the reporters. As if silence wasn't the only possible refuge during such a wait. Had O'Caoimh said nothing, Tim might have had a bit of respect for him.

'I urge them to take this present moment for itself without worrying where it might take them, without looking too far forward or perhaps giving into the temptation of looking backwards and wishing things were otherwise.'

The last thing people in difficult situations needed was to be advised to battle every human instinct, to be made to feel that their worry was counterproductive, that they were somehow doing it wrong.

Watching Nina's family deal with their grief, Tim had wondered how his own parents would have handled it. If they, too, would have tiptoed around them. But his parents had died years earlier, his connection to home long gone. A fact made more real by the strangeness of his uncle and cousins at the funeral. The loss of his parents gave an odd comfort. Nights he couldn't sleep, he would imagine Aisling in heaven, being spoiled by her grandparents. In his imagination, heaven looked a lot like the local playground.

'One step at a time,' Dr O'Caoimh was continuing. 'That's the key.'

Where did that leave readiness, that bracing of the body and the mind against the worst? Hope needed some small area to flourish.

In the pause between questions, Tim heard the low chant coming from outside, where someone had started the rosary again. No doubt they thought it was a comfort to the families, there would be much mention of community spirit. If he closed his eyes, he would be able to picture their faces. Pity. Gratitude. There-but-for-the-grace-of-God-go-I. The self-serving sympathy for which the lost were supposed to thank the lucky. Community. The clawing hands of strangers. People clutching at him or avoiding him, either too close or too far away. Forever splitting groups of friends into those who could and were, and those who couldn't and therefore weren't.

They had heard them all. The more catastrophic the occasion, the greater the number of such clichés that people rolled out, believing that to say anything was better than saying nothing: 'You were chosen for this because you are strong'; 'God never made a burden that he didn't make the back to bear it'; 'No cross, no crown'. The countless ways in which people swallowed the first and most natural reaction, their relief that it was not them.

Dr O'Caoimh made way for the garda liaison to update on access and security for the vigil planned for that evening. Tim glanced out the window at the darkening sky. With winter well underway, nature itself was working against them.

When the doctor passed him, followed by Nina, something in her face prompted him to turn and leave the room with them.

'The majority of people who have undergone trauma will carry it with them,' Dr O'Caoimh was saying. 'There's a certain theory that traumas – particularly those which severely breach our emotional boundaries – manifest on our external boundaries, literally appearing on our skin.'

They glanced down at Nina's arm, where her hand stopped in mid-scratch. 'Eczema is very common,' she said, pulling her sleeve down over her wrist with a tight smile.

'Excuse me, Doctor,' Tim said. 'Nina, could I have a word?'

'Is it to do with the corruption rumours?' she asked, when the lift door closed and they were alone. 'I was going to come and ask you, but then I got caught listening to that fool.'

He smiled despite himself. 'I thought he might have that effect on you.'

'So, tell me.'

'Tell you what?'

'The planning issue. Is it true that the engineer who greenlit the rezoning was the brother-in-law of the contractor?'

'Where do you get this stuff? You shouldn't believe everything you read on Twitter.'

She shook her head. 'Ben told me. I'm not on any of those sites, you know that.'

He did know. She purged all of her accounts one evening without saying anything. The first he knew of it was Facebook notifying him that his wife no longer existed.

'I don't know anything about the engineers or the planners or any of it,' he told her. 'Hardly our priority today.'

She rolled her eyes. 'Yes, yes, lovely party line, consider yourself unsullied. So, what did you want me for?'

He shrugged. 'It looked like an uncomfortable conversation, I thought you could do with an out.'

'Oh.' A flash of her smile. 'Whose idea was your man?' She jerked her eyes upwards.

'I'm sure some of them will find him helpful.' Loyalty to the team, he supposed. Or something defensive. They used to be on the same side.

'You would have found it helpful, would you? All that bullshit about how grief belongs to society rather than the individual? A burden shared? That would have comforted you when it was us? When it was Aisling?' Her voice broke.

'Jesus, Nina.' He looked at her for a moment. 'Are you okay?' The question was out before he could stop himself. She would hate it, would hate him for asking. 'It's cutting a little close to home.'

'Save your rescuing for the people who need it, why don't you?' She pushed the door to the media centre and re-entered without looking at him.

It never occurred to her that he was asking for help, not offering it. She was always territorial about her grief. She used to stiffen perceptibly when they visited the grave and found someone else's offering, as if their sorrow somehow encroached on hers. While she tidied the grave – often gathering the offending item into a large black bag brought for the purpose – he would bow his head and pray.

On the bad days, it infuriated her. A difference in belief that started out as playfighting when they met first. Before it mattered. Theoretical arguments over a bottle of wine morphing over the years into a more bitter divide.

'You and your bloody God,' she spat at him once, vodka splashing her fingers as she poured.

What she didn't understand – then or now – was

that it was less about the search for comfort than about finding the strength to keep going.

* * *

'You have to hand it to them,' Leo told Tim, 'they have every angle sewn up.'

They watched as a priest moved through the crowd, his soutane parting the people like a staff. The two laypeople helping him passed him bottles of holy water and waxy dead-skin-coloured candles from incongruous sports bags. Tapers followed, passing carefully from hand to hand, the wind already cast out by the mass of bodies. The swell in the number of people suggested that Dr O'Caoimh was accurate in his estimation that the vigil would serve a purpose for the local community.

'What are we doing about the protesters?' Tim asked Leo.

'They're being asked to move back before the families come down.' He grimaced. 'It's the ones claiming Alina O'Reilly was involved I'm worried about. The rest are just the usual conspiracy guff.'

Tim nodded. 'It's being fuelled online as well, crackpot bomb theories and the like.'

Leo swore. 'The situation isn't even under control yet and here we are wasting time on this nonsense.'

'The Chief has asked the Defence Forces to sit in on a press briefing to shut it down.'

'They're sure it wasn't anything... sinister?'

Tim raised an eyebrow and Leo shrugged apologetically. 'What could be more sinister than money?'

People, property, the environment. The safety-management system dealt out its protection in that order. It had always bothered him, that inclusion of 'property' ahead of 'environment' despite the fact that one was clearly replaceable. The same kind of half-arsed thinking that had everyone obsessed with buying houses instead of renting like the rest of the world. Except the English, but where did they learn that madness only from each other?

Well for him, the more pass-remarkable might say, with his feet firmly under Deb's unmortgaged table. With Nina buying him out of their place last year, he was, by Irish standards, luckily debt-free. A unicorn among his peers.

He stayed where he was for a minute or two longer, watching the faint light of the candles growing with the hint of evening. He remembered his own incomprehension as a teenager going with his father to join searches for the lost at sea, thinking that surely something could still be done after sunset. It wasn't the dark ages, after all. But it was easy to judge from the outside, less easy to balance the needs of the many and the few.

Right now, the families of those few stood at the edge of the cordon waiting for the vigil to begin. He might have told Nina he understood the need for it, but seeing them there, bewildered, it seemed no more use than offering a bottle of aftersun to a third-degree burns patient.

NINA

Nina watched the families during the vigil. Sometimes a moment of eye contact was all it took to establish a connection. People might have been chanting anything, such was the power of a solemn crowd. *Hail Mary, full of grace.* The simplicity of the prayer shook her heart up into her throat.

March 13th: Aisling was born. Half past four in the morning. No sunrise was ever more beautiful.

March 15th: they took her home. A blur of worry about car seat straps and heating. Nina herself in the back seat with the baby. The quiet of the living room when they closed the front door and found themselves, all of a sudden, a family of three.

March 19th: heel-prick test. The first evidence that the world could hurt her daughter and all she could do was stand by and let it happen.

March 21st: Tim went back to work, his week's holiday over. She and Aisling figuring out their new world, together.

The counting of days, cataloguing of moments in her memory, absorbed her, drove out the noise of the other vigil. When the crowd began to disperse, she waited where she was, smiling at anyone who looked her way.

'I know you,' the woman said, stopping in front of her. 'Nina Cassidy, isn't it? From the TV?'

The woman was of a certain age, as the French said, and fighting it all the way. Her make-up was poured deep into her eye sockets, her hair frozen in place. Normal people feared the march of time.

'Nina, please.' She held her hand out and the woman shook it.

'Pat Phelan. Patricia, I mean. Patricia Phelan.'

'Lucy's mother,' Nina said and the woman nodded. 'Would you be willing to talk to me for a few minutes?' Nina asked, resisting the urge to tilt her head to one side, to place a sympathetic hand on the woman's arm.

'Would there be a camera?' Patricia asked.

'Not if it makes you uncomfortable,' Nina said.

'No, no, that's fine. I just need a minute to get ready.' She turned away, taking a mirror and mascara out of her bag.

The families were moving back towards the fire station, where they would wait, and then wait some more. Don't hate the limbo, she wanted to tell them. Sometimes it's better than the alternative. Tim walked with them, a little apart. He had gained back the weight he lost, after Aisling. She wanted to run after him, to grab his arm, to ask about his woman. Whether she took away his tiredness. If she made him happy.

He glanced up as if he felt her eyes on him. She held her smile while she turned away, letting it fade from her lips a millimetre at a time in case he was still looking: such things are the pillars of perceived wellness.

You are all surface, Nina, don't pretend to be shocked at yourself. Didn't the three days in the hospital with Aisling prove that you couldn't live anywhere but the surface of the world? Your rusty prayers, the deals you made with a god you didn't believe in, your shallow faith that changed nothing. Your fake smiles and congratulations when people texted to tell you about the fundraiser they were doing for the meningitis research foundation for the hospital, the children's ward. Yes, you lied, it would be wonderful if some other baby was saved by their 10K run. Their climb to the top of some fucking mountain. Yes, you agreed, their achievement would dwarf her loss. Yes, indeed. Yes.

Three coats of mascara and a dusting of powder into the wrinkled suede of her cleavage and Patricia pronounced herself ready.

'Mrs Phelan – Patricia – your daughter is one of the bus passengers involved in today's accident,' Nina began.

'My Lucy, yes,' Patricia nodded. 'She texted me early this morning to say that she was on her way home on the early bus.' She paused, then dabbed at her eyes. That was the first layer of mascara gone. 'She tells me everything, you know, we're more like sisters than mother and daughter.'

Nina never understood why women prized this statement. Parents were one category, friends another, children a third. The overlap was incidental, surely, rather than sought-after. Keep the child safe, that was head-and-tail of the job.

'Does Lucy usually take the early bus?' she asked. To be random was to be universal, everyone saw themselves there.

'No, never,' Patricia shook her head, playing her part to perfection. 'She was out last night and stayed with a friend, so she was just on her way home to get ready for work.'

Nina nodded, let the silence sit.

'She should have been at home in the safety of her own bed.'

'Tell me a little bit about Lucy,' Nina said, when Patricia had wiped her eyes and cleared her throat. Second layer of mascara gone. 'What is she like?'

'She's warm and… and fun-loving. Smart, you know, forever stuck in a book. It's always been just the two of us. Her father was a dead loss, wanted nothing to do with the responsibility, just walked away and washed his hands of her. We're better off, I told her. A father who doesn't want to be there is worse than nothing.' Patricia began to cry and Nina signalled to Ben to stop filming.

It was worse than nothing, sometimes.

Tim had suggested they go away for a weekend. 'A chance to get our heads clear,' he said.

Nina couldn't help but think of it as a weekend of trying. She planned the dates to coincide with ovulation, telling him she had to work the weekends either side. That meant four days in the office with little to do, but a few hours of online browsing would be a small price to pay for another baby. For a fresh start.

The first hour of the journey was bumper-to-bumper and they sat in silence, letting the radio do the talking for them. The open road was no better, the heat of the car and the winding roads joined forces to turn her stomach. The bump-bump of the rumble strips on the way into the car park was the last straw and she crouched beside the car, retching into a border of French lavender while Tim walked ahead of her down to the beach. As if privacy had been renewed between them, turning them back into strangers.

The place was almost empty, the sand boggy and

grey, a bold dog's paradise. The sea seemed far away and she fell for the grand illusion of it, walking out too far and getting caught by a stray wave. The sting of wet jeans around her knees was nothing compared to Tim's voice as he told her he couldn't do it any more.

'I'm sorry,' he said. To give him his due, he looked straight at her. 'We're just… we're not us and there isn't anything else left.'

'There could be.'

'It wouldn't be fair to bring a child into this mess.'

When she cried, he kissed her head and whispered into her hair. And when her hand, the hand that was stroking his arm, moved around to pet his back, sweeping into the waistband of his jeans, he didn't stop her, easing himself around into her palm.

When jeans and socks and pants lay tangled on the sand at their feet, it felt like redemption. But his sad smile as he pulled out early told her that he was serious, that it was over, there would be no more talk of a family, a future. Somewhere in the last days or weeks, while she had been anxiously counting backwards and forwards between her last period and her ovulation date, trying not to do the excited dance of if-I-get-pregnant-this-month-then-the-baby-will-be-due-on-that-date-and-that's-perfect-because-, he had been dreaming of a future without her in it.

She followed his footsteps back to the hotel, placing her shoes inside his prints, watching the scuff on the inside left where his fallen arch had dragged the sand with it. His feet were always easy to read.

'I'm sorry,' Patricia wiped her eyes and cleared her throat. 'It's just that she's the most precious thing in the world to me.'

'I know,' Nina said. Something about the way the other woman squared her shoulders and lifted her chin made it personal. 'Is someone here with you, for support? Family?'

'My sister is on her way down from Limerick.'

'What time will she be in at?'

'Not for a good while yet, she has to get the connecting train from Dublin. She didn't want to get the bus.' She caught Nina's eye and they laughed together, harsh and helpless.

'Are you okay in the meantime?'

'I'll be fine,' Patricia said, and Nina could see, suddenly, the steel it must have taken to raise her girl by herself. 'I'm going to go back upstairs and get a coffee, see if there is any news. Thank you.'

Nina watched her walk away, unsteady on heels an inch too high for her, like a tower block built by a child. The poor woman. Hopefully her sister would be here shortly, nobody should go through this alone. Easy to wish family on others. If their positions were reversed, she might well prefer solitude over the burdensome concerns of others.

Tim, of course, was not alone for long. Smart, good-looking, a hint of damage – he was snapped up quickly. He phoned her when he started dating. He didn't used to be so concerned with doing the right thing and she wondered how long his guilt would last at having left her. Not long, she guessed. Men had a capacity to compartmentalise, to move on.

'It's a small city, I didn't want you to hear it from someone else,' he said. As if she spoke to anyone outside of work. Or listened when anyone spoke.

'Is it serious?' Giving him the opportunity to tell her

no, of course not, sure, they were still at the dinner-and-a-movie stage.

'I think so.'

Did he remember telling her, thrilling her, years before, with the same careful words: 'I think this might be serious,' whispered in her ear as he walked two-armed with her down the quays after a long night of talk and quiet? If he had forgotten, she remembered it well enough for both of them.

'At our age, what isn't?'

To which 'our' was he referring? Was he the serious one, chasing some flighty twenty-something barely out of college? Or, worse, still going?

'I've met her children,' he said. 'Well, not children exactly. Teenagers, almost. A boy and a girl.'

'That's nice,' she said.

Later that night, the real words spilled from her throat, thick and heartsick.

'Already?' she spat at the empty armchair across from her own.

'A ready-made family, how convenient,' she sneered into the silence.

It was not his cruelty she cried over, but the return of his hope.

She saw them together once or twice. He was right, it was a small city, although she had to go a little out of her way to do it. She was not young, his new – his new what? Lover? Partner? It would be three years before Tim could file for divorce, so she couldn't have much by way of formal status.

She was not young, but that didn't mean she was too old. She had teenage children, everything in tormenting working order. Nina began to brace herself every time the phone rang, waiting for the call in which he would tell her – with halting words unable to mask his joy – that their family was growing. Theirs, not hers. Her family seemed capable only of shrinking.

'You the reporter?' The kid's voice startled her. Lost in her own thoughts, she hadn't noticed him approaching. He was a stubby teenager, the kind that made people shudder and remember the horror of their own teen years, all spots and gawky self-importance.

'Nina Cassidy.' She held out her hand for him to shake. If she made him feel respected, then he would open right up; teenagers were oddly dependable.

'Declan Rafferty. But my friends call me Dec.'

'Do you know someone involved in the accident, Dec? Can I call you Dec?' She smiled at him.

'My friend? Paul? He's one of the people on the bus. I thought it might, like, help people to know more about him?'

'Is there a parent or someone with you right now, Dec? Someone I could check in with to see if it would be all right to interview you on camera?'

'My dad picked me up at school and dropped me in. He's over there talking to Mr Teegan, Paul's da. Hang on, I'll get him.'

Dec's father was a smiling version of his son. A man who wore short sleeves in all weathers.

'Sure, as long as he wants to do it. You want to do it, do you, Dec?'

Dec nodded. 'It's Paul, like.'

'All right, so. Just watch your language or your mam'll kill the pair of us.'

'So, Dec, tell us a little bit about Paul, he's a good friend of yours?'

'My best mate since we started secondary, ya,' Dec nodded. 'We live in the same park and we always do everything together, like.'

'Do you usually travel to school together?' Nina asked.

'We used to get the eight o'clock together every morning, but Paul started getting the early bus a few weeks ago.'

'Was he going to school early to study?' Nina knew this was unlikely, but it might loosen Dec up a little bit, get him to stop glancing at the people around him to see if they were watching.

Sure enough, Dec hooted with laughter. 'Paul's no swot. He's down in pass maths with the rest of us. No, this girl started stalking him, like, so he was trying to avoid her.'

'A girl?' A man behind Dec cut in. 'What girl?'

'His… I suppose she was his girlfriend for a while. Should I say her name?' Dec asked Nina.

She was more interested in Mr Teegan, the angry man from earlier, the one that Tim had been urging upstairs. If she changed tack now, though, she would lose Dec, possibly for nothing. She could approach the father afterwards, see if he was willing to talk. 'Probably better not to,' she told Dec, with one eye on Mr Teegan. 'It might not be respectful.'

'Right, well, this girl he had a thing with—'

'A thing?' Paul's father's voice was loud. 'I can assure you that my son did not have "a thing" with any girl.'

'Jason, please.' A woman with him placed her hand on his arm. 'Let Declan talk, he's not doing any harm.'

'Ya, so, they just got together once, like, at a party?'

Dec continued. 'Then she wouldn't leave him alone, always texting and wanting him to be her boyfriend, but he wasn't into that. He was all, like, "Get in line, girl"—'

'This is simply not true. Turn off your camera,' Mr Teegan turned to Nina. 'Paul was brought up in a good God-fearing home. He wouldn't engage in lewd behaviour. We never met any girl.'

'Jason, calm down,' his wife said again. 'He did mention a girl to me once, but in a nice, respectful way...'

'What girl?' But Paul's mother lowered her head.

'It's true, I swear,' Dec said. 'But it was at a party so maybe he was, like, you know, a bit buzzed or whatever—'

'Buzzed?'

'That's enough now,' Dec's father pulled his son away by the arm.

'Girls? Drinking? Pass maths?' Jason rounded on his wife. 'What are these lies?'

'That's not quite...' his wife said. 'There was a girl. And, yes, he gave up higher-level maths a little while back. But you know Paul, he was always such a good boy.' She turned to Nina. 'He still notices if I am wearing something new. Imagine that for a teenager!'

Her eyes were sad and eager. Nina smiled at her.

'He sounds like a lovely boy,' she said.

'You know what they say about boys and their mothers.' She leaned in towards Nina. 'It was all true in our case. All true.'

Jason put out his hand, cutting his wife off. 'I would have thought you media people would have been trying to find out the real story about what happened here. That woman

105

that got out? That Muslim and her so-called miraculous escape? That's what you should be looking into.'

'What are you suggesting?' Nina asked, knowing full well what he was suggesting but wanting it on camera.

'Terrorism in your own back yard and you're here flapping your mouth about some girl that my son probably never even met. Do we have to tell you how to do your goddamn job?'

Behind him, his wife began to cry quietly.

'Now look what you've done,' he shouted. 'You've upset my wife. As if she hasn't enough to worry about today. You delete this, all of it, you hear me?' He reached out as if to take the camera from Ben.

'Mr Teegan?' Tim's voice was welcome. 'We're asking all of the families to come inside, please.'

'Make them delete it!'

'Please. This way now, Sir.' Tim glanced at Nina and she nodded slightly, thanking him.

'He's worried about Paul, that's all,' Jason's wife said to Nina, her face anxious. 'He's not usually like this. He's under a lot of pressure at work… The important thing is Paul. He was a good boy. He is a good boy.' She gripped Nina's hand, 'A mother knows these things. A mother always knows.' She let go of Nina and hurried after her husband.

'Poor lady,' Ben said from behind Nina. 'He's an asshole, no doubt about it. Work pressure, my backside. He looked like he was going to hit one of us. You okay?'

Nina, too, had wondered if he might lash out. She almost wished he had, it would have spared her Mrs Teegan's words. *A mother knows these things.* The words left her feeling oily and raw, as if she might slide right out of her own life and into the endless past.

You might not have known everything, but did that make you less of a mother? You want to run after the woman and scream at her. Tell her that sometimes you still cradle your arms as if she is held within them.

'I'm fine,' she told Ben. 'Why don't you head on inside? I'll go and grab us a couple of decent coffees and meet you in there.'

That bought her a few minutes peace but meant she had to head towards the town square, where the small supermarket would surely have a decent machine. She recognised the same homeless woman the moment she turned the corner. The woman sat on the footpath, licking powdered soup out of its small packet. There was a whole layer of people living in a parallel world, invisibility the tax they paid on whatever circumstances had led them out of their lives. People talked about small towns as if their lack of anonymity conferred a kind of security, but, in reality, self-interest lived everywhere. Any other day, it would be a piece she could drum up interest in.

On a whim, she ordered a third coffee and a scone with the works, and handed them to the woman sitting down on the ground beside her, tucking her knees awkwardly to avoid flashing her knickers at passers-by. Unlikely, she realised after a minute or two. Most gave them a wide berth.

The woman placed the half-finished soup packet into the plastic bag at her feet, glancing sideways at Nina as if she might try to grab it and run. Nina looked away, up into the sky, searching for clouds, for rain, for a face peering down from heaven. She went to Mass with Tim once, watching the reverence on his face as he took the host into himself, the sheer voodoo of it all. Hearing the priest promise she would see Aisling in the next life made her feel dizzy and hateful.

But oh how you would love to be wrong.

'Lovely afternoon,' the woman said. They might be at a tea party, except for the dirt under her fingernails and the smell of outdoors that clung to her clothes. 'I'm May.'

'Nina.'

'It's a sad thing.'

'It is,' Nina agreed. No matter that she didn't know the specifics or the generalities, whether life or a paper cut. Sadness was everywhere.

They sat side by side and drank their coffees. The footpath was hard on her backside and the coffee tasted faintly of its plastic lid, yet there was more comfort in it than any rosary. Tim found their daughter in talk, in prayers and groups, and families; she carried her inside, needing only silence to hear her clearly.

'Let me pay you,' the woman said, suddenly, placing her empty coffee cup on the ground as if it were glass.

'No, please, there's no need.'

'I insist.' From within the plastic bag, she drew out a sheaf of papers, removed one, stroked it fondly and handed it to Nina. It was a page from an online shopping order, culled from who knows where, someone's rubbish bin, or a spilled sack trailing the back of an early-morning bin lorry.

'Will that cover it?' May asked, with odd dignity.

'More than enough, thank you,' Nina told her. She took her cue for dismissal and rose to leave, awkward on sleeping feet.

Of all the documentaries and think pieces on homelessness, none ever quite answered the question of why. Or, more accurately perhaps, who? What differentiated the person led straight off the edge of the cliff from the person who veered harmlessly along the grassy verge? There but for the grace of God, Tim might say, easy inside the security of his new, more grown-up family.

Noel's phone call saved her from going back inside.

'They've agreed to an interview,' he told her.

'They?'

'The bus driver and the woman that got out.'

'Richie Murray and Alina O'Reilly.'

'That's them. They're still at the hospital.'

'What about the scene?'

'You wanted the people, this is the people.'

'Okay, I'm on my way.'

'The backlash against the woman is getting nasty. All nonsense, according to the Defence Forces statement, but see if you can get a reaction from her.' His tone softened. 'Can you handle it?'

She could. Of course she could.

She looked for Tim as she gathered Ben and her things. *I have to go to the hospital*, she could say, *I have to go back*, and the feel of his eyes on her as she walked away would be enough to straighten her spine. But that privilege was no longer hers. Instead, she let Ben drive her there, fiddling with her phone under the guise of getting the latest on the comments against Alina, then telling him to follow her inside when he had the gear assembled.

She walked across the hospital car park in the faded light of winter's early dusk. Or perhaps the whole world had dimmed. Her heels clicked and crunched on concrete and gravel, as solid as if a real person walked in her shoes. It was two years since she came out the door of this hospital and got into a waiting hearse – she on one side, Tim on the other. They might have been returning from holidays, were it not for the tiny coffin on their laps, lighter than hand luggage. Heart luggage. The words rose like a giggle in her throat.

The pinkness of the casket was an affront, you knew the moment you saw it. But you hadn't wanted any part in choosing it, had been too busy giving in to your grief, indulging the weeping and the hysterics as they came. So you sat in the back of the car, ashamed at how wrong it all looked. Ashamed of saying goodbye to your girl in what amounted to nothing more than a monstrous jewellery box, one final betrayal at the moment of her leaving the world.

No. Wrong. She had already left the world, left you. That was simply the moment of her leaving your arms.

This is your marketplace, this cattle call of souls, if any part of you believes in such a thing. You traded the lightness of your child's body, the barely-there weight of her in your arms as she died, and you took that weight into your heart. You traded her fine wisps of hair, smoothed back from her face by sweat, for lines on your face and in your soul. The death of your child aged you with its small irreversible indignities. Hair turned grey, face creased with pain, these things do not return to themselves when you close your front door on the temporary mourners.

In here, you do not look out of place.

Nina stopped, breathed. The automatic doors opened and sucked her in.

'Welcome, Ms Cassidy. I'm Victor Griffiths, Hospital Director.' A tall man came forward to meet her.

'Nina, please,' she said, shaking his hand.

'If you'd like to follow me, we have our interview room ready for you.'

He led her down familiar corridors, her breath held until they passed the stairs to the children's ward and moved safely beyond it to the well of the lifts.

'How are Mr Murray and Mrs O'Reilly?' she asked.

'I can't tell you that, Ms Cassidy, Nina, as you well know.' Victor twinkled at her. 'But I can say that I wouldn't be letting you in here if they weren't up to it. All the rest they can be telling you themselves. Far be it from me to steal their fifteen minutes of fame!'

Ben was already inside the room, setting up, and Nina busied herself with her preliminary notes, while waiting for Victor to stop hovering.

'It's good to have you back under better circumstances,' he said, in a low voice. 'I hope you are doing well in yourself.'

Nina smiled, stretched it out for long seconds. There were few questions a bright smile didn't answer.

'We'll start with a few questions for you, Victor, if that's all right?' she said.

'Of course, Nina,' he said, delighted, before excusing himself for a few minutes to prepare, as she guessed he would, giving her a break to gather her thoughts.

The room was pale grey with one turquoise wall, an effort to combine hygiene and homeliness. A large painting took up most of one wall. 'Donated in memory of Lydia Costelloe', the little plaque underneath announced. The painting was a woman, half-sitting, half-lying, four children cluttered around her. She looked beatific or exhausted, one enormous breast hanging out of the front of her dress, held firmly by the child nearest to it, his own pendulous belly mirroring her breast, one growing the other. Poor Lydia Costelloe, whoever she was, was lucky she couldn't see it.

The extension of that symbiosis beyond your pregnancy shocked you, you were both consumed and renewed. Your old life, your old self, pushed out with the afterbirth, like being in a witness protection programme, your old identity no longer available, a new one all ready and waiting for you to step into. Relearning the world together.

In labour, with each contraction your heart expanded to accommodate your daughter. Shed like excess weight, your heart was left with folds that hang empty, too big for the little that was left.

The door opened and Victor stood to one side, shepherding people in ahead of him.

'Here we are.'

'Good afternoon, Mr Murray, Mrs O'Reilly.' She stepped towards them and back into the world, the perennial hand out in front of her, 'I'm Nina Cassidy. Thank you for agreeing to share your story today.'

ALINA

Seán insisted on pushing Alina's wheelchair to the interview room himself, leaving the orderly to walk crossly beside them. She saw the same look on the faces of the small boys in their housing estate who sat on the kerb and waited in vain for their turn to be the goalkeeper and thus to join the game.

When the hospital director opened the door and ushered them in, Seán was the first to step forward and greet the lady reporter. 'I'm Seán O'Reilly and this is my wife, Alina.'

She admired him in that moment, so tall and well-spoken, so sure that it would all go well. When, though, had the word *wife* lost its thrill?

'Alina was on the bus,' he added. 'Richie here got her out.' He placed a large hand on the bus driver's shoulder and rocked it backward and forward.

The man's belly shook like pudding and Alina swallowed a giggle. Was it a good idea to do this, she wondered, when she felt so unlike herself?

Seán leaned forward and took the woman's hand again. 'I read about your daughter. At the time, I mean. I wanted to say that I'm – we're – sorry for your loss.'

Alina watched the woman's face. She did not look as if Seán's sympathy was welcome.

'We don't have little ones. Not yet anyway,' he looked at Alina and squeezed her hand. 'But I can imagine.'

Alina pitied his foolishness. How could he think it possible to imagine the loss of a child without ever having had that child? If the woman reacted, she hid it well.

'Thank you. It means a lot when people remember.'

While Seán continued a conversation he should have known to end, Alina glanced at Richie. His head was dipped low, showing a bald spot the size of a two-euro coin. She wondered if he knew it was there.

'Seán,' she put her hand on his arm, 'could you get me some water, please?'

'Are you okay?'

'It's been a long day, that's all.'

Time moved in strange bright jerks. One minute sipping her water, the next sitting in a semicircle. The woman, Nina, sat opposite them. The spotlight behind her threw shadows onto her face, making it hard to read her expression. That must be normal, they seemed to know what they were doing.

'Thank you all for making the time to come down and have a chat with me, I know it's been a long day.'

There was something obedient about their laughter. The performance had already started, it seemed.

'Now, folks, everyone is anxious to hear your story, this amazing rescue, and we'll get to that in just a couple of minutes. I'm going to ask Victor a couple of quick questions first, just background stuff. You'll see it's nothing to be worried about at all. Think of it like a chat amongst ourselves.'

The men spoke first, but Alina found it hard to summon any offence. Margo would have done better in her place.

Richie mumbled his answers, making it hard to hear

114

him. She must remember not to do that, to speak out clearly. *So that they knew she could.* The thought was gone almost before she could register it.

'You're being hailed as a hero, Richie. Tell me, how does that feel?'

'Ah, sure, you know,' he said.

'I spoke to a woman this morning who told me she is often on your bus,' Nina said.

'It'd be hard to know,' Richie said, without waiting to be asked anything.

'She said her name was May,' Nina added. 'She might be a bit... troubled.'

'The old lady,' Alina said. 'She was on the bus when I got on. She walked up and down the aisle. Up and down. Up and down.'

Seán's hand squeezed hers and she stopped talking.

'She told me you always let her on the bus,' Nina smiled at Richie.

'She showed me a bus pass,' Richie said. 'She doesn't mean any harm. She only talks to herself, not to anyone else.'

'Everybody sat in the back because she was at the front.' Alina said. They were afraid of her, but Alina didn't say that. The woman had done nothing wrong. The fear was theirs, not hers. Dangerous people didn't wear it so much on the outside.

'Did you sit in the back as well?' Nina asked her.

'No,' Alina said. 'I was in the middle.' Her mother's advice: sit where the driver can see you, that is how you avoid trouble. How many days had she got on and followed that advice without ever wondering how her mother came by that knowledge? Without going to her and saying, *Mama. Tell me.*

115

'I was lucky to get to where Mr Murray could help me to climb out. Otherwise I would still be in there. Those poor people,' she added.

'Indeed. What prompted you to help Alina, Mr Murray? We know at this stage that the road collapsed still further almost immediately afterwards, you must have had mere seconds to decide. Can you talk us through that?'

'They were reaching down to help me out. I heard her – Alina – asking for help and I gave her a hand up. It was as simple as that.'

'I see.' Nina shuffled her papers and cleared her throat. 'This lunchtime, Mr Murray, a report stated that you were recently suspended from work for an incident that was claimed to be racial in nature—'

Richie looked at the ground, his hands rubbing one against the other. She wanted to lean forward and explain it to him. To tell him that the question might be directed at him but it was really about her. The colour of her skin complicating what he had done.

Richie coughed. 'There was an incident, all right, but there was no racism involved.'

The story stumbled out of him. As if it was something new. A work night out. Drinks, lots of them. Pints of beer. Shots of whiskey. The teasing turned sour. A comment passed about Richie's wife. Alina was surprised to hear the word wife; he didn't seem married. There was something about him, a messiness, or a desperation, maybe, that a wife shouldn't permit.

'Do you want to tell me what he said?' Nina asked.

'I wouldn't repeat it.' He lifted his head up as he said it and caught Alina's eye, ducking his head again and flushing.

'You were defending your wife's honour?'

'It was the wrong way to go about things, whatever I thought I was doing.'

'Sure, how could the man be a racist?' Seán cut in. 'Didn't he pull my wife out of that bus?'

She was grateful to Seán for taking away one kind of awkwardness. She was. But he had taken it from Richie only to hand it to her.

'Alina, can you tell us a little bit about your own background? You're Lebanese, I believe?'

Always her past. Always. The largely unremembered years of her earliest existence destined to forever be the most singular thing about her. Never the life she chose for herself, an Irish life.

'I have lived in Cork since I was six years old. I'm a naturalised Irish citizen, as are my parents. I'm married to an Irish man. If we have children, they will be Irish. Yet the moment anything goes wrong, I am Lebanese. A blow-in, a johnny-come-lately, a radical, exotic. Jokes that are not jokes.'

The light was hot on her forehead. She put a hand to her head, felt her hair. Giving up the veil, it seemed, didn't make her the same, any more than wearing it had made her different. She took the scarf – a silk square that Seán had given her for her birthday – from the back of her chair and improvised a veil, letting her hands remember for her. Seán tensed beside her, while the others watched wordlessly.

'This morning, for the first time in a long time, I saw the face of Allah,' Alina said, gesturing to Richie.

'I take it your beliefs are very important to you, Alina?' Nina asked.

'Not for many years and I regret that now. Today... all this? I am thankful for my life.'

117

'You believe that Allah spared your life today?'

'If not him, then who?'

'Richie, are you a religious man? Do you believe that some higher power was at work this morning?'

'I wouldn't say I'm religious,' he said. 'But I understand what Alina is saying. God between us and all harm, my mam always said, and she always believed it too.'

'Exactly,' Alina said. 'Allah chooses who to home and who to go to him.'

'We're not a family of faith,' Seán said. 'What Alina means is that this sort of thing makes you think. It would make anyone think. More importantly, we wouldn't want to take anything away from the brave actions of this man here.' Seán laid his hand on Richie's shoulder. 'But just because Alina and Richie were lucky doesn't mean that someone wasn't at fault. Politicians, builders, the government, the bankers, they're all stuck in it together, they have everything sewn up. The ordinary, decent man can hardly get approval to build a new barn and these cowboys are killing drainage with their car parks. It doesn't take a rocket scientist to see it. They should be compensating the families—'

Anger turned so easily to blame if there was nothing to filter it through. In the days after 9/11, she kept her head low, bowed down by the weight of her veil and other people's looks. After school, she bumped into a girl in the supermarket, a girl who had been in her class but left early to have a baby. Not a friend exactly but someone who had shown her casual kindnesses, offering a spare seat, sharing a book. She had her baby with her and Alina went over to congratulate her. 'I have nothing to say to your kind,' the girl snapped and walked away, leaving her basket of nappies and baby formula in the middle of the aisle. Sixteen, unmarried and with a baby, yet she felt Alina was the one who should be ashamed. Perhaps she was right, Alina thought. She certainly felt that shame.

Two years later, or maybe three, she read Bin Laden's statement that it was the bombing in Lebanon that had made him decide to carry out the attack on America, so that what had happened to the women and children there would not happen again. The statement was buried in the foreign news pages that nobody important read. None of her new college friends ever mentioned it, but the idea that he was protecting her made her feel dirty again. Perhaps that girl with whom she had once shared her Friday Twix was justified in walking away from her.

'So often when we talk about blame we put it in the wrong place,' she said. 'But it is not about blame, it is only about the actions of those involved. The righteous are saved and so those that are not saved are not righteous. These things happen because we make them so.'

She hoped they were watching, those girls who took all they had for granted. The men they married, the interchangeable pints-and-football men that their teenage years had promised them they were due, their babies. They should know the fear they created, the helplessness. She hoped that they stepped outside the front doors of their four-bedroomed detached houses and carried their responsibility with them, loaded into the boots of their big cars.

Seán was looking at her, his mouth loose with fright, as if she had turned into someone else, instead of finally finding a part of herself missing all along.

'Alina, are you suggesting that the victims, the people still trapped in the bus, somehow brought this on themselves?' Nina's voice was careful.

'Of course not. She's in shock,' Seán said. 'She's not even... I mean, she doesn't even go that often...'

He didn't realise that he had taken his hand from hers.

'Nothing is an accident. The righteous have nothing to fear.'

'Something like this, the shock of it,' Seán tried again. 'You understand...'

But they didn't understand. They never would.

* * *

'Sacred Heart, Alina child, what a fright you're after giving us all.' Seán's mother ushered Alina in the front door as if she owned their house. Talking talking talking, like it changed anything.

'I'm sorry, Annie.' What else could she say? She was sorry, as it happened. Even though her only crime was to get on a bus and survive a crash.

'We were half out of our minds with worry, you know.' Annie scolded Alina as she prodded her along the hall and into the kitchen. 'I have the kettle on, you'll be wanting a cup of tea.'

'Alina's exhausted, Mam,' Seán said. 'I think a lie-down would be best.'

He had been like this since the interview finished, tongue-tied, speaking only to tell her how tired she was, how she would feel like herself again in a day or two. He did not mention what she said and neither did she. Her certainty under the lights had given way to a sort of numbness. She doubted if she could decide on a pair of shoes to wear.

'Thank you, Annie. Tea would be lovely.'

Another lie. A kind one, the sort she became practised in after meeting Seán. Forcing down many cups of milky tea when the sharpness of lemon was what she wanted. It started innocently, a step towards being accepted by Seán's mother. Already put off by her skin, her beliefs, her failure to gossip, Annie needed no further ammunition against her. Rude refusal of the customs of her tea might have been a fatal blow. Seán, for all that was wonderful within him, used up much of his courage in bringing her home. She was not sure he could withstand a strong attack on their relationship by his mother.

'We saw the pictures on the news,' Annie continued, taking tea things out of cupboards with great familiarity.

Full milk, white sugar, the things Alina only kept in her kitchen for Annie's visits. The biscuits were already on the table, arranged on a plate as if they were food. Dark, sticky jam in between mounds of whipped sugar, turning a single cup of tea into a child's birthday treat.

'Jesus, Mary and Joseph, weren't you lucky?' Annie touched her forehead, then her chest and each shoulder, marking a cross on her body. It had the wrong dimensions, pushed out of shape by Annie's short neck and broad chest.

'Very lucky,' Alina agreed. She was out before they even knew she had been involved, what need for this great drama? But that was her mother-in-law's way, to make something out of nothing, to hold life's horror up to the light, the better to admire her own place of safety.

'I told Seán – didn't I, Seán? – that you have no

business on those early buses. Not at that hour of the morning. It's a car of your own you need. Didn't I say it, Seán, not a month ago? Oh, I know' – she held up her hands as if warding off a crackpot theory – 'the planet and all that.'

Little point in explaining it again. In winter, Seán took the car and she the bus. Spring and autumn, he cycled and she drove. In summer, when university let out, they decided day by day.

'It was muggers you were worried about, if I remember rightly.' Seán rolled his eyes at Alina behind his mother's back.

They used to make her feel special, these gestures he made without his mother seeing. The two of them together. When she told her mother, laughing, happy to show that Seán could protect her, her mother didn't share the joke.

'How can you trust that he is not making these faces also with her behind your back? Someone who laughs at others is simply someone who laughs at others.'

Her mother's words burrowed under her skin and hid in the place where her insecurity lived, coming out when she and Seán argued. When she wondered if he only married her to seem less boring to other people. To himself, maybe. If he believed her perceived exoticism was somehow catching. Never mind that she grew up here, went to school here, froze with Jack on the *Titanic* and ran across America with Forrest, knew all the words to Baz Luhrmann's sunscreen song. Never mind that she was the same as every Irish girl he had grown up with. The same in every way but one.

It shamed her when he introduced her to work colleagues and she heard a boast in his voice. It shamed them both when she wondered if he was more racist than any of them.

'I knew it wasn't right,' Annie said now, clicking her tongue against her teeth when Seán put the milk carton on the table. She took a jug from the cupboard, washed the dust away and placed it on the table. Click, click, click, went her busy tongue. How tired it must be at night-time. 'I had a bad feeling about it all. Nobody should be going around that hour of the morning that doesn't have to.'

Here it came, what she was building up to, the real problem.

'Why you can't go and say your few prayers in the Sacred Heart chapel when it's only across the road, I will never understand,' Annie said. 'It isn't even a church, if that's what you're worried about. It's a perpetual chapel, no tabernacle. They couldn't say Mass in it even if they wanted to.'

'Mam.' Seán's voice was a warning.

'Sure, God can hear you wherever you are,' she said, with a sniff.

'It's about more than that, Mam, and you know it. You wouldn't go to the mosque on Sunday mornings instead of Mass, would you?'

'That's different,' Annie said.

'Different how, Mam?'

'I wouldn't know what to do in one of those places,' Annie said. 'It's different for Alina. She's been inside the church plenty of times, she knows her way around it. Isn't that right, Alina love?'

Alina smiled vaguely. How could she describe the feeling of peace when she got on the bus, knowing that she would shortly slip in the side door and join the community of women, the warmth that settled inside her. Studies said that regular attendance at religious services increased feelings of well-being, but sitting among those strangers was more than simple calm. It felt vital in some way. She was spared the betrayal of her own reply by Annie bowing her head.

'Bless us O Lord as we sit together. Bless the food we eat today...'

The words, heard so often, floated in the air before settling on her tablecloth. She would have to wash it, she realised. Bleach it of its foreign meaning. She wished she could cover her ears with her scarf, but she had removed it in the car on the way home, anxious to be rid of the tag rubbing against her ear. Some Muslim, she, to reject such small discomforts.

'I think I might need to go and lie down,' she said when the prayer ended.

'I'll be here if you need anything,' Annie said. 'I told Seán I'll stay for a few days until you're back on your feet.'

'Thank you, Annie. Thank you, Seán.'

'You know how hard it is for me to take days off in term time,' Seán's voice was apologetic.

'It's fine. Please don't worry.'

It was not fine. Something he should have known. As her husband. As a human. She pretended to be asleep when he came in to kiss her goodbye before leaving for his evening lecture. Every year, she memorised his timetable, calculated how long it would take him to walk from the lecture theatre to his office, gather his bag and coat, collect his bike from the rack – or the car – and leave the city behind, so that she would know when to expect his key in the door. She almost always got it right, except on days when he was accosted by a student with a question or a colleague or, on the brightest days, when he went straight from the lecture hall to their house, surprising her with an extra twenty minutes of the evening together.

She wondered if his mother would go with him, grabbing with two hands at the chance of time alone with her son. But after the front door closed between them, she could hear Annie moving around, the whirr of the handheld hoover as she gathered up the coconut flakes from those poisonous biscuits. The hoover was the wedding present she liked least and yet used gratefully every day. That, alone, should have told her… but she couldn't remember what it should have told her.

Had she fallen asleep or not, when Annie pushed open the bedroom door without knocking?

'Alina? Your friend Margo is on the phone. Will I tell her you're sleeping?'

'No, it's okay.' Alina held out her hand for the phone and Annie handed it to her before going to stand in the doorway, not even pretending not to listen. Was it good or bad that such pretence was gone? Did it mean she was as close as family or inconsequential as a stranger?

'Aren't you the one for the high drama!' Margo said.

She wasn't sure if she was expected to answer. Or what she might say if she did. 'Hello, Margo. How are you?'

'Run off my feet, thanks. Doing the work of two people while you're at home napping and eating biscuits. Isn't it well for some?'

'I won't be out long, Margo. The doctors said to rest for a day or two, but I'll be fine then.'

'Don't worry about it,' Margo's voice softened. 'People will still be breaking their hips and needing to order plastic replacements next week. Just don't be listening to the nonsense on the radio. People are terrible, they would depress you.'

'What are they saying?' Alina didn't know why she was asking. She could already hear the whiteness of their words.

'I'm hardly going to repeat it, now am I?' Margo said. 'Didn't I just tell you not to listen?'

* * *

'I hope she wasn't pressuring you to come back to work?' Annie came to take the phone.

'She's just being practical.'

'She might as well be getting used to doing without you.' Annie winked at Alina. 'You rest now, you might be needing your strength sooner than you think. Days like today make us all think about the future, about the important things in life. About family.'

Annie's hints were never subtle. When asking her to stop didn't work, Seán told Alina to simply ignore her, to pretend she hadn't understood.

'You're right, Annie. I should rest now. Thanks.'

She placed the phone beside her on the bed. It was spiteful, she knew, to take the thing that gave Annie such a sense of purpose.

'I just need to give Dympna a quick tinkle,' Annie would say, settling herself at the table with a pot of tea and the inevitable biscuits.

Seán was delighted. 'Isn't it great that she can use the phone here and we don't need to worry about it? I hate

126

to think she's worrying about the phone bill in her own place at her age, after everything she did for me.'

Who could argue with that? She did indeed raise Seán, a fine son, a fine man. If she had not yet let go of him, was that the worst crime?

Without the phone, Annie turned the radio up loud, that awful show she listened to every evening, a man with a loud voice encouraging other loud-voiced people to phone him and discuss the things they found important. Things that required shouting and the casting of aspersions. The application of slights to others.

No matter which way she turned in her bed she could hear the voices, low enough that she had to concentrate to make out the words. It made it worse to have to work so hard to hear such filth. They talked about the bus crash. Some idea that builders were to blame. Or the planning board, who gave land to underground car parks so that the river came in and washed away the road.

'There needs to be criminal prosecution,' a woman insisted.

'But for what, Noreen? For what?' asked the interviewer.

'For murder, if necessary,' she said.

'Surely that's a bit strong, Noreen? We don't even know if there are victims yet.'

'There will be,' said Noreen, grimly. 'I feel very strongly about this. People are getting away with far too much for far too long.'

'I understand your frustration, Noreen, but—'

'I speak my mind,' Noreen said.

She sounded like Margo, who, too, asserted her right to speak her mind. Rudeness and cruelty were permitted under this guise, it seemed. If their manager asked Margo to do something she didn't agree with, she watched and waited for the chance to make it all go wrong. Whenever she managed to shout him into doing something her way and it still went wrong, she would tell him smartly he should not have listened to her, the boss should make up his own mind and be a man about it all. So the failure of her idea was someone else's fault too. Sometimes Alina thought it must be comforting to be Margo.

On the radio they talked about Richie, his suspension from work, the time Nina Cassidy asked him about. Alina believed what he had said: it happened and he was sorry. He didn't seem capable of lies. He was too sad. Too sweaty.

'He's not racist at all,' some man insisted. 'It's the other side of it I'd be worried about.'

'Tell us what you mean,' said the interviewer.

'He pulled her out, didn't he?' said the man. 'Before anyone else? For all we know they knew each other.'

'Now we can't know anything like that,' the interviewer said. 'There are no reports yet of any existing relationship between Richie the bus driver and the lady he says he rescued.'

'Maybe they were in it together, the pair of them. Maybe she had him brainwashed. That's how their religion works, it's all brainwashing and extremes.'

'I'll remind our listeners again that the Defence Forces have ruled out explosives as the cause of the crash,' the interviewer said, quickly.

'These terrorists are years more advanced, the guards would be only trotting after them. Look at that shoe bomber...' the man continued. 'He lives alone, that Richie does. Put his mother in a home, I heard. Maybe he needed her house to do his plotting.'

'Everyone is entitled to their opinion,' said the interviewer, 'but, again, we have no evidence yet to suggest anything of the sort.' He stopped there to take an ad break.

Everyone was entitled to their opinion. They could not exactly say that she had an affair, that she was a terrorist, but they could wonder it out loud in front of the whole country. It should be funny that her beliefs should be held to such high standards when they had all but disappeared from her life. The vitriol in their voices shook her. How could they hate her, these people whose religion was their culture, this vast love for their books and their god? These people who celebrated belief and St Patrick the converter, who gave their god a legal place in their lives. That they should accuse her when she had let her life be filled up with weddings in churches, christenings in churches, Christmas and Mass and the tight lips of her mother. They had not stopped her family at the airport when they arrived but neither, it seemed, had they really let them in.

Her father in Saturday-morning shirtsleeves, scrubbing graffiti from the gate of their house. 'Young people and their pranks, my dear, it is nothing,' he told her, his smile the same smile as always.

Her mother had different words, bitter and fearful, 'At home we saw our neighbours take up arms against each other, only days after they had eaten together.' Her hands in fists, pounding flour.

'We come from a place where people report each other as informers, people vanish overnight.' Her father's voice was firm. 'Can you really believe that some paint is the worst thing?'

Alina turned away from the sight of her father's arms around her mother's shaking shoulders. Those arms could no longer hold anyone. But her mother was still here, would know to say the things he could not. She could not pick up the phone and call her. Not yet. Not until she needed her less.

She had chosen Seán's life over her own. *I do*, she said, agreeing to it all. To putting his mother before her own. To dinner every Friday evening, their heads bowed over the table as if it was something for which they were grateful. Lunch every Sunday after Mass. A fuss made of Christmas, as if they were children. The meal and presents spoken of for weeks before.

'She's still disappointed she missed out on our wedding,' Seán said each time she brought it up.

'We had a wedding, Seán. You know this, you were there. She was there.'

But their civil ceremony, their great compromise, disappointed everybody but her father. He cried with joy, while, beside him, Alina's mother nodded patiently and Annie complained that a priest's blessing would have been nice. Seán's mother might have forgiven him for marrying outside the faith if Alina had given her the wedding she wanted.

'How many years until we have made this disappointment right for her?' Alina asked.

Time was not the issue, of course. Only a new little Catholic would undo the wrong done to Annie.

'You're properly Irish now,' Seán had said to her, laughing, the night they got back from their honeymoon to find Annie had hung a papal wedding blessing above their bed. And despite her heart, despite the veils boxed in the attic of her mother's house, despite the Irish passport safely tucked into her handbag, she, like a tongue-tied foreign fool just off the boat, believed him.

* * *

Alina woke when Seán got in from work, his idea of closing a door gently being to push it from a distance of ten centimetres instead of forty. She could hear his voice in the kitchen, which meant his mother was still here. While she slept, her neck had stiffened, as the doctors warned her it might. The pills they gave her were in the kitchen and she resigned herself to the stiffness. Better pain than any more tea.

Her own mother's tea was a sudden ache of memory. Lemon-fragrant, drunk in silence. Her mother spoke less and less after they moved to Ireland, her speech replaced by sighs and soft smiles, shakes of the head.

'How will Alina ever be truly Irish if we do not speak English at home?' her father had scolded, and her mother nodded her agreement, left another part of herself behind. At university, Alina's psychology module made her wonder if her mother ate to keep her mouth occupied, to stop the forbidden language from slipping out. Mai's fear expanded alongside her waistline. She became afraid of the narrowness of the bus doorway, the heaving incline of the steps. She preferred to stay at home, she said. Where nobody would comment, she did not add.

Her mother's silence would be understanding, complicit, full of the knowledge that passed through blood. Some day she, too, might share that with a daughter, God willing. *Inshallah*. Her mind, long accustomed to the Irish way of invoking luck, brought forth her father's word.

'What are his beliefs, this young man of yours?' her father had asked when she told them, shyly, that she had met someone.

'He is a good man. We love each other,' she answered. She burned at the memory of her pride at her own integration, her ability to look at the person instead of the accidental heritage of their birth. How quickly the heart reprogrammed the brain. Chemicals, she supposed.

Caught up in her new love and her new life, she ignored the unquiet parts of her heart. She hugged the memory of Seán to her and thought that a love so clearly meant to be was not so different from a divine plan.

'I do,' she declared in front of them all and told herself that her words, her life, were hers to give.

But clinging tight to the bus driver, Richie, she was lifted up and up, above the glass and the other people. She was lifted right out of the skin she tried to fit into, exposing her centre. Where, it seemed, Allah waited all along, unfolding like the paper hat hidden inside one of Annie's Christmas crackers.

The pain was too much. She sat up and eased herself out of bed.

In the kitchen, she found Seán and his mother sitting over cups of tea, a fresh currant cake on the table between them.

'Well, the dead arose and appeared to many,' Annie said. 'You didn't think you'd be able to sleep at all, you said, and here you are six hours later. Didn't I tell you?'

What to do with such a statement? As with so much of her mother-in-law's conversation, it was best to simply smile. To pretend she meant no harm.

'How are you feeling, love?' Seán asked, getting up to usher her over to the table. 'I'm not long home, I didn't want to go in and wake you.'

'I'm fine.' Alina did not say she heard him come home half an hour ago. He was powerless before his mother's ambushes. Conversation and cake, her weapons of choice. 'Are they out? Did they get them out? The others?'

Seán shook his head. 'They tried to take a crane in, or a cherry picker, but the road wouldn't hold.'

'What are they doing now? They must be doing something.'

'The news said something about moving rubble by hand. Nothing seems certain.'

Alina sat down. She had slept and slept and all the time they were still in there. 'You have to eat something, child,' Annie said. 'I'm after making a nice currant loaf for you. I popped another couple into the freezer, it was nearly empty. You'd have been living on ice soon.'

Alina took the knife from the table and started to cut herself a slice of cake. Soft and warm from the oven, it went with the knife, leaving her with a slice that had a normal top but no end. She laid it carefully on a plate. It wasn't a slice at all.

'Let me.' Annie took the knife from her and pointed the tip of it down at a forty-five-degree angle to cut a square so neat it might have appeared in a maths book. 'There's a knack to it,' Annie said. She didn't gloat. She didn't need to, her slice of cake did it for her.

'You're not to listen to a word of that nonsense on the radio, the awful things people are saying about you—' she continued.

'Mam!' Seán's voice warned.

'I'm not the one saying it,' Annie's tone was injured. 'Haven't I known Alina for all the years? Sure, she wouldn't hurt a fly. That's what I said to that reporter that called as well. "There isn't a pick on her," I told her. "Where would she hide a bomb?"' Her laugh was too loud. 'If you were brainwashed by one of them, wouldn't we know it?'

'Mam. Enough.'

Because only brainwashing brought someone to her religion. No legitimate grievance could be admitted. That they created such a thought in her head was shocking. She who never believed that violence was the answer to anything! Within the space of a single day, her own family had put her on the opposite side of us-and-them. She was as Irish as they were. Until they decided otherwise. Because her family didn't pick potatoes, because they didn't live and die by this tiny-stoned land, because she bore no grudge to the East, she could have nothing more than formal citizenship.

'I'm not the one saying those things,' Annie said. 'Everyone wants to get their spoke in, is all.'

'Can you leave your spoke out of it, please? Alina has enough to think about at the moment.'

'I'm only saying there's a lot of crackpots out there. I don't mean you, Alina love.'

'I should phone my mother,' Alina said. She stretched out a hand as if it was someone else's and stroked Seán's cheek. How deeply he believed he struggled to keep the peace. As if apologising behind everyone's back was enough.

'I phoned her earlier,' Seán said.

That was not easy for him, her mother's deference had a way of sucking the natural easiness out of him. 'Thank you.'

How much simpler if those were the only two words available. If, for everything a person did or did not do, there was simply a thank you or nothing.

In her bedroom, she dialled her mother's number.

'Mama?'

'Alina.' Her mother's voice was warm and cool in just the right places.

'How lucky we are,' Mai said. 'Baba was looking out for you.'

'Have you been listening? Did you hear?' For a moment she thought she might cry.

'I turned it off. They will let anybody say any awful thing they want to, with no reason. I watch the shopping channel. There, they smile and dress nicely and say only good things about the world.'

Alina tried again. 'They're saying—'

'Just because they are saying it does not mean you need to listen,' her mother said firmly.

Mai prized certainty. It was her mission to create it where there was none, in her small orbit around the neighbourhood. Her faith in the *ijma* was unshaken. The consensus of the community was the principle Mai lived by, even in a place where that made her an object of suspicion. Her mother's life was forever delineated by the expectations of others.

Alina herself had longed for a world with infinite possibility. At university, finally, she found acceptance, or the convincing pretence of it. Everyone with their gay friend, their musician friend, their political activist friend, their foreign friend. The uniform of political correctness they wore as if it was individuality. She gave her opinion loudly, shared her history freely, before realising that she was only asked that they might claim her comments as their own understanding. She had presented her whole self for their skin-deep acceptance. Shown off, once again, for visiting teams. She nodded to descriptions of potholed streets as 'downtown Beirut' – *so true!* she laughed, swallowing the prick of betrayal in her throat. She joined in their outrage at the single-image portrayal of Ireland in English soap operas and American films – *so unfair! so limited!* she raged, thrilling at her inclusion.

If things had remained that simple, if she were more grateful, might that have bought her peace?

'The neighbours have all phoned to ask how you are,' her mother said. 'They are praying for those poor people.'

'They are still in there, Mama.'

'It is a terrible thing.' Her mother paused for a moment. 'But you, my daughter, did not die and that is something to be grateful for.'

It was her mother's way to be grateful. Each was given enough, if he looked hard enough. *We must not be ungrateful for what fortune has given us because it has not filled the measure as full as we expected.* That was Plutarch. And her father.

'It could have been me,' she said. The words shivered through her and she was grateful for her empty stomach.

'It was not meant for you,' her mother replied. 'This was not your day.'

Alina closed her eyes. So many times she explained to her mother that she had the expression the wrong way around. That here in Ireland to say that it wasn't your day meant that you were unlucky. Yet her mother persisted in her own interpretation, every day lived was another day to be thankful for.

'Will you come?' Alina asked. She knew the size of the request. Mai did not like to be out of her own house, away from her things, her safety blankets. But even the thought of her mother nearby made Alina feel stronger. Annie was intimidated by Alina's mother, by a silence she did not understand.

'Of course.' Alina heard the air sigh out of her mother as she sat down.

'Can you bring my chest?' Her mother had watched her as she put away the emblems of her former life, her engagement ring winking in the sunlight, and closed the lid. Such a small box, to carry a whole past.

'Your father watches over you still,' Mai said, by way of goodbye.

* * *

'Are you all right?' Seán asked, when they lay in bed, tucked together in their familiar half-spoon.

'I'm lucky,' she said. Maybe she would convince him, help him to feel as she did now.

'So very lucky,' he agreed. His thumb traced her arm and grazed the side of her breast, almost by accident. 'Are you too sore?' he asked her.

When she shook her head, he turned her over and began to kiss his way along her neck.

'I asked my mother to bring my chest,' she told him. 'You know, when I stopped wearing it, I never said it was forever.'

He didn't reply but moved her onto her back.

She thought about how wearing it made her feel separate, but in a good way. Pure, almost. Her family's observance when so many others did not. These things might once again be good things to feel. These old thoughts might be good things to think. A secret between her and the prophet.

'It feels like the right time—'

'You don't need to explain anything. It's your decision, Alina, it always was. I'm happy with whatever choice you make, you know that.'

'My hair will be for you alone, like it used to be,' she said, stroking his back. She did not add that her thoughts would no longer be his.

In the light from the window they moved slowly together, and she could see the hope on his face. The hope that had been written there for some months now, the bright wish that tonight might stretch out its arms to the future. That when those arms came back to them, they might cradle an infant.

Let it be a girl.

If they were to have the baby he wanted so badly, let it be a daughter to whom she might give the gift of secrets. The gift of silence inside her head, one sacred space in this unholy world.

RICHIE

Niall Tóibín came to wheel him to the interview room. He looked delighted with himself and Richie wondered if he volunteered for the job. Maybe he was always delighted with himself, some people carried on like that.

'You're not the first hero I've wheeled down here.'

What was he lowering his voice for? Did he think some old woman passing by with her handbag high on her arm might run to the press? He had a sudden memory of his old mam stepping up the aisle to her usual spot for Sunday Mass.

'The one piece of advice the big fella gave me... and I don't mind telling you since it's yourself...'

Richie had no idea who the big fella might be or whether his advice was something that should be minded or avoided.

'... is to look at the camera as if it was your dog,' Niall finished. 'And don't be looking around too much, it makes you look shifty, but, sure, every cat on the street knows that.'

By the time Niall pushed him down a corridor to the interview room, Richie's head was spinning. What did Buddy have to do with anything? He ran his tongue over his lips. His mouth was dry as a piece of toast. He wondered if it was possible for all the moisture in his body to move to the palms of his hands. Anyone looking to shake his hand had better have a tissue handy.

Alina was at the door already, with a man that must be her husband. He looked as Irish as Paddy's pig. What did she say his name was? Did she tell him? He should remember or they'd think he was badly reared. His poor mam would die of shame.

Anxious to avoid handshakes, Richie was only half-listening while Alina introduced her husband, in such a way that he still didn't know the man's name after all that. He clamped Richie's shoulder and said something.

After that, it was the interviewer, Nina. She seemed nice at the start. Then she asked about all that business at work. Richie's tongue swelled – or maybe his mouth shrank, it was one of the two anyway – and words were hard to come by. He was relieved when the focus turned to Alina, although she seemed to have got a bit more into the whole religious bit since earlier. While she spoke, Richie realised with a shock that when the guards had brought up gear bags and agitation, they had been asking him about terrorism. He shivered. It was like the bad old days in the North.

When Niall returned to wheel Richie back to his room, he could hardly remember a word that had been said. Maybe he had sat there like a mute, he panicked. But no. The hospital fella would have made a fuss if that was the case.

'Ah, have it your own way, so.' Niall was annoyed that Richie wouldn't tell him anything.

Let him join the queue.

'Are you sure I'm ready to go?' Richie asked the nurse as she helped him with his shoes and socks.

The stiffness had settled deep in his bones, reminding him of going camping as a boy. He used to wake at first light, cold and rigid as roadkill, his father dead to the world beside him, filling the tent with snoring and farts.

'We wouldn't let you out if we weren't sure.' She straightened up without so much as a hand on her back. Nurses were always fairly nimble, everyone knew. That's why they were popular in the pornos.

'It sounds like you two were the lucky ones,' she continued, solemn with bad news. 'The radio is saying that things are pretty serious, they won't have them out tonight anyway.'

'Christ.'

The miserable string of an orderly appeared to wheel Richie to the door. Niall must really have the hump. On ER, they would only release patients to the care of a loved one – there were often grateful tears involved – but the orderly deposited Richie in the foyer next to a bright yellow wall-mounted telephone.

'Pick it up, it connects you to a taxi company,' he said. 'Can you sit in one of those chairs by the wall? I need to get this one back to the ward.'

Richie watched him amble back down the corridor, pausing to flick the hair out of his eyes before turning the corner to the lifts.

The taxi driver was all chat, none of it bright.

'Desperate, isn't it? Desperate altogether, hah?' he shouted into the rear-view mirror, bobbing his head up and down to catch Richie's eye in between the felt branches of the swinging air freshener.

Keep the head down, Richie-boy, don't give him a good look. Jesus, would he ever shut his trap?

The fake pine smell turned his stomach and he opened a window. They must give them out in taxi-driver school, instead of a cert. Congratulations, may your taxi always smell fresh. A laugh bubbled up from his throat. Christ. Maybe those painkillers were stronger than he thought.

He watched out the window as they left the city behind. Twenty minutes or so and he would be in the comfort of his own home. A hot shower and a cold beer were almost within touching distance. They said no drink, but, sure, fuck it, he had nowhere he had to be.

He undressed and rid himself of the borrowed scrubs.

Straight into the bin with them, don't mind the wash basket, Richie-boy.

The shower was awkward. They told him to put a stool in there, to take the weight off his knee while it healed, but he forgot until he was already in. An old shampoo bottle of Sandra's threw him. The brain was a powerful thing, all the same. Like those tablets. Mighty little yokes, they were. He was flying. He could run a mile. He could climb Croagh Patrick, naked as a jay-bird. Bare feet and all.

It took him a while to get downstairs again, a slow one-two on each step with the crutches. The house was against him, that's what it was. The dark, narrow hallway tightened his throat. The echo of his mam in the kitchen, griping that the milk was sour. How could it be sour, he had it for his breakfast. Was that only this morning? Jesus, fuck. It was against him, though, that

142

was the long and short of it. The holy all of it. Maybe that was enough painkillers for the moment. He should stick to the soft stuff, beer and the likes.

The silence was a killer. He turned on the telly. An hour and nothing. Only the clench of his belly every time an ad break ended, waiting to see his own face and some headline. Some breaking news. Some something.

It was a relief when it came, like finally vomiting out a bad Indian.

'Attempts earlier this evening to move the rubble by crane only worsened the situation as the road collapsed further around the crash site. The Gardaí and fire services are working with experts on site trying to ascertain the best way to proceed with the rescue attempt. Six passengers remain on board and they have been identified as...'

Richie watched the faces on the screen. With the travel cards these days, most people just walked past him to the metre. But he recognised them, all the same. There was the teacher who wore the same thick tights and carried the same big handbag no matter the weather. The woman who looked like she had been out on the tear. The boy with the headphones surgically attached to his ears. Tony, who wore his tracksuit pants so tight that Richie could nearly tell if he was hanging symmetrical. The little Down's girl, Orla, whose mother had come to talk to the drivers when her daughter was learning to use the buses. She had asked them all to look out for her. *To keep a special eye out for our special girl*, she had said. Hard words to forget. The older gentleman, who wore an old-fashioned hat, the kind Humphrey Bogart used to wear. Looking at him now, Richie wondered, as he always did, if someone had once told the man he looked good in a hat. Alina, of course. Her big eyes in the picture looked gentle – the half-madness was only recent, so. His own face was there too.

'Our reporter, Nina Cassidy, spoke earlier to Richie Murray and Alina O'Reilly—'

He muted the sound and hobbled to the kitchen for another beer.

Even if his mam saw it, she mightn't connect it to him, please God. On a bad day, she thought he was still in short pants. To her, he was always Richard, like his father. Richie Murray the bus driver might not shake anything loose in her. He should ring the nursing home, just to be on the safe side. Not with drink taken. He would wait till the morning.

'In the meantime, you can go live to the scene on our website…'

He sat forward in his chair, forearms resting in the hollows worn there over the years. Over the closing credits they ran a set of images from throughout the day: the ambulance taking him away, teams of emergency personnel watching a tiny unmanned camera, the crowds gathering, the man with the GPR machine, the crane. It beggared belief that, despite it all, they were still in there. That he was out here. Only for the crutches, nothing at all might have happened.

Throughout the footage, parts of the emergency response statements were added. A man in a suit made comments that turned out to be only hot air and hope when put against the whole day together. More men in the background. The same pair, often. Calm-looking, the kind you'd want in a crisis. The real heroes.

He'd be lucky if anyone ever got on a bus with him again. Even if he was only a fucking passenger. That

144

was assuming he still had his job. The world and his cat saw Crazy May on the news earlier, 'He lets me on the bus when the others don't.' Probably a firing offence right there. Wouldn't that HR bitch just love to have him back in front of her again? It nearly killed her to lift his suspension the last time. He could say he didn't know the bus pass wasn't hers. That he didn't know she was homeless. That he thought she had Alzheimer's, maybe. Good call, Richie-boy, all those hours in the nursing home could come in handy. He could talk about Alzheimer's all right – sure, didn't he know it like his own pocket?

Five or six beers later, he couldn't bear any more of it. He reached for the phone on the table beside him. He kept the landline on when most gave it up, remembering his old mam saying it made her feel like she lived in a place to have a phone there. Wasn't it just as well he did, with his mobile in smithereens somewhere on the bus?

He dialled Sandra's mobile number from memory and let it ring until he heard her voice on the voicemail. Her posh voice, the one she used on the reception desk at work. Whatever he might have to say, he wasn't stupid enough to think it would bear recording. He considered ringing the phone in the flat, but it wasn't really Sandra's phone there, it belonged to that bastard. Didn't everything? Even Richie's own wife. Legal was legal, though. She couldn't belong to that bastard for another two years and however long the divorce court stuff took. Until then, Richie was still her lawful family. Still had the high ground. Didn't the Constitution itself say the family was the moral centre of the country? They'd get no argument from Richie on that score.

He slept on the couch to avoid the stairs, wishing he had thought to bring a blanket and pillow down after his shower. He pulled the phone jack out of the wall. Let it ring, he wouldn't kill himself getting up to answer it. Sandra would see his missed call and probably think his old mam had finally gone. Let her think it. Let her be upset. It might be one less rut that bastard would have out of his wife. Let him keep it in his pants for one night while she cried for his mother. Let him pretend to be supportive, shifting sideways in the bed when he got the horn at the sight of her in her short nightie. Let her call him a disgusting pig with only the one thing on his mind. The image of her in her nightie stirred him, and he pulled away at himself for a couple of miserable minutes before giving it up, too drunk or too distracted. Pathetic, Richie-boy, can't even be bothered with yourself. It's no wonder she left.

It was too quiet. His own voice in his head was the only thing he could hear. He turned the telly back on.

'I'm telling you now, she knew more than she let on,' the man insisted.

'What do you mean?' asked the host, egging him on.

'How come she was the only one sitting up near the front?' said the man. 'Answer me that!' A note of triumph. 'She must have known.'

'It was only luck that she got out at all,' the host said. 'The driver pulled her with him, emergency services said earlier.'

'Maybe there was a pair of them in it.'

'Are you suggesting an act of domestic terrorism?' the host asked.

This frightened the man. 'Well now, I don't know. I'm just saying that there's been no official statement that it wasn't a bomb.'

A terrorist, Richie-boy. Jesus. Lovely. A fine end to a fuck of a day.

'I should point out that there was a statement earlier from the Defence Forces...' the host clarified.

The news bulletin claimed it had breaking news about a planning scandal, some kind of political corruption that might be to blame for the road collapse. 'More to come after the break,' they told him, as if it was a soap opera and not people's lives.

He knew there hadn't been any gear bag of guns. Nobody with a big coat and a bomb under it. Was that even what people did, outside the movies? Did that mean it was the planners' fault? Was it something he did, somehow, to the bus? The question that circled all day, the one he ignored.

He lay awake to hear the news, but his eyes were heavy and he dozed off, caught by the beer and the day. He dreamt of fires, floods, his mother's eyes, only there was glass where her eyes should be, her arms out, 'Please, Richie'. She turned into Sandra in his arms, the pair of them buck naked, and he woke up pulling himself raw until he came in a burst, then slept curled around the wet patch like a cat.

* * *

The doorbell woke him. Three sharp rings, a break, then three more. She knew how to get her own back, Sandra did.

'How are you feeling?' she asked, pushing past him in the doorway like she still had a right to.

'A bit stiff,' Richie said, closing the door behind

147

her. Whatever she had to say wouldn't be improved by being shared with the neighbours. 'Nothing a few days at home won't fix, they said in the hospital.' He followed her into the living room, his head hurting with every step.

'Have you someone to come in to you? To give you a hand with things? Since your mam…'

'Since I've packed Mam off to a home for the bewildered?' Richie said. He usually threw the finger commas around when he said that to people, but he needed two hands on the crutches. If she had to help him up off the ground, he wouldn't be able to hide the stone and a half he'd put on since she left.

'You know that's not what I meant,' Sandra sighed. 'Everyone knows she was too far gone for you to mind her any more—'

'I have a few dinners in the freezer.' Richie cut her off mid-sentence. 'They'll see me right.'

'Put some trousers on, I'll make tea.'

The stain on the couch glowed as if it was radioactive. Had she seen it? Smelled it? Christ, she would think he was pathetic. He nodded towards the kitchen. 'Can we have the tea inside? I need food with the tablets.'

He struggled into his jeans, listening to her hum as she opened cupboards for teabags, sugar, marmalade.

'I can pop in, if you want?' she called. 'Bring a few things over, run the hoover? It wouldn't be any trouble.'

'Lover-boy wouldn't be happy with that,' Richie muttered.

Sandra walked over to the window. 'Never miss a chance, do you, Richie? No fear the crash would have made you grow up any bit.'

'You sound like your mother.'

'Don't talk about my mother,' Sandra said, turning her head so fast he wondered for a minute if it might keep going all the way round. 'Wasn't she right, anyway, my mother? She told me we'd never last.'

'She was a long way off,' Richie said. Didn't they make it to fourteen years? The old bag wouldn't even give him credit for that much, no doubt.

Sandra breathed in, he could see the ten-count in her shoulders, the way the therapist showed her. A million years or more since they laughed about it, the pair of them breathing and counting together. He breathed the last three with her, even though she didn't know it.

'Do you want my help or not?' she said.

Richie pictured her in the kitchen of that shiny apartment, making sushi or caviar or whatever fancy shite that bastard ate for his tea, before putting the leftovers into a Tupperware box to bring over to him in the poky corners of his mother's house.

'Just because he took my leftovers doesn't mean I have to take his,' he wanted to say.

'That wouldn't make us equal,' he wanted to say.

That would send her nuclear altogether.

Instead he sighed and hoisted his leg onto a kitchen chair. 'No need,' he said, 'but thanks all the same.'

Her shoulders relaxed. 'Do you want me to put the heating on for you?' she asked. 'It's after taking a real dip these last few days.'

'I have it on a timer,' he said. 'It's daylight robbery any other way.' He didn't add that it was only part of the reason. That he was afraid he would forget to turn it on some night after one too many and wake to burst pipes in his kitchen. If he woke at all.

'True for you.'

'It's handier anyway for when I'm on the late shift.'

'It's a new breed of cold,' Sandra said. 'Climate change or what have you.'

They didn't sound like her words. They might be that bastard's. Or maybe it was the legacy of the recession talking. The new Irish, cynical and apathetic at the same time, the worst of bar-stool politics. It didn't make a jot of difference that it was true that even the weather had turned against them. The new cold of winters, the army called in to defend its citizens from Mother Nature. The new shortness of summers, the golden days of his childhood and shirtsleeves from April to October long gone. A sunny bank holiday weekend the height of it. Believing that was all they deserved. That it wasn't climate change at all, but human change.

'Do you know those lads, Richie?' Sandra said, pulling the lace curtain back a bit to see better.

'Who?' he pulled himself up, holding in the sigh of his weight, and peered out the kitchen window. Over the garden wall, he could see a few heads peering in. 'Local lads, I think.'

'Looking for your autograph,' she nudged him gently.

'A likely story.'

'It was on the news, you know, about you pulling that woman out to safety,' Sandra said. 'They called you a hero.'

'Go on out of that.'

He saw her to the front door and watched her walk down the little path in front of the house and out onto the footpath. The gang of teenagers, five or six of them identical in matchstick-man jeans and hooded sweatshirts, sat on the kerb across the road. Their eyes followed her down to the parking bay where she'd left her car. Why wouldn't they? She was always a handsome woman, even back when she was carrying the extra weight.

When the doctor told them there would be no children, they didn't talk about it much. Sandra would pull out the crisps and biscuits at night in front of the telly, 'to cheer us up', as she put it. Neither of them told his mam. Her disappointment, couched in grim novenas and the offers of relics, would have made reality out of it.

Hard to say if a child would have kept them together. The poor thingeen might only have dissolved under the weight of the responsibility.

Hard to imagine having to explain to a child about Sandra's new apartment, about the part that bastard was to play in its life. About their new fucking daddy.

They were better off the way they were, most likely. *Que sera sera*, as his mam would say.

Sandra's car pulled away and he had barely lowered his arse to the couch when a crash broke the silence. It took him a second to realise what it was: a stone hitting the front window. The little fuckers. It didn't break the glass, though, nor did the next one. Third time's a charm, wasn't that how it went? He was left standing in the smithereens of his own living room, the hole letting their words in along with the blasts of icy air.

'Where's your girlfriend now?'

He was confused at first and thought they meant Sandra. Had she said something to them, told them to get on home?

'Where's your headscarf?'

'Terrorist.'

'Osama bin Murray.'

At this last comment they doubled over laughing and

ran off before he could pull it together enough to say anything at all. If he could run, he still wouldn't have caught them, greyhounds that they were. Kids raised on McDonald's and the absence of a slap. He'd have been pawing the air behind them like a bear after salmon.

Fifty-two years old and he wanted his mother. No. Thank God his old mam wasn't here, the shock would have killed her. Not in her younger days, mind, when anyone that dared to look sideways at him got the hard edge of her hand and words that stung and kept coming. He couldn't have gone after them, sure, look at him, stiff as a board and on crutches to boot.

'You're a cartoon, Richie-boy,' he said out loud.

He had to wait for his hand to stop shaking before he could call the police. They would be able to do fuck all about it but they might board up the window for him. Keep some of that expensive heat in, if nothing else.

PART THREE – OUT

IN THE BEGINNING WAS THE WORD

If it were a film, the camera would hold for a long moment on the hush of the scene, moving from mourner to mourner against a backdrop of some gentle instrumental piece. No. Nothing instrumental, nothing that would make a person want to sway. Something darker, with the hoarse sorrowful tones of love lived and lost. A woman, an American, someone with sky and scale in their voice. The kind that could never come from a small, wet island that rarely saw the two ends of the sky at the same time.

There would be a montage of grief. Picture the sort of thing. Inviting unity. Pseudo-art on the universal nature of sorrow. Hands clasping. Tissues and phone numbers moving from one pocket to the next. Fingers digging warm on shoulders.

In real life, there are no montages. The isolation that comes from knowing little or nothing doesn't play well on-screen.

In real life, the hush of the scene is real, the machinery quiet, the only movement coming from the fingers of the crowd. Type, click, read, react. Refresh.

@elliepk1 Thinkin of all ur families. #staystrong #corkbuscrash #pray

@pickitoutside Oh my god. How cud dis happen blame the planners. #corkbuscrash #staystrong #protest

@rachdaddy1 Pipes should be replaced periodically. Not done here. Where did that money go? #corkbuscrash #staystrong #answers

@margaretshanahan03 Why are they not doing something? They've been in there all night. God love the poor parents. #corkbuscrash #staystrong #dosomething

@littleredridinghood Dey must all be ded else dey wud be doin sumtin. Lies lies lies. #corkbuscrash #liars @conspiracy

@mxnoonan Easy to judge, not so easy to do. Don't know how they do it #corkbuscrash #heroes

@stfinbarrschurch It is the families we must help now. Prayer service tonight at St Francis Church. #corkbuscrash #letuspray

@bartsimpsonspants Nuttin happenin cos waitin for bomb sqad. No coincidense she got out. Must of known it beforhand. #corkbuscrash #sendthemhome

@ciarantimm Two of the council 'helping police with enquiries' after they found them at the airport. Disgrace. #corkbuscrash #answers #shame

@rachdaddy1 RT@ciarantimm Same old thing. Watch, they will be back at airport and gone in 24 hours time. #corkbuscrash #answers #shame #disgrace

Type. Click. Read. React.

Refresh.

Refresh.

Refresh.

TIM

'Deb? Everything all right?'

'Everything's fine. I just wanted to check in, see how things are over there.'

Tim felt a flicker of annoyance. She should know better than to think he had time to chit-chat. He reminded himself that things like this brought everyone's heart a little closer to their mouth. The call was a sign of her big-heartedness.

'It's slow but steady. There's a lot riding on the contingency planning.' The party line felt strange on his tongue. She wasn't part of it, though. She wouldn't know which or whether.

'I saw the last statement,' she said. 'It was solid.'

'Good.' He cleared his throat, tried for something warmer. 'Good to know we're covering our bases.'

'I'm glad you're not taking any notice of the nonsense,' she said.

No fear she would come right out and say that the radio gobshites were wondering if they had any fucking clue at all. She would never just ask if they really had ballsed it all up earlier. He was so sick of this twist-mouthed country. The cynicism of the politicians seeped into everything. The bitter passivity they bred. Everyone a victim.

'We need to get these people out before we start looking around for people to blame,' he said, his voice wound tight as thread on a spool.

'I'll let you get back to it.' She paused. 'Fuck the begrudgers.'

The unexpectedness of her swearing made him laugh, but she was already gone.

* * *

He was a million miles from laughter when night fell and they were no closer to an end. An island nation with plenty of ships and lifting machinery and every one of them seemingly too heavy. Throw a stone on a normal day and you'd hit a builder, yet it took three hours to find one and get the machine in position. It lasted less than a minute before the cracks radiating out from the hole began to advance and spread. The machine retreated, leaving the road like something out of an Indiana Jones movie.

They were doing their best and coming up short. Every time. Every fucking one of them.

'Should I congratulate you on your scoop?' Nina was coming out of the bathroom, her head down, focused on her phone. Who was she texting this late at night? 'I suppose you're feeling very pleased with yourself.'

'Excuse me?' She looked up at him.

'You certainly made a story out of nothing,' he went on, anger making him reckless. 'That poor Alina O'Reilly, suffering from shock, and you had her cocked up in front of the whole country putting on a headscarf and talking about Allah. I didn't take you for a racist, whatever else—'

'Get a grip,' she said, sharply. 'Nobody put Alina in any kind of position. She is as entitled as anyone to talk about her beliefs. Nothing could have been less racist. And what did you mean, "whatever else"?' she went on. 'Whatever else, what?'

'Whatever else you might have asked her,' he said. He heard how flimsy it was.

'Things must be bad if you're out here picking fights,' she said.

How much of their marriage was spent in this space, where the slightest thing could deepen a fight, or dissolve it entirely. It was the phone that tipped the balance. The way she slid it into her pocket as if it was of no importance and stood facing him, her eyebrows raised. 'I'm here,' those eyebrows said.

'Off the record?'

'Of course.'

'The Coast Guard helicopter did eight or ten passes with a thermal-imaging camera. The surface material is heat permeable, so they should have been able to pick up heat signatures of anyone alive in there.' He stopped, swallowed.

'Fuck. Does that mean…?'

He spread his hands wide, palms to the ceiling. 'Not necessarily. We just don't know.'

'Those poor people,' she said.

Anyone else would have thought she meant the six souls trapped under the earth. He knew better. He could see the stories of the families written all over her face. He had a sudden urge to go home, to say goodnight to the children.

'I didn't know she was going to say any of that,' Nina said. 'Alina, I mean. Nobody did. Her poor husband was terrified.' She looked away, as if the question was casual. 'Did she really believe it, do you think? That people bring it on themselves?'

Tim couldn't help it, a snort of laughter escaped him. 'Pretty convenient, considering she got out,' he said.

'Do you believe it?' Her eyes were back on his.

'No sane person, no matter how devout, believes in the existence of a divine balance sheet,' he said. 'Rest assured of that.'

'I hope they're asleep,' Nina said.

She spoke so softly he wasn't sure he heard her right. '*Le Repos des Âmes*,' he said. 'That *Repose of the Souls* painting we saw years ago, remember?'

She shook her head.

He had been so moved by it that he didn't see a single other thing in the exhibition. It was simple, sombre. A sky full of souls, all watching over one house. Like guardian angels. He forgot about it shortly after, but then, after Aisling, he remembered and looked it up online. There was something comforting in the idea that people could still watch each other when they were gone. See how it all turned out.

'I have to go,' he said.

'Of course.' She lifted up her hand as if to touch his arm, then let it drop back down to her side.

He took the stairs two at a time. It was night-time, the roads were quiet. He'd be home and back in forty minutes. A quick hug, if they'd let him.

* * *

They were in the kitchen when he got to Deb's house – home, he corrected himself. Laura was bent over

159

her homework, while Deb tapped away on a laptop beside her. Brendan was standing by the sink, slurping cornflakes out of a bowl. Would he be able to tune it out better if Brendan was his?

'I didn't expect to see you,' Deb said, getting up to kiss him hello. 'Is it over?'

He shook his head. 'Flying visit, that's all.'

He bent to kiss Laura's head. 'What are you working on?'

'You smell funny,' Laura said, wrinkling up her nose.

'Funny how?' He made a show of sniffing himself to make her smile.

'Like when the tumble dryer is left on too long,' she said.

'You're right. There are oil heaters in the meeting room. I smell just like them.'

'You were on the news,' Brendan said, between bites.

'We're falling over news crews. It makes everything that bit harder.'

'The public have a right to know.' Brendan had a thirteen-year-old's self-righteousness.

'They do,' Tim said, evenly.

'I mean, all afternoon all anybody talked about was safety and then, the next thing, the crane cracks the road.'

'It was hardly a stamp of confidence,' Tim agreed. 'But what was the alternative? We had to try. That's what we're trained to do.'

'Some training,' Brendan said. He put his bowl in the sink and left the room.

'How did it happen?' Laura asked, her face tight with worry. It was hard to tell if it was the bus or the tension. Everything worried her. Would Aisling, too, have grown up carrying the weight of the world on her soft shoulders?

'We're not a hundred per cent sure yet, but it looks like the run-off from the river, you know the way it's been flooding a lot in the last while?' He waited for her nod. 'All that extra water might have stayed in the ground and washed away so much of the foundations of the road that there was nothing to hold it up.'

'Then the bus was too heavy and broke through it,' Laura said. 'Like ice.'

'Exactly.'

'The driver and that woman are okay, right? That means the others are more likely to be fine too, doesn't it?'

Tim's throat closed for a second at the idea that these questions were in her head. That she had to know these things happened in her world. He nodded. 'We're optimistic.'

'What happens next?' Deb asked.

'We might have to do things the old-fashioned way,' he said. He took a sheet of paper and sketched a chain of emergency workers, smiles on their faces and a pile of stones behind them. Propaganda at its finest. The safety chain, the Dutch called their safety management system, a series of steps to tether one thing to another. Straight-talking people, the Dutch.

'Will you be one of them?' Laura pointed to the little stick figures.

He felt rather than saw Deb stiffen. She had told him early on that if he was still on the front line she wouldn't have agreed to the blind date. She could never have a relationship with an active firefighter, she said. It wouldn't be fair on the children. He told her she was right. That firefighting was a young man's game, there was a reason they offered early retirement. He didn't tell her that there was also a reason so few of them took it.

'They need me outside,' he told her. 'To keep track of everything that's going on.'

'I'm glad,' Laura said.

He wished he could be sure that it was worse to be on the ground, facing the ball of fire, instead of outside, spinning it.

* * *

'I'm not sure she should know that much about it.' Deb folded clothes in their room, neat his 'n' hers piles on the bed. He had a sudden urge to fling them everywhere.

'She obviously heard it on the news during the day. I didn't tell her anything she didn't already know, except how we're going to get those people out.'

'Even still. It's not what she should be thinking about before bed.'

Was this what it would be like? Tim wondered. Having to run every conversation past Deb first? Perhaps he should ask her for a list of approved topics. That way he could be sure not to offend. 'Should I have refused to answer?'

'Don't be silly. It's just a bit morbid for her, that's all.' She began to put clothes into drawers.

'As a child, I lay in bed the night before my thirteenth birthday, waiting for twelve o'clock,' he imagined telling her. 'When it came, I was so relieved that I wouldn't die before I became a teenager.'

But her sunny disposition – one of her most attractive

162

features, he reminded himself – wouldn't admit the possibility. 'It was probably a thought you had much later,' she would tell him. 'You're rewriting history.'

Nina would be tolerant. No morbid imaginings of his could touch the darkness she lived in.

Finished, Deb stood and stretched, her T-shirt rising above the waistband of her pants, the softness that spoke of her contentment. He went to her, ran his finger along the line of winking skin, and she turned to face him.

They were red and breathless, like teenagers fumbling in the back of a car, when Deb stopped.

'Laura's crying.'

She had been sick, there was vomit stuck to everything when he led her out to the bathroom, the sour smell of her reminding him of nights pulling drunks from crackling hallways and rivers.

'I have to get back,' he said. 'I'm sorry.'

'I know. It's fine.' Deb kissed him and closed the bathroom door. He could hear her running the bath for Laura, her voice a constant reassuring stream.

* * *

In the dark, everything was strangely quiet. The vigil was long over, the crowds scattered to their homes for the night. No doubt they would be back at first light. He didn't know Nina would be there, but as soon as he saw her standing at the barrier, he felt he had always known.

'Is it too early to say good morning or too late to say goodnight?' she said, without turning.

'Couldn't stay away?' he asked.

'I'm like one of those ghouls,' she said. 'Hanging

around to see if bodies are brought out under cover of darkness.'

He wondered if he looked as tired as she did. If, once again, they had matching purplish shadows under their eyes. Like Halloween bookends they were, once upon a time.

'What do you think the day will bring?' she asked.

'I wish I knew.'

'Now is the hour of faith,' she said.

When he looked at her, she shrugged. 'The Church doesn't get a monopoly on it,' she said.

He moved to the side and sat on the edge of the footpath. The air was still, a rare moment of quiet in the city.

'*Le Repos des Âmes*,' Nina said, coming to sit beside him. 'I lied yesterday when I said I had forgotten it.'

'You called it creepy, if I remember right,' Tim said, nudging her arm.

'I couldn't understand what you found so comforting in it at the time. But now...'

'Less creepy?' Tim offered.

'Less creepy,' she allowed.

'You okay?' he gestured at her hand, running its track up and down her arm as if battery-powered.

'It's a little bit worse than usual,' she said. 'It'll pass.'

'Can I see?' He took her arm and pushed the sleeve up gently, exposing raw, scaly skin. 'Do you have anything to put on it?'

She made a face. 'Did you not hear our friend yesterday? It's all in my head.'

They laughed at that idea, that stress could be imaginary. The luxury of it. The sheer stupidity of people.

'I joined a grief group,' Tim said, suddenly.

He didn't mean to tell her. So many people had advised them to go, telling them that meeting others who had gone through the same thing would lessen their burden. They both baulked at the idea. Tim because he couldn't bear the idea of talking about Aisling with strangers. Nina because she rejected the idea that the burden should be lessened.

'Don't look so shocked,' he said. 'I've only gone once or twice.'

'How come?'

'It all felt a bit… staged, or something. A lot of them had been there for a while and there was this real sense of one-upmanship there, like everyone's grief was graded.'

There was a couple there, their teenage son the victim of a hit-and-run. That mother was the real yardstick in the group, her shock and grief open like a vein the length of her arm. The father sat silently, his grief pale beside hers. In a child's life, fathers got to be heroes just for being there. In a child's death, they got second billing for reasons everybody knew and nobody understood.

'Seeing as we're confessing…' Nina nudged his arm as he had done earlier.

'No way! You too?'

'One session. They thought I was a stuck-up bitch.' Her laugh was a hurt bark. 'A woman asked me one day if I thought I was better than them, just because I didn't want to go into the ins and outs of how Aisling died.'

He understood the impulse to stay silent. He had felt it too, a reaction against people's greed for the story, the horror. Himself and Nina the cautionary tale that everybody dreaded. He could see how withholding it would feel like a small victory. If he was being honest, he could also understand the confusion of those other nameless grief-stricken parents. Nina had a way of making her mourning seem better than anyone else's, made purer somehow by the fine filigree of her grief. When they – the they that peopled their lives back then – suggested cremation as a way of keeping Aisling with them, Nina was furious. 'It's not the same,' she kept saying. 'I didn't carry ashes.'

'Do you go alone?' she asked. 'Or…'

'Alone,' he said. 'I haven't told Deb. Yet,' he corrected himself. 'I wanted to see if it was likely to stick before I said anything.'

'Don't tell me how to grieve and I won't tell you how to grieve,' she said, and he smiled at the quote.

'How are you doing?'

She didn't answer the question. Instead, she said, 'Do you remember last Halloween, that old woman whose dog was killed?'

'Tied to a firework. We were called out to it.' It was a grim scene, one of the worst, in a way.

'I interviewed her a couple of days later. No big deal, it was just a dog story, you know?'

He nodded.

'To me a dog is just a dog, but I could have sworn I saw some of the same grief in the woman's eyes. We sat in this dirty little living room, with one square of window at eye-level with the street and it was the first time something else felt real. Since Ais.'

'I'm not waiting to see how the grief group goes before telling Deb,' he said, without knowing he was going to. 'I'm afraid she will want to come with me, and I don't want her to.' Support would pale beside true understanding. He didn't want to see if that was something they could withstand.

'We never stood a chance, did we?' Nina asked. 'All those social workers telling us that fifty per cent of couples whose child dies end up splitting up.'

'Hard to tell if they were warning us or egging us on,' Tim agreed.

'Did we only last the year to try and prove them wrong, do you think?'

'No.' Of that he was certain. 'We got each other through that year, we helped each other to survive it.'

'And you, how are you?'

I'm afraid, he wanted to tell her. I'm afraid that I've made the wrong choices. That I'm with a wonderful woman I don't love enough simply because she's everything that I'm not. Everything you're not. That her children will never accept me fully and my second chance at fatherhood will vanish into dust. I'm afraid that I've given up the job I love and taken a lesser version because I feel it's all I deserve. I'm afraid I'm only moving misery from point a to point b. I'm afraid that when Aisling died, my best life died with her.

'I'm still a step away from the blue plastic bag,' he said and wondered if his smile looked as sad as hers.

They had gone for a walk early one evening, trying to get the hospital smell out of their noses. Or the reality out of their lives, maybe. Waiting at the traffic lights, they saw a Pakistani man walking along. It was not his Pakistani-ness – if that's what he was – that made him memorable. It was the blue plastic bag tied around his head, tucked neatly under his chin, the handles tied on top of his head, twisted together with a black wrap-tie like some sort of avant-garde style from the catwalk.

From that designer who did the *Fifth Element*, Tim said. Gaultier, Nina said at the same time, and they laughed, delighted with themselves, until they remembered their daughter, attached to machines.

The man fascinated them both for some reason. Maybe because they didn't know if it had meaning, this strange headpiece. If it signified anything more than his own gentle disconnection from the world. He became their private shorthand for madness. 'I'll be only a step away from the blue plastic bag,' they would say to each other when things were bad with Aisling. And then, when things were worse, without her.

Rain began to spatter down lightly, flecking her cheeks. 'I like this weather,' she said.

He remembered. Gentle rain was honest, she used to say. Not like that false, spitty, bastarding kind of rain that drowned a person without their noticing and ruined them for the rest of the afternoon.

In his pocket, his phone buzzed. If he ignored it, would it mean there was something more left to say?

'Leo?'

'The engineers say the water pipes are compromised.'

'I'll be right in.'

When he stood outside a burning building, not knowing how a rescue was going to go, everything was simplified: it was just breathe in, breathe out. The gaps to think were so tiny that only the inconsequential things squeezed through: a song he learned from the radio to impress a girl; the U-14 semi-final they won; the shirt he wore to his grads with the little pleats down the front, his mother complaining that it was a nuisance to iron.

Later, he would realise that he ran towards this building without a thought in his head.

* * *

The tech guys had made a good job of the visuals. Tim watched the image on screen, layers of grey gravel like bubble wrap being pushed away by a bright blue stripe of virtual water, leaving nothing but a thin black line under the model bus. He felt for the little bus as it broke the surface and fell into the hole. Then an agonising five-second wait before the network of pipes in the surrounding area crumbled, with water beginning to creep towards the bus.

Leo sighed. 'At least they didn't put any model people in it.'

'Or the camera footage.'

'Christ. Don't.'

Earlier, they had sent the camera back in to assess the situation. Breathless from his sprint from the site, Tim joined the cluster around the monitor hoping for... what? A bird's-eye view of people sitting in a circle singing cheerful songs?

The view was grainier than before, the camera not penetrating as deep as it had previously, the rock and rubble blocking most of the side panel of the bus. It took a few seconds of fiddling with the settings to realise that it wasn't grit smearing the lens, but water. Coming in slowly, but coming in nonetheless. It was impossible to say how long before it would flood the bus. The geologists were hunched over their calculations: the absorbency of various rock and soil types, the rate of water flow.

Manpower was the only solution. The teams were already assembling and suiting up. For all that Tim had cheerfully told Laura they would move the rubble stone by stone, the reality was more complex, with the likelihood of a rockfall dogging every move.

'Donnellan wants to visit the site.' The Chief slammed the receiver down. 'The caring face of the government in the run-up to the election. He wants to be seen wearing a helmet. Jesus fuck.'

'We can refuse,' Leo said.

The Chief sighed. 'We'll give him five minutes, Leo, while you brief the team for entry. Tim, can you take him to the family centre then, let him shake a few hands before we send him over to the media. With any luck they'll eat him alive.'

That would go down like a lead balloon, Tim knew. The last thing the families needed was to have politicians paraded in front of them. But it wasn't his decision. He would just have to keep it as short as possible.

When the Chief brought Donnellan and his entourage back in from the site, Tim met them at the door.

'Minister, this is Tim Kelleher. Tim was part of the working group that tested the framework before it was adopted. Tim will take you in to meet the families. I'm needed elsewhere, I'm afraid.'

'Are the media in there too?' Donnellan asked.

Tim gritted his teeth. 'No. We like to give the families their privacy.'

'Can't win them all,' Donnellan said. 'Smart move, Tim, watching it all from in here. The front lines are a young man's game!'

He wasn't any better in front of the families.

'I wanted to come and visit the site and meet with yourselves,' Donnellan started. 'And offer you my assurances that the government fully supports the rescue effort and sympathises with your situation.' He stopped, seeming intent on making eye contact with every individual in the room. 'I have met with the coordination team on site and I understand that they are in good possession of the facts of the situation and I share their confidence that a rescue is imminent. And a happy outcome for you all, please God.'

Blowhard. Saying the one thing the team had so far managed to avoid. The implied promise that none of them could stand over.

'What I think we can take from the situation so far is the strength of the coordinated response from the principal emergency services, the kind of coordination that is the lynchpin of the major emergency framework brought in by the government...'

It was no place for useless politicking, but cutting across a minister was above Tim's pay grade. Deb would be well able for him. Heading people off at the pass was one of her specialties. The open-hearted could speak with a bluntness forsworn by others, they were assumed to have no hidden agenda. She would tell him anyone could do it, that a path only became a path when someone else walked it.

He cleared his throat.

'Minister Donnellan, I'm sure you'd like to meet some of the families now,' he said, when the man stopped to draw breath.

While the minister made his way from table to table, a young woman appeared at Tim's elbow.

'Loretta Keaveney, Media Liaison for HSE South,' she said, shaking Tim's hand. 'Alison told me I would find you here. We're close to entry, she said, so I wanted to come over and talk through the next stage with you.'

'Next stage?'

'Media centre at the hospital, who takes point on statements once the action moves over to us, that kind of thing.' She clicked the lid of her biro, ambition fairly crackling off her.

'Of course,' Tim said. 'Just give me a few minutes to finish up in here.'

Donnellan was on his final round, giving it the two-hands double-pat of sincerity, when Jason lost his temper.

'More fucking suits?' he shouted. 'What we need is more men on the ground. Does nobody understand that?'

'The response to this situation is part of my department's strategic—' Donnellan began.

'Strategy? You're joking, right? What you need is more tactical. More guys willing to get in the goddamn hole.'

Tim intervened. 'Mr Teegan's son, Paul' – thank Christ he always had a head for names – 'is one of the people on the bus.'

'I understand your frustration,' Donnellan said, 'I assure you everyone is doing everything necessary to get your son out.'

'Everything necessary? You're joking, right? Tell me you're joking. Am I going to have to go in and get him myself? Because I tell you, that's the way it's looking to me right now.'

'The rescue team are being briefed as we speak,' Tim said. 'They'll be in there in the next few minutes. They're nearly there, Mr Teegan. It's nearly over.'

'Is it really?' Jason's wife, Elmarie, asked him. 'Is it really nearly over?'

God damn Donnellan for putting him in this position.

'It really is,' he told her. He held his hands in front of him, resisting every impulse to cross his fingers.

'Thanks, Tim,' the minister chuckled, when they were safely back in the lift. 'Not an easy situation in there.'

'It's a tough day for them,' Tim agreed.

Part of him believed it was toughest on the fathers, the men reduced to sitting on the sidelines overcoming their own urge to pull the child out themselves. People talked about the ferocity of the maternal instinct, the ability to lift cars for their offspring. The ferocity of fathers had to be contained, channelled into holding back, supporting, a simmering presence.

Aisling needed a lumbar puncture to confirm the diagnosis. The nurses were apologetic about it, knowing its bad press, but almost certain wasn't certain enough. There was no time to waste, they had Nina gowned up and ready before he even thought to ask, 'why you?' He was answered with a row of pitying smiles, as if it was self-evident: his job was to wait. He stood outside the door and wondered why the assumption that she was a good mother outclassed anything he might have done. Through the door, he heard her sing the silly songs that made Aisling smile when she was conscious. He was a good parent, although he would not have thought to sing. Nina, when they came out, was pale. 'What happened?' he wanted to ask, but he couldn't put her through reliving it, so he held her hand in wordless sympathy, the not-knowing burning a hole in his belly all the while.

For a sudden, savage minute, he admired Jason's angry bluster, his refusal to parent silently.

* * *

Leo texted, 'Starting final run-through', and Tim went to the crisis centre, flicking through the early news stations while he waited. 'Taking the pulse,' they called it on the Media and PR Diploma he did as part of his training for this job.

'Of course, this part of the county is notoriously marshy,' a commentator's voice boomed out. 'So there's nothing really to say that this kind of erosion isn't happening in other places. This might be just the first weak spot, given its proximity to the channel of the river.'

Jesus. He paused again on a particularly teeth-grating segment about the will of God and thought immediately of Alina. How was it that people heard her statement as somehow frightening, when it so closely mirrored their own? So much of it was just habit. Although, he had noticed, after his father died, his mother started invoking his dad's name instead of God. As if having been awarded his seat in heaven, his father had some kind of clout up there. The idea would have made his dad laugh. He would have looked at Tim's mother with affection, finding her oddnesses endearing in the way he always did.

He missed them both, but securely, with a kind of nostalgia for all the good years he had with them. They didn't make marriages like that any more, built to last, no matter what. In the aftermath of his and Nina's separation, it took his moving out to really recognise the quiet achievement of his parents. Forty years together, with little fuss or fanfare. It was the way of their generation, coming together in pairs and groups, family, neighbours, community, friendships made up of blood and geography, the concerns of a small coastal town. Finding enough comfort in it to keep going. On the rare Saturday mornings after a boat lost at sea, they would line the beach, him and his dad together with the other men and boys, watching the waves for the body to wash back in. Behind them, the families would wait in the car park, afraid to look, afraid to know. Feeling their eyes on his back and knowing that he would spend his whole life trying to make sure that fewer faces like that had to exist in the world.

'It's a good thing you do,' his dad said to him once, careful to hold onto his words until he was standing in the doorway and could walk away from the drift they left behind.

Neither of his parents ever knew Aisling. His father never saw Tim's own face become the thing they stood shoulder to shoulder to keep out.

'That's why I don't fly Ryanair,' a listener confided to the presenter. 'I'm always sure that if I pick my own seat, that'll be the one that gets ejected or that's fatal in a plane crash.'

'So instead of picking your seat, you feel like you're picking your fate,' said the presenter, 'I see.'

Surely the whole point about fate is that it cannot be chosen, it just comes. God spare him this crap.

'Are you listening to this, Dad? Can you have a word with someone?' he said to the empty room.

Even after shutting off the radio, the woman's fear stayed with him. She sounded so exposed. He found himself dialling Deb's number.

'How's Laura?'

'She's fine. She didn't eat much, her stomach was still a bit tender, but she went off to school no bother.'

'Maybe she should have taken the day off.'

'You know Laura, it would kill her to miss a day of school.' Deb laughed.

'Even still.'

'Tim. She's fine. I wouldn't let her go if she wasn't.'

There it was again, the chiding tone. The I-know-better. Laura was too thin already, he knew, but he was afraid to bring it up with Deb.

He dropped his phone onto the desk, activating his laptop. The screen saver was an image he liked of a man sitting in a tiny lamplit caravan at the foot of a giant wall. He never decided to his satisfaction if the man was safeguarding whatever was inside that wall or if it kept him out. Either seemed plausible, depending on his mood.

There was scuffling outside his door and it swung open to reveal Leo, pushing a young man inside ahead of him. 'We caught this fool trying to get through the perimeter. He says he wants to go into the hole.'

'She's in there,' said the man. 'I have to get her out.'

'All you're doing now is preventing us from getting in there,' Leo said.

'Our job is to go in,' Tim said. 'Why don't you sit down and tell me what you think we need to know? Anything could help.' He drew a notepad towards him and clicked his pen.

Leo mouthed a thank you and headed back out to the real work.

Sitting and quiet, the man was older than Tim first thought. Early thirties, probably, with a newly shaven head.

'Aftersun works wonders on the rash,' he found himself telling the man.

'What?'

'I had the same thing the first time I shaved my head. A charity thing, you know.'

The whole unit did it, caught up in their own big-man-ness, cocksure that their ten thousand euros would be the sum that would change the world. Nobody told him about the spots, how vulnerable and ugly his head would look.

He got up and poured a paper cup of water for the man. 'Drink this.' Sometimes they just needed something to focus on. With one hand taken out of play, he would be less likely to make a bolt for the door. 'I'm Tim,' he said. 'What's your own name?'

'Kieran. Kieran O'Halloran.'

'Who were you trying to get in to, Kieran?'

'Lucy Phelan, my girlfriend. Ex-girlfriend. Girlfriend.' He put his head in his hands. 'I'm not sure.'

'You're not sure she's in there?' Even though Tim knew she was. Lucy Phelan, twenty-eight, postgrad student. Only daughter of Patricia, she of the high heels and running mascara.

'I'm not sure she's my girlfriend. We were together two years, nearly, and then she broke up with me for no reason, out of the blue, like, and I heard she was seeing someone else. Some big businessman. A married fella. I bump into her in the city from time to time, like Wednesday night, she came back to my place when the pub closed and I thought, I thought...' He slumped a bit in his seat. 'She left before I could ask her if we were back together or what.'

Somehow Tim doubted it. If she was creeping out before he woke up, then that told its own story. Something about the way Kieran insisted that he met

Lucy by accident didn't ring true. Easy to imagine him gathering titbits of information about her, hanging around in the hopes of meeting her in a vulnerable moment.

His eyes darted sideways as he talked, casting upward and left most frequently. Tim heard the voice of his media instructor telling them that this was one of the body's most consistent 'tells'.

'Nine times out of ten looking up and left means a lie,' he had said. 'People look up because it's instinctive when you're thinking. There's no good scientific reason for why they look left, but it seems to hold true all the same. To outsiders, looking up seems sincere, it's looking down that seems to generate mistrust. One of life's many little quirks.'

'What do you do if you're the exception?' Tim asked. He liked this kind of stuff, knowing it made him feel more interesting somehow.

'Learn to retrain yourself and bloody fast, before you're on national TV looking shifty.' They all laughed together.

Nothing about Kieran suggested he had invented this relationship in order to garner sympathy. Not like some of the others who turned up to the site or phoned the hotline. Still, there was no telling with people.

'Tell me about Lucy,' he said to Kieran. This wasn't his job, not really. The guards already had enough information from her mother, but the longer he kept the man in here, the less chance he would disrupt Leo's final run-through.

'She's my whole life,' Kieran said. 'Life with her was perfect. We used to sit together and talk for hours, you know? We really understood each other.'

Tim knew. He had felt the same about Nina, as if they fit together perfectly. Before Aisling, he had kept her passport photo pinned inside his helmet, touching his finger to his lips then to her face each time he got into the rig.

'She can't die,' Kieran said. 'Not when I only just got her back.'

'The team are doing everything they can to get everyone out safely.'

'She doesn't even know how much I've changed,' Kieran said. 'All the things that annoyed her before. The things she left me over. I don't do any of them any more.'

Tim nodded. Let the poor fool believe it if he needed to. Older and wiser men knew that women didn't share the things that annoyed them most intensely.

'Seriously, man, I've changed,' Kieran insisted. 'I can be who she needs me to be now.'

Lord spare them all from a man who thought he had changed. What, he wondered, would Deb choose to modify? Who did she wish he was? The social cache of him, such as it was, hadn't quite worn off yet. He could still see a little burst of pride in her when she introduced him to friends, told them he was with the fire service. Nina was the same. Then it began to wear away, a mouse nibbling on a wire, a little bit here and a little bit there. Until suddenly the fuse box was gone, seemingly out of the blue, and no one but the mouse any the wiser about what had happened.

'Have you someone you can call to come down and take you home?' Tim asked.

'I want to stay here,' Kieran said. 'Please. I want to be here when she gets out.'

179

'If you go anywhere within spitting distance of the cordon, then I'm going to have the guards take you into custody until it's all over,' Tim warned him. 'Nothing surer.'

'I swear, man. I swear,' Kieran said.

Tim walked him to the edge of the crowd, watched him skirting the emptier spaces to take up a position at the back. He saluted Tim, who made a 'V' of his two fingers, pointing them from his eyes to Kieran's face.

Kieran nodded, pointing at himself then at the ground.

One of the private television stations was doing a piece to camera while they waited for the rescue to begin. He walked over closer to listen in, careful to stay out of the range of the camera.

'The Tánaiste and the Minister for Transport were unavailable to join us this morning,' the reporter said. 'But they have assured the families that they are doing everything they can to resolve the situation as quickly as possible with regard to the safety of those concerned.'

Doing everything they can. Everyone's official line. Instead of saying they were sitting on their arses in an office at the other side of the country, spitting out soundbites.

What better could be said of himself, he wondered, as Leo gave the signal and the units went in to lay the struts. To the watchers, this would look humdrum. He was one of the few that knew those two-by-fours would mean the difference between life and death for everyone who went into that hole. He might be in an office, he might only be passing information from one side to the other, like misery's errand-boy, but he was no sideline gawker. He knew the cost of every decision made.

NINA

Her heart beat to the sound of Alina's words. She breathed them in and out. When she washed her hands, the water sang them. She walked and they crunched under her feet. 'Nothing is an accident,' Alina had said. 'These things happen because we made them so.'

It felt like falling and landing at the same time. Finally, someone had said it out loud. Not the empty comfort of everything-happens-for-a-reason fatalism, but the hard fact of individual responsibility, the indisputable hand of people in their own fate. The thing that nobody dared to say to her before now: this thing happened because you made it so.

Nine months and four days waiting for Aisling.

Eleven months and nine days with her.

Twenty-two months and thirteen days without her.

And counting. Always counting.

These numbers that replaced the ones that tormented and comforted you by turns when you walked the hospital floors waiting to find out if Aisling would live. Then, it was the limits of time, chances, percentages. Then, the song you hummed was twenty-four-hours-and-. ten per cent-chance-and-. The prayers of science over your daughter's tube-tangled body while you stroked the side of her arm, the side of her face. Sideways touches the only kind permitted.

This thing happened because you made it so.

* * *

Leaving the hospital after interviewing Alina and Richie was a blur. Ben might have talked on the way back to the crash site, or maybe not. She couldn't have said.

She sat in the media centre with her phone in her hand, scrolling news feeds with a studied frown. Around her, the room hummed with gossip and rumour. Every time someone went to the bathroom, it seemed, they came back with a wilder theory as to what would happen next. The only certainty was the crane that had been brought in. People huddled around makeshift dinners of Pot Noodle and coffee, and an almost perceptible cheese and onion crisps vapour hung in the air. Outside, evening had fallen, slowly at first and then all of a sudden, as if someone had grown tired of holding up the sky. Everywhere Nina turned, she looked without seeing. Was she even real?

'I need the loo,' she said to no one in particular and stumbled to the door.

On the other side of the door stood Tim. For a second, she thought she had imagined him.

'I suppose you're feeling pleased with yourself,' he said. 'Parading that poor Alina O'Reilly around, making a mockery of her. I didn't take you for a racist.'

She could have reacted angrily, she would have been within her rights.

'The scarf was a nice touch,' he added.

She wanted to tell him that the scarf was the one

thing she understood. The drive to wear something that symbolised belief. She wore a locket around her neck, precious with a lock of her daughter's hair. It was the one thing she could bear. Having never been a living thing, Aisling's hair was no more dead in the locket than it was on her head.

She wanted to ask him why he felt the need to be mean. But when she looked up to say it, his eyes were bloodshot and it might have been the day after they turned off the machines, so close did she feel to him.

'Things must be bad if you're out here picking fights,' she said.

Something in him crumpled as he told her that the thermal-imaging camera had picked up no signal.

'I didn't know Alina was going to say any of that.' It was the only comfort she could offer him. Or maybe it was comfort she was looking for.

'Do you believe that people bring things on themselves?'

He sighed. 'Faith is faith, Nina. It's not some kind of divine balance sheet. This isn't the Middle Ages.'

'Or the eighties.'

He blinked, confused.

'AIDS,' she said, by way of explanation. That got the ghost of a smile and she watched him take the stairs two at a time. Once upon a time, he wouldn't have needed her to explain anything, he would have followed her thoughts as surely as Theseus in the cave of the minotaur.

'You should go home,' she told Ben, when she went back inside. 'Nothing much will happen now until daybreak. I'll see you back here before the early news.'

* * *

At home, the sense of unreality persisted. Nina found herself, bizarrely, performing somewhat. Putting an extra something into her movement as she baked a potato in the microwave and crumbled some cheese over the top. Humming a little here and there. Exaggerating her gestures with a light self-consciousness, as if others' eyes were on her.

When she went upstairs to change her clothes, she went instead to Aisling's room and lay on the floor beside the cot. If Aisling had been a little older, perhaps there would have been a toddler bed here that she might have curled into. It was not the worst 'if'.

The room was warm and cosy. The radiator was timed to match the rest of the house, a tiny private memorial in the monthly heating bill. It was her equivalent of going to the grave. In Aisling's room, she could feel the warmth of her blood, the bubble of her laughter. Here, there was neither stone nor earth between them.

In the early days after it all, lost in the flurry of bravado and life-goes-on that flooded into the sudden space in their lives, she and Tim had a drink with everyone that came to the house. 'To celebrate her life!' they cheered, clinking their glasses at every mention of her name. Her baby as a drinking game. The memory made her shudder.

Weeks later, after everyone had gone and they were left with the reality of their twosome, she continued to drink. Night after night, the wine poured in and mean words spilled out, a sour displacement. Tim's patience wore thin.

'She can't keep doing this to herself,' he told the social worker. 'She isn't moving on. The drinking is only driving her backwards, to relive it all.'

You marvelled at his earnestness. His ignorance. How did he not understand that backwards was exactly where you wanted to be? Backwards was closer to your baby. You wondered how you ever suited each other well enough to believe in a life together.

'We'll get through it,' he promised. That proved the distance between you: he already wanted to be beyond it while you would have given anything to remain forever stuck. He held your hands and cried into your hair and you thought about the fact that fifty per cent of couples who lose a child stay together. How was it possible that so many made it through?

She stopped drinking. The acid stayed inside her, breaking out through her eyes in unguarded moments, boring into his back, making him feel exposed. Who could blame him for seeking ease somewhere else?

* * *

She was watching TV with the sound turned off when her mother phoned. The *EastEnders* credits were her cue to call and discuss the events of the episode.

'We've been watching it together since she was a teenager,' she told strangers, in the conversations she started in supermarket queues and dentists' waiting rooms.

Her mother was not a stupid woman. She must have realised that these conversations about TV characters had replaced any talk of her daughter's own life, yet she held onto them as evidence of progress.

With her mother, she talked about fictional people. 'I can't believe she's going to marry him after everything he did.'

With her father, she talked about current affairs and the state of the nation. 'A vote of no-confidence wouldn't help things now, they just need to get on with it.'

She watched the phone until it stopped ringing. *You used to talk together about Aisling all the time when she was alive. That was the thing with talking about loss, it wasn't safe. No matter their best intentions, people's tolerance had a shelf life. They couldn't help it. Eventually, there was a first cut-away of the eyes, a faint hint that they were indulging the same old story. There was simply no way back to meaningful conversation after that. It made you hard, loss did. Hard, and self-reliant.*

The less you talked about what you lost, the more you thought about it. That was where the real danger lay. In the comfort of the past. In earlier times, they understood, using bloodletting to release the diseases of mania and depression. It would be a lie to say you hadn't thought about it, looking at the small, childless freedom of the razor carelessly left on the edge of the bath. But it was never a real possibility.

Without you, who would remember Aisling?

The phone stopped ringing and Nina exhaled in time with the creaking house. There were so many little noises that had been masked by Tim's presence. Never noisy, he nonetheless had a way of filling up the space, of warming the air. An impression of safety, even today, when she was no longer entitled to feel it.

At the time of Aisling's death, she and Tim had been trying again, a little soon for the perfect two-year gap between siblings, but she hadn't wanted to overshoot the window, so they started early. It had taken her five months to conceive Aisling, they reminded each other, breathless with freedom after almost a year of fettered, condom-punctuated sex.

They kept trying for a while afterwards, pushing themselves towards each other in search of a moment of forgetting. Until that arch of forgetting began to seem a betrayal of the highest order. How could she call herself a mother if she sought out moments away from the memory of her girl?

Would another child have healed the rift between them? The social worker was careful not to disaggregate those particular statistics. Perhaps he or she would have bowed under the weight of all that expectation. Little Fergus or Aoife, doomed to live forever in her imagination.

* * *

'Is it too late to ring?' she said, when Irene answered the phone. 'Sorry about earlier. It was one of those days, you know.'

'I've just been watching it on the news. Jesus, Neen. It's like something you'd see in a third-world country.'

'Tim's here. I mean,' she corrected herself, 'he's there. He's some kind of communications liaison or something.'

'That's weird.'

'Not really. It's his job now. If anything, he was more surprised to see me intruding into his world. Besides, I haven't even seen him that much. Just at the general press briefings.' She wasn't lying, exactly. It was just that there was nothing to be gained from telling her sister about the roil and joy and dread between them. 'How's the little man?' There was no surer way to deflect Irene than asking about Dónal Óg.

187

'Full of beans. He's busier than myself. It feels like there's a blasted birthday party every weekend.' She couldn't conceal her pride at his popularity.

'And you? How's work?'

'There aren't enough hours in the day,' her sister sighed. 'If I could only knit myself a few more!'

You wish for fewer hours in the day. You will the days smaller, so that on your next birthday you might find you had skipped forward a year or two or ten. You, the non-believer, hoping for the miracle of being nearly finished.

'Mam wants me to drive her to some reunion on Sunday,' Irene said. 'I would, but three hours in the car is too much for Dónal Óg. It doesn't seem fair.'

'I'm sure he won't mind.' Nina sidestepped the gap in which she was meant to insert her own offer of help.

'I don't suppose there's any chance you could take him for a few hours?'

Nina flinched. Soon after the water park debacle, she had tried again. She met Irene and Dónal Óg in the city centre one Saturday morning for coffee. First, Irene told her, they had to get his hair cut, it was the only appointment she was able to get. It was an involvement she was unprepared for. She had to remind herself that her sister meant well.

In the hairdresser's, she watched as his hair fell to the floor in chunks, all of his messy, careless, beloved hair. In the space of ten minutes, it seemed, her baby nephew was gone and a different child was in his place. A changeling story brought to life.

'There, now,' Irene said, pleased. 'Look at you with your big-boy haircut, all ready to start preschool.'

'It's a sad day, Missus, how fast they grow up,' the hairdresser said, and Nina had to clench her hands on the back of the seat or she would have slapped her with the alternative.

Dónal Óg looked painfully new, his face framed against nothing. How could he ever survive the world? In the coffee shop, he swung his legs and ate his muffin and she looked at the tough haircut, the softness beneath, and it broke the last little bit of her heart.

'Nina? You still there? Can you take him, just for a few hours?'

'I don't think so,' she said, slowly. 'With everything going on at work right now, it's going to be full on for a few days. I'd hate to say yes and then have to let you down.'

'They'll have them out shortly though, won't they?'

'Once they're out, it'll only get busier. Noel has me covering the family angle.'

'They must be in bits.' Irene paused. 'You're minding yourself, Neen, right?'

'It's not like I'm down in the hole.' She heard the snap in her voice, but there was no way to take it back.

'I just want you to be safe,' Irene said. 'I only want the best for you. We all do.'

We love you. We want the best for you. Code for *enough now*. Time to get on with things. Time to move on. As if love and concern somehow made their judgement acceptable. She tried, she really did. After all, she loved them too.

'Promise me this time you'll tell Noel if it gets to be too much?' Irene demanded.

At the back end of last year, she had interviewed a woman whose son died of leukaemia years earlier. He wasted away to nothing; his mother showed her the pictures.

'Every starving child I see on the television has his face,' the woman told her, as she loaded up lorryloads of food and medicines for a charity campaign.

They ran the interview next to a segment on wedding diets, the bride-to-be on a ketosis kick, receiving eight hundred calories a day through a tube in her nose. Nina blazed into Noel's office, pinching at her own scrawn and calling it the dead baby diet. He asked her to take a month's holiday before she said something he wouldn't be able to overlook.

'I'll tell him,' she said.

'Nina.' Her sister's voice was half-plea, half-warning.

'I promise,' she said.

Upstairs, she took off her outside self with relief. She laid out her clothes for the following morning, brushed her teeth, climbed into her side of the bed. Tim's side remained resolutely his.

On every channel, they showed footage of the crane advancing into position, then the great roar from the crowd as it retreated. For a moment they showed the faces of those other parents. They stood by the barrier, suspended between two versions of their lives, their children just outside of arm's reach.

Beside her, the baby monitor glowed, crackling lightly with the proximity of her silent mobile phone. The noise comforted her. Souls above, looking down, Tim said.

How much lighter your days might be if you could be sure of seeing her at the end of it all. If years were to pass, would she recognise you? In the years since her death, you have worn the same perfume, kept your hair in the same style and colour. And Aisling, would she still be the age she was that night or would time have moved on there, too? Might you be given the gift of seeing your daughter grown up?

Every child has his face, that other grieving mother said to her.

No child has Aisling's face. You know because you never stop looking.

* * *

Nina woke sweaty and trembling. She sat up and tried to identify the sense of wrongness she felt, her body heavy seconds ahead of her mind.

Aisling.

Her name stretched tightly across Nina's forehead, a hairband made of pain. In the early days of her pregnancy, she used to go to bed early, lying with her hand on the curve of her belly, just the two of them. Now, it was mornings that were theirs.

She closed her eyes and ran the steps in her mind, the well-worn memory of that last night with her daughter.

You bathed her together. She was still baby enough that her bath was a delight neither of you would forgo. You rocked her in the chair, reading her a story while she had her last bottle of the day. She wasn't even that interested in the bottle any more, she spent more time putting the lid of the bottle off and on than she did drinking from it, applauding herself each time. You let her, it was an excuse for one last cuddle after the day.

You placed her in her cot, kissed each of her three soft teddies in turn before kissing the little lady herself and pulling the door almost closed behind you.

Did you do anything differently? No. At eleven months old, her routine was well-established.

Did you notice anything unusual? No. She was a little warm, maybe, but she was just out of the bath.

Was Aisling upset or trying to climb out of the cot? No. She lay quietly – too quietly? – a teddy in each hand, the little music box emitting wave sounds.

But you were so tired. Always so tired. You were back at work, with a baby to look after in the evenings and a life to live. Could you swear that her cheeks weren't the faintest pink, the infection signalling its intent? Could you swear that some little part of you wasn't itching to pull that door behind you and escape to the quiet of your living room, to the Valentine's Day dinner and glass of wine that were waiting? Your answers were untrustworthy, the carpet of your mind worn thin with retracing your steps.

It tormented Tim, the way she would lie in bed running the steps over and over. Unable to get up until she had gone back through it all.

'You have to stop,' he said, in the initial months. 'It's not your fault.'

Then, 'If you don't blame me, then how can you blame yourself?'

Because I'm her mother, she wanted to scream. *I'm her mother and where was I?*

By the end, he was swinging himself up and out of the bed, unable to bear even being next to her while she silently replayed the careful choreography of her daughter's last evening.

'How nice it must be to forgive yourself so easily,' she said to his retreating back one morning. There it was, the unsayable said. The imbalance of their burden. Where he saw punishment, she saw penance.

He moved into the spare room that evening. There

was one last spike of hope. Their social worker suggested they take a day away together, somewhere meaningful. They went to the beach, the scene of Tim's marriage proposal lifetimes ago, in search of the couple they once were. Their flimsiness was no match for the sea. There was nothing left to say. Nothing left to save.

'We deserve more,' he told her. 'After all we've been through.'

He took only an overnight bag, coming back for the rest of his stuff the following week while she was at work.

In truth, it was nice to have the house to herself. Her memories spread out and breathed a little more easily without someone else's watchful eyes.

Nina pulled on her clothes in the dark, fumbling in the drawer for clean underwear. It seemed too personal, somehow, to leave it lying there overnight, exposed in the darkness of her bedroom.

She drank her coffee in the rocking chair in Aisling's room. She was reminded of the time Aisling was sick. It was nothing much, just some vomiting bug, but she refused to drink anything. Nina sat with her in the corner of the room and rocked her to and fro. When her little hands tried to fight off the bottle, Nina pinned her arms with one hand and used the other to force the bottle into her mouth, squirting the teat into her throat over and over, keeping up a light sing-song all the while.

'You were like your man out of *Reservoir Dogs*,' Tim teased her afterwards and they laughed and laughed.

Aisling recovered after a day or two, the way babies do, and Nina forgot all about it. Her hard hands on the soft little body. Her lack of gentleness.

The mothers she met yesterday would have memories like these. They, too, would look at every little action through a funnel of regret, every fragment broken open to the elements.

* * *

The car brought its usual relief. In the weeks after Aisling's death, she drove in circles at night, unable to sleep but afraid of the release of sleeping tablets. There was something intoxicating about the quiet and she would drift slowly through red light after red light until the darkness began to lift.

She drew up at a set of lights once, to find a woman in the car alongside, a toddler asleep in the back seat. The woman smiled and shrugged in a what-can-we-do kind of way. Then, her eyes cut to the empty car seat behind Nina and she turned away.

She drove the seductive open length of the quays as carefully as if Aisling was in the car with her. *Le Repos des Âmes*, Tim had said earlier, and it jolted her. He was so taken by that painting, dovetailing neatly as it did into his then-unexamined idea of an afterlife. She had teased him, then put it aside as something that had no bearing on her life. She thought of her little performance in the kitchen earlier. Did part of her secretly believe Aisling watched over her? How Tim would laugh if he heard her doubt.

The radio replayed soundbites from government ministers on the previous night's panel shows. They used up their few minutes asking to please not be interrupted, to be allowed to finish the point. It was never anything worth hearing in the end, only the promise of a full investigation and an official report. The Malteser approach, she and Tim used to call it – sweet words around an airy lack of substance. Its predictability, the sordid, deniable, back-slapping, dirty hole-and-corner-ness of it all angered her. Instead of going into the media room, she went to the barrier and stood there, looking at the site itself.

'You deserve better,' she said aloud to the pile of rubble. The words left blood on her teeth. She must have been chewing on her bottom lip while listening to the radio.

It had started with picking at her split ends in the hospital. She sat next to Aisling's cot for long hours, needing something to do with her hands that didn't involve slapping anyone. By the day of the funeral, she was chewing on the tips of her hair. She moved onto her nails some weeks later, after flick-reading an article about a woman who had a two-pound hairball removed from her gut.

But nails were too visible. Her hands, after all, were a vital part of her job, her means of convincing the world that she was calm, ready, on their side. Her lip, by contrast, was private, her own tongue the only guest. Sometimes, at night, she imagined chewing away until there was nothing left, erasing herself bit by tiny metallic bit. Guilt, it seemed, tasted like iron.

* * *

She would have known Tim's footsteps anywhere.

'It's too early to say good morning yet,' she said.

'I couldn't sleep either,' he replied.

'Ghoulish, I know,' she said. She wasn't surprised to hear that he had gone home. He used to crave the release of sex whenever work was particularly intense. They both had. They used to joke that holiday sex was the worst they had.

What was it his woman did? She was some kind of number cruncher, that tiresome kind of person whose life was governed by month end and year end. There was a small satisfaction in knowing there was little need for release there.

'What's the plan for the morning?'

'It's a work in progress,' he said.

'Now is the hour of faith,' she said. At his sharp look, she added, 'The Church doesn't get a monopoly on hope, for goodness' sake.'

When he moved to sit on the footpath, it felt like an invitation.

'I lied,' she said. 'I didn't forget the painting.'

He nodded. 'I thought as much.'

'I think I get it now.'

He said nothing and she thought maybe she misread his intention. Tiredness could have driven him to sit, maybe he didn't want to talk at all.

He caught her hand, stopped it in its path up and down her arm. 'Let me see.'

'It's all in my head,' she joked. 'Wasn't that what the psychologist said yesterday?' They both laughed.

'I joined a grief group,' Tim said. Then, with a note of apology, 'I've only gone a couple of times.'

It was the one piece of advice they had rejected. Neither of them felt it necessary to share their grief with strangers. They had each other. They believed that was enough.

'I went once myself,' she said. 'It's fair to say I didn't warm to it. Nor they to me.'

It was the polite fiction of it you hated most. Sold to you as a place of honesty, you sat and vomited out your loss until you were red raw, unwilling to spare anyone any detail when you weren't spared yourself. The lie became apparent when you had to listen to people who had lost their elderly parents and pretend that their loss was the same. You were expected to sit and be grateful when people heard your story and chimed in. Everyone knew someone who had had it. They held these stories up to you as if they could compare. As if some other child's eventual survival was relevant. They believed themselves helpful when they told you they could imagine what you were going through. How could they, when to you it was still unimaginable? It was better, far better, to carry your daughter inside yourself, a lifelong first trimester of grief. What little you had left went to protecting yourself from having to soothe others' distress at your sad story.

Tim was the only one who might have understood. But you were on separate sides of a living divide. Neither of you had the energy to shout yourselves hoarse about every tiny daily thing when even the smallest whisper took more than you had to give.

'Only once? I win,' Tim said, and they shared a smile.

'I don't know whether to think it's strong or sad that we only went when it was too late for us.'

'Given that we both hated it,' Tim said, wryly, 'it's fair to assume it mightn't have helped matters.'

'My enemy's enemy is my friend?' she offered.

'Smile and smile and be a villain,' he countered.

'Did Deb go with you?' She hated herself for asking.

'I didn't tell her I was going. I wanted to… see what it was like.'

'Don't tell me how to grieve—'

'And I won't tell you how to grieve,' he finished.

Love flared and she swallowed it back. 'I covered a story at Halloween. That woman whose dog was tied to a firework, do you remember?'

He nodded.

'Listening to that woman talk about her grief, I felt like it was the first real conversation I'd had since Aisling died. She got it, in a way most people don't. Does that sound nuts?'

He looked at his hands, folding his fingers together. 'I don't want Deb to come to the group with me,' he said. 'It's not her loss.'

'We never stood a chance, did we?' she said. It was true. There was something about seeing their joint life's work crushed as if it were nothing. It took past, present and future with it.

'We survived it.' His hand gripped hers, warm and strong. 'And I'd say we're both still a step away from the blue plastic bag.'

She smiled at their old code. Then his phone buzzed and he let go of her hand.

'That's Leo,' he said. 'There's a problem with the pipes. I have to go.' He paused. 'Are you coming?'

'I'll stay here for a minute or two longer.'

'To enjoy the rain?'

'To enjoy the rain,' she agreed. She closed her eyes and listened to him walk away.

* * *

The crowd returned when the rain stopped. The protesters with their banners kept to one side. 'End corruption' and 'Jobs for the boys' waved alongside 'Asylum seekers out' and 'No room for Allah here'. Here and there people ate breakfast, taking small guilty bites of croissants and rolls in white waxed paper from the deli nearby.

May, too, was back. Nina watched her stalk the perimeter, her lips and hands moving to some internal conversation, her plait twitching with every rock of her heels. Was it for warmth she kept it long, Nina wondered, or was there some other reason? For women, after all, hair was a semaphore of mood. 'Is she still washing her hair?' her mother used to ask Tim in the weeks after the funeral, reading the smell of shampoo as a badge of her willingness to live in the world. She was right. Nina continued to wash her hair every morning, pulling and dragging her fingers through it, willing the post-pregnancy hair loss to end.

'It's still fucking falling out!' she cried to Irene in desperation.

'Do you think it's alopecia?' Irene asked, her hands over her mouth with horror. 'As if things weren't bad enough.'

You wished that your hair would fall out until it was all gone, how savagely you wished it. Baldness would have marked you out.

May stalked the eaters like a cat, watching them drop thick unfinished packets into bins, then darting forward to paw them back out. The hypocrisy of her, claiming that people were better off dead when she herself fought for every hard day she got. She skittered off to a corner and stood with her back to the wall, cradling the food as if was the most precious thing in the world.

You got to hold Aisling when the machines were

turned off. You would have a few minutes, they told you both. As if warning you to pack a lifetime of love and wisdom into its shortness. 'We'll make it meaningful,' you promised each other and it was just the next in a line of promises shattering.

You were paralysed with all that you should say. More aware of yourself than of Aisling. Should you focus on memories, on mental snapshots? Or should you tell your daughter about the world she was leaving, the life she might have lived within it? To your shame, your arm tingled, already tired of the dead weight.

It was supposed to be special.

It was supposed to be everything.

But it wasn't your girl. There were no gurgles or giggles or screams. She was a giant grotesque doll, the essentials all there but painted on, lacking animation. So unlike Aisling that it was hard to believe in your own grief while you held her.

Afterwards, confronted by her absence, it was all too easy to find evidence of her passing. Life and its little ironies. Fuck it anyway.

* * *

The job of shoring up the mouth of the hole was complete. Wooden struts were placed with precision, crossing each other over and down in a bid to stop the hole closing in on the rescuers. Here and there, gaps were left for the firefighters to gain access. She imagined them resting on the planks, like the games of KerPlunk she used to play with Irene, pulling out one stick at a time until the marbles all went crashing in a great pile to the bottom of the tray.

'They're not rushing it. They've learned from their mistakes,' she overheard a man in the crowd saying, before he bit into his burger.

Everyone loved a bit of drama near them, loved to pull their chair up close to the bad in life and lean forward in the knowledge they could pull back whenever they wanted to. 'If there's anything I can do,' people said, through the safety of borrowed tears.

'Don't they look like a calendar, though?' A woman nudged her friend and they laughed and took photographs.

'It won't be much longer,' Nina told Noel on the phone. 'Minutes, if that.'

'Once they're all out, I want you over at the hospital with the families. No hanging around doing any kind of state-of-the-nation crap. Leave that to Mark and the political team.' He paused. 'Unless they're all sent to the mortuary. Then I can get one of the others to go.' He hung up before she had a chance to reply.

No matter. When Aisling died, a lot of people gave her their grief to carry, but not Noel. After the funeral, he followed her and Tim back to the house and sat with them until midnight came and they had survived the day.

'You should be at work,' she said at some point.

'Today, the world can fuck off for itself,' he said, and his awkwardness was more moving than all the careful condolences of strangers.

* * *

The firefighters remained in their huddle and the noise rose a little as the crowd began to shuffle restlessly. What was all the time for, all the consideration of alternatives, all the technology, when, in the end, it boiled down to people taking one breath at a time?

The families stood together, knuckling the barrier. Mothers stood shoulder to shoulder; the breadth of a wish would hardly slip in the gap between them. It was a hard place, that in-between world. Once that world came knocking, it was yours for keeps, like a strange parasite brought home from a holiday.

'Here we go,' someone said beside her.

It would go on to win an award for the photographer that captured the moment from high on a rooftop across the river: the women and men walking onto the site, clear purpose on every face.

Behind the crowd, where the road curved towards the centre of Kilbrone, six ambulances waited in a holding area. Emergency medical teams stood by their open doors, jumping in and out, opening supplies and kits. The injured would belong to them.

'We want to be screaming through with the siren on,' an ambulance driver told her at a party, years before it mattered. 'It means there's still a chance.'

RICHIE

'Those little bastards,' the glazier tutted while he worked.

As far as Richie was concerned, he could keep his sympathy. Patronising fucker. He was glad, suddenly, that nobody local was able to do the job out of hours or it would be all over the parish. Richie Murray, the soft touch.

'They're cold, these old houses, I'd say,' the man said. 'Little enough insulation.' When Richie didn't answer, he carried on undaunted. 'Would you not consider getting the double glazing in throughout? 'Twould make a power of difference in the wintertime.'

'Maybe. We'll see.'

'Have to ask the missus, is that it?' The man laughed the easy laugh of someone whose wife liked him well enough to stay.

'No,' he said. 'I wouldn't want some cowboy putting me on the spot for a decision on something like that.'

That softened the man's cough for him. He finished up in silence and accepted Richie's cheque with poor grace. Richie had the cash to hand, but he left it in his pocket. Let the prick pay his taxes like everyone else.

* * *

Richie parked under the wispy stand of trees in the nursing home car park. They were miserable at the best of times, never mind in the depths of November. 'Landscaped' the brochure called the place, but the trees were lonesome-looking, convincing nobody. Like the last few strands of hair combed across a bald dome.

The doctors told him it was very highly thought of, but, sure, they knew he had little choice. It was this place or somewhere in the city. At least here he could get in to see her every day. Truth be told, he was relieved enough to let them talk him into it after his mam's last bout of wandering, when she walked into a barbed-wire fence and opened the veins of her hands trying to claw her way through to God knows where. The blood and her rolling eyes put him in a panic and he finally agreed that the Alzheimer's had advanced to the point where she needed more minding than he could give her.

He packed her few things and handed her over to them. Passed her on like a worn-out shoe. Pigs would fly before his old mam would have shirked her responsibility like that. She stood for him all the years he could remember. Packing his lunch, checking his homework, slipping into the space between his face and his dad's fist the odd night when there was a drop too much taken.

'Go on up to bed now, Richie, your dad isn't feeling well,' she would say, beckoning him to cross the room behind her, while she held his father's eyes with her own. He never knew what happened after he went to bed. 'My brave man,' she called him, when he fell and cut his knees, but he wasn't so brave at night with his head under the pillow for fear he'd hear anything. The following day, he would always find a treat in his lunch box: two Rich Tea biscuits stuck together with butter, or, when his dad was out of work and money was short, a slice of bread doubled over, with sugar sprinkled inside.

He leaned his crutches against a tree, gauging the level of cover before unzipping and pissing onto a clump of grass. Between the window and everything else, he forgot to go before he left home. He couldn't use the toilets in this place. He'd be literally peeing on the work that some younger version of his mother broke her back to clean. Let the security cameras film him all they wanted, it would give them something to look at.

'Been in the wars?' the manager asked, gesturing at the crutches.

'Something like that,' Richie said.

'Won't she be delighted to see you?' she added, while he signed himself in. 'She missed you yesterday.' She made a show of thinking, 'You might find her in the lounge, I'd say.'

His mam was always in the lounge. Morning and night, the same arses in the same seats. Her back to the window. He asked them once if they could turn her to see outside – she used to love her garden, his old mam did – but they told him it made her agitated. There had been an incident of some kind, the extent of which was never made clear, but the sight of people coming and going in the hall was more calming for her, they said.

The easy-wash tiles of the hallway give way to the easy-hoover carpet of the lounge. It was put down recently and there was only the odd stain here and there. One of them might be his mam's. All of them, for all he knew of what she did day in and day out, beyond sitting with her hands folded across her lap like some big old mangy cat, with one eye closed and the other watching the door.

'Hiya, Mam, it's only me.'

For the first few months, he added his name. 'It's me, Richie, your son,' he used to say, hoping it would jog something in her. It never did and he stopped telling her who he was. If he didn't tell her, she could be forgiven for not knowing. 'Hello.' Her smile was as bright and false as the one she used to wear for the neighbours the morning after his dad's voice was heard the length of the street. She said nothing about the crutches. Around here, he supposed, supports were nothing remarkable.

He looked at her carefully. There had been a period of weight loss when she first came to live here and refused to eat, but that seemed to have settled down. She seemed well, although there was something... he couldn't put his finger on it.

'No rain today, thank God.' He sat in the chair next to hers without kissing her hello. These days, if anything came too close to her face, there was a risk she might rear up and lash out.

'Thank God,' she agreed. 'The summer won't be long coming in now.'

'True for you.' It cost nothing to be kind. She taught him that. 'Any news?' he said.

He liked to give her the chance to get her spoke in before he filled the half-hour with harmless chat designed not to upset her. Sometimes, if the weather was fine, he took her out for a turn around the garden. No matter how good an idea it seemed, it was always worse out there. Walking at snail's pace, her arm looped in his, concentrating on keeping his steps small enough for her. Where did this shuffling creature come from?

This old hag that stole his mam's face and her dressing gown but cast her memories aside like the outgrown carcase of a spider. Oh, but that was life, Richie-boy. It came for everyone.

'How are you keeping?' she asked, bringing the words forward with effort.

'I'm grand, thanks.'

'And the family? Are they all well in themselves?' Her manners were always perfect.

He was spared answering by a commotion on the other side of the room. An old woman half-stood, shrieking and slapping at the old man sitting beside her.

'Help! Help me!' she shouted in a thin, girlish voice.

The man stood with his two hands held up like he was in a Western and two nurses rushed in.

'Are you all right, June?' one of them asked the lady.

'I'm sorry,' the man said. 'I don't know what I said to set her off.'

'I know,' the nurse said. 'Let's give her a few minutes to calm down and then you can come back in and visit for another while.'

The man nodded, defeated, and watched them lead June out of the room.

'Help me!' she continued to say, but her voice got softer and lower with each telling.

Richie smiled at his mother and moved his eyes quickly down to the carpet before she could read any challenge into them. Was it a full moon, maybe? One of the nurses had told him, cheerfully, that the myth was true. 'Batten down the hatches, there's a full moon tonight!' she warned, with a dramatic roll of the eyes.

His mother's feet caught his eye and he noticed she was wearing new shoes – trainers – glowing white under her navy slacks. That was the source of his unease. The absence of the flat shoes she wore all his life. Court shoes, she called them. They were as much a part of her as her mother-of-pearl brooch, or the smell of tea and lavender.

She leaned in close to him, grasping his forearm with her papier-mâché hand.

'Some of these poor women don't know their arse from their elbow,' she whispered, loud enough to be heard in the car park.

It shocked him to hear her cursing, after all the times she smacked him around the head for so much as a stray 'Jesus' when he was a teenager.

'Will we turn on the television?' she asked. It was already on, but he turned it up, grateful to have something to do for her.

'I'll go and ask for a cup of tea,' he said, but her eyes were fixed on the soap opera on the screen.

This was the best place for her, no question. All the medical advice, the doctors and the social workers said so. But that didn't mean he had to like it. She gave him everything, his mam did, working two and three jobs so he could finish school. What's more, she did it with grace. She was never one of those Irish women who had children as an extra place to put their grudges against the men in their lives.

She wanted him to join the civil service when he left school, but he couldn't do what his father had done.

'Tell her you want to come in with me on the bus training. What can she do? She'll never kick you out,' Sully advised him.

A small power, maybe, but it was all he had. She hid her disappointment poorly when he refused to take the exam. But he pretended not to see it, ashamed of himself for denying her that bit of pride, the peace it would have given her.

Back in the lounge, he nearly dropped his cup of tea when his mam pulled at him in excitement, pointing at the television.

'Look!' she said. 'Lookit!'

The news was on and he watched the footage of the bus crash site.

'Wait now. Wait. Whisht!' She shushed him, although he hadn't said anything.

His own face flashed up on the screen and she pointed in triumph. 'There!' she said, 'Look!'

For a moment Richie's heart lifted. 'Mam—'

'I'm sure I know him from somewhere,' she said, frowning. 'Did he live on our road, I wonder?'

He kept smiling as if she was joking.

'I never forget a face, you know,' she confided, with her old smile.

'That's me, Mam,' he said.

'Go on out of that,' she said. 'Stick out your tongue till I check is it black,' she cackled. 'He pulled some woman out of the bus, you know,' she said. 'A hero, they were saying.'

He sighed. 'I heard that too.' He took a gulp of tea. Everything in this wretched place tasted of disinfectant. On the screen, a reporter talked into the camera. Behind him, Richie's face appeared again, beside that of Alina.

'You chancer, trying to let on that you're him, and you hardly even able to get yourself ready for school if I'm not there to do it for you,' she said.

'True for you, Mam. I'd be lost without you.' She knew who he was in that moment. That was something.

'But you were always my boy. My Richie,' she said, her tone fond.

'I know, Mam.'

They listened to the reporter talk about an investigation in short order. The word hit him like a slap. He would be forced to go over every grunt and groan until he hardly knew his own name. He reminded himself sharply to be grateful. Wasn't he out when the rest were still trapped underground? It would be a foolish man who'd let a gift like that pass him by. Whatever she might be now, his mam didn't raise him for a fool.

'Those poor families, Mam,' he said. 'Aren't we lucky we still have each other, you and me?'

But when she turned around, her face had gone blank again, her eyes like a window she walked away from.

'Sit up straight,' she ordered. 'Your mother would be ashamed of you.'

He managed to sit a while longer, letting the television do the work for him even though he would hate himself for it later.

She hardly noticed him going. 'The man that was on the telly grew up on our road,' she said excitedly to her neighbours. 'I used to know him.'

Who would have thought his dad's heart attack at barely fifty, there and gone, would be the more merciful way to go?

'I used to know him,' she insisted, though nobody had contradicted her. He had an awful feeling nobody even heard her.

He used to know you too, he thought, and let his wave of self-pity carry him down to the front door.

It was too late to turn and pretend he hadn't seen

Sandra getting out of her car, a white plastic box in her hand. That was all he needed, to pick up the fight where they left it earlier. Her smile threw him.

'Twice in one day, imagine. People will talk.' She raised her eyebrows and smiled.

'I was just leaving.'

'How is she?'

'Same as ever.' He couldn't help himself saying it, 'I didn't know you came to see her.'

'She was always very good to me, your mam,' Sandra said, simply.

'Was it you brought her the sneakers?' Richie asked.

'She mentioned a couple of weeks ago that her foot was sore and it turned out she had the start of a corn on her toe. The sneakers give her a bit more room.' She smiled and shrugged as if it was nothing. With the lift of her shoulders, he caught the evening smell of her, her heavy perfume worn down by the day's work. He knew without looking that she would have a damp patch under each arm despite the cool winter.

'She never told me,' he said.

Sandra smiled again. 'Girl stuff,' she said.

They got on well from the start, Sandra and his mam. He would come upon them gossiping in the kitchen about this neighbour or that and never think to wonder at his luck. His mother liked the bit of female company. With Sandra in the house, she was happier than she ever was in his dad's world of bike parts in the garden and matches on the telly. Where, even on the best days, an outing meant going down to the local pub and sitting at a low table by herself while he stood at the bar with the men.

'She told me my mother would be ashamed of me,' he said, surprising himself.

Her laugh was wide and warm. 'You should hear her talking about you when you're not here. She is forever telling me that she would introduce me to her son, only he's too good for me.' She winked companionably. 'Pure lies, obviously.'

'Obviously.' He pulled a laugh out of somewhere.

They fell silent, but neither of them moved to leave.

'She has it the wrong way around,' he said.

'Oh, Richie,' she said. 'You know I'm with someone else now.'

No point in asking if she was happy with him. He could see it in her, in the weight she shed so casually at last, as if all those years of struggling into her clothes were nothing at all to leave behind. Why would anyone want to get on this ride again?

He gestured at the Tupperware in her hand. 'Any chance you'd have a box of that for a sorry old bastard?'

She laughed. 'I could hardly let our hero waste away.'

Only if it won't get you in trouble with Lover-boy. He barely resisted saying it. His mam needed her too, he couldn't forget that.

'I'll bring something over to you later on for your tea.'

He dropped his eyes while she talked, not wanting to see the past reflected there. That last Christmas party made for an ugly collage: the free bar proving too much of a temptation, her dancing alone, himself propping up the bar. Then everything went south. He woke up the next morning in a pool of vomit and found her gone. He was no better than the father he swore he would never turn into.

'Phone me if you need anything,' she said. 'If Alan answers—'

'I can be civil,' he said. 'I can manage that much.'

'Don't sell yourself short, Richie,' she said, and patted his arm.

He watched her walk away from him. The sway of her sparked something in him. Nostalgia for the old days. For the old Sandra-and-Richie.

For a moment he wanted to shout into the air after her. 'I think about you,' he would say.

But tell the truth, Richie-boy. Tell the truth and shame the devil.

The truth was he only ever thought about her when she wasn't there.

* * *

The pub was empty when he hobbled in. Only Pitch Flynn was in his usual seat, his back to the wall for fear anyone would creep up on him.

Behind the bar, Fran made a show of giving him a round of applause. 'Well, if it isn't the man himself.'

'Leave it out, Fran,' Richie said, feeling foolish. He sat down at the opposite end of the bar to Pitch. 'A pint of your finest, please.'

Fran hummed while he worked the taps.

'Is that a thing that men do,' he found himself asking. 'The humming, I mean. Do all the men hum where you're from?'

'Our cosmopolitan friend,' Pitch said sourly. Legend had it that he had a wife once and she ran off with a foreign fella. A younger man, if the stories were to be believed.

Richie ignored him and whatever fucking point he was trying to make.

'Everyone hums round our way,' Fran said, putting the pint down in front of him and waving his money away. 'This one's on the house. It's not often we have a real-life hero in our midst.'

'I just meant that we're more of a nation of whistlers,' Richie said, to cover his embarrassment. 'You'd go from one end of the year to the next before you'd hear anyone humming.'

Fran shrugged and began to take down the miniature Pringles boxes to dust them off. They had all warned Fran it was a fad that would never take off here, but he didn't listen. Whenever a stray tourist wandered in by accident and bought one, he left the gap there for a few days, to be sure everyone saw it.

'He's a man of the world now, is Richie Murray.' Pitch finally had his thoughts gathered and ready to share.

Fran rolled his eyes and kept on dusting.

'He has a little Iraqi friend now, you know. A new Muslim friend, isn't that it, Richie? They do their TV interviews together and everything.'

He shouldn't respond. He should know better. Offer it up, as his mam would say. 'Wrong on both counts, Pitch. She's Lebanese, not Iraqi. And I'd hardly call her a friend. Sure, I've met her for all of five minutes.'

'If you saved her life and she's not a friend, that must mean you'd give me a kidney if I asked for one.'

Fran shook his head.

'You'd have left her to die, Pitch, would you?' He heard his voice coming out too loud and he took a swallow of beer, sloshing a bit of it onto the counter.

'I wouldn't have let our own behind.'

'There wasn't much time to look around and pick someone, Pitch. It wasn't a fucking darts team I was after. Between the broken glass and the petrol, there wasn't time to ask her to give me a few bars of "Come Out Ye Black and Tans".'

'Would she have done it for you if the situation was reversed, that's the real question.' Pitch nodded into his pint.

'Leave the man alone Pitch or I'll have to refuse you any more.' Fran placed a coaster under Richie's glass, the spilled beer disappearing as if no mess was ever made. 'Richie here is on the side of the angels.' He winked at Richie, as if they were in it together.

It was the wink that did it. Richie downed his pint and picked up his crutches, muttering a goodbye over his shoulder.

Co-conspirators in what the fuck, exactly? Did all the angels have dark skin or something?

This time, he made it upstairs to his own bed, but he still couldn't sleep. Not in the kind of way where he woke up every hour on the hour the way Sandra used to the night before a flight, but more that he couldn't drift off in the first place. At the slightest hint of a noise outside, his body tensed up as if a shadow had passed below his bedroom door. Telling himself that those little stone-throwing bastards were locked in at home did no good at all. The fear simply wasn't willing to listen. Was this what it was like to be Alina? If she were a man, he might have asked her. She might laugh at him, or – worse – tell him he knew what it was like to walk in a woman's shoes and reduce it to a feminism thing. A woman wouldn't understand the... *un-manness* he felt. He knew they used a better word on the radio, but he'd be fucked if he could remember it.

He couldn't meet Alina anyway. They were funny about meeting men in public, weren't they, and it wasn't

215

like he could invite her here. If that gang of thugs were to see her coming to his door, well, it wouldn't be his window they'd be looking to break next.

At 1 a.m. he was sure he wasn't responsible for the people left in there. Or for the person he pulled out either.

At 2 a.m. he would have sworn he wasn't racist, but neither did he want his country overrun with Muslims. The Catholic Church might have its problems, but, still and all, it was their own.

At 3 a.m. he knew that although he wasn't responsible for the bus crash, he was responsible for something. Maybe Emmanuel was right to call him racist the night of the Christmas party. Could he honestly say – hand on heart, like – that he would have swung for Sully or one of the others if they said the same thing?

At 4 a.m. he phoned Sully, knowing he would be up for the early shift.

'What do you want with Emmanuel's phone number?' Sully sounded suspicious. As if he thought Richie might phone him up and scream obscenities down the line.

'I want to talk to him.'

'You're not after finding fucking Jesus or anything are you?'

'I'm not, no. No worries on that score.'

He had enough sense to wait until a more reasonable hour. When the news started on about the rescue, he changed the channel. He didn't want to chicken out and go about his business as if nothing had happened. It was like he told Sully: he hadn't turned religious or anything, he just wanted to get a couple of things off his chest. Make amends. Like in AA, only without the alcoholism or the side order of God-bothering.

In the end, though, he bottled the phone call and

sent a text instead. 'Can we meet and talk? No funny business. Richie Murray (from work).'

* * *

Emmanuel kept him waiting. Richie was the bigger fool, sitting in the window like a girl on a blind date. He'd forgotten how much the little prick liked his power plays. Even when he arrived, he sat at the table beside Richie's, as if he was afraid of him. Breakfast time in a busy coffee place, what did he think Richie was going to do? Shake sugar at him and turn him into a diabetic? Jesus wept.

He needed to focus. He had a reason for asking him here.

'Thanks for coming,' Richie said. 'Can I get you a coffee or something? A bun, maybe?'

'I don't want anything from you.'

Richie couldn't help it. 'Why did you come?'

'Everybody at work said it was you in the crash yesterday. I thought it was your typical exaggeration until I saw the news.'

'It was real, all right.' Richie pointed to the crutches leaning against the window. 'I have the injuries to prove it.'

Emmanuel looked at the cast on Richie's leg. 'Perhaps I will have a cup of tea after all,' he said.

The little feck sat and watched while Richie crutched to the counter and ordered the tea, then limped down to the table with it on one crutch before limping back up to the counter to get the second crutch. By the time he sat back down he could feel the sweat seeping through his shirt.

'It is an awful business, this crash,' Emmanuel said. He seemed prepared to talk now that something had been satisfied by Richie's humiliating show of hopping. 'Of course, there is corruption at the heart of it. Tell me, did anybody ask you to change your story about what happened?'

'No,' Richie said. 'They came and took a short statement yesterday, that was it.'

Emmanuel nodded once, knowingly. 'I expect they will come and talk to you again.'

'You and your conspiracy theories,' Richie said. He might have been trying for jovial, but it fell flat.

'You and your blindness,' Emmanuel replied. He stirred his tea without looking at Richie.

At the Christmas party, Sandra had marvelled at his sweet-rough accent. She leaned in too close and told him it was like a strawberry milkshake with the seeds left in for a bit of grit. When she lurched off to the ladies', Emmanuel watched her walk away, shaking his head. 'I bet she go down easy, hey? Like ice cream. The big girls always do.'

Richie's fist had made a surprising mess of his face. He didn't think he had it in him, truth be told, but he was after a whiskey or two. Oh, he was his dad's son, right enough, the whiskey making puppets of his fists.

'Why did you ask me here?' Emmanuel asked. 'What purpose is all this' – he waved his hand in the air – 'to serve?'

He could keep his superiority complex and his vowels. There was no way on earth Richie was going to ask him how he walked around unafraid. He must have been mad to think he could ask him. It was the lack of sleep that had turned his thinking around.

'I wanted to apologise. In person, like,' Richie said. It sounded lame in light of the apology he had been forced to write before being allowed back to work. 'To clear the air.'

'You are looking for my forgiveness,' Emmanuel said, in such a way that it wasn't a question.

'I only wanted to clear the air,' Richie said again. He was tempted to add, 'I want nothing from you,' but he held it in.

* * *

The joy of knowing he wasn't racist followed him to the car. Emmanuel was a jumped-up little prick, pure and simple. No one, whether black, white, blue, yellow or any damn colour, got to talk about his woman – his ex-woman – like that. That, as his old mam would say, was the holy all of it.

The radio cut through his relief.

'The bodies of all those trapped on the bus have now been recovered—'

He snapped it off and drove home, unable to recapture the feeling.

Racist. Hero.

All words.

All bullshit.

LUCY

'Lucy?'

'Yes, Orla?'

'Do you think they'll come to get us soon?'

She knew she should be positive, if only so she could say it afterwards. Modestly, of course. Think aw-shucks-it-was-only-what-any-living-saint-would-do. Princess Diana sauntering across a field of landmines.

'I'm sure it won't be long. It might take a while to clear away all the rocks and stones you see. That's probably what they're doing.' She didn't add that the noise would be unmistakable when it came. If it came.

'Will it be scary?' Orla said.

'It will be just like being on a roller coaster.' It was her best guess.

'I never went on one. I was always too scared.'

'When you get out of here, you'll be well up for roller coasters. Look how brave you are!'

'Do you think my parents are wondering where I am?'

Lucy breathed in and out twice before answering. Imagine, it took two years for that term of yoga classes to pay off. Great and all as it was that Orla had warmed up to her, she needed such constant reassurance that there was nothing left to spare for Lucy herself. The panic was in the post, she could feel it. Pretty soon there would be no stopping it.

Was this what it would be like to be a parent? If there was a little blue cross on the pregnancy test in her bag? The one she put there on Monday afternoon when she finally admitted the possibility. It must have happened the night of the party, which was mostly a blur of poker and tequila. In all honesty, she overdid it a bit that night, relieved that James showed up. She had planned in secret for two full weeks before casually letting it slip that she was having a few friends over on one of his unscheduled nights. Already tipsy by the time he got there, she all but ignored him, flirting shamelessly with everyone, male and female. He had pushed her into the bathroom and leaned her against the sink while she watched them in the mirror, smug that her hold on him had not yet eroded entirely. She usually made him wear a condom, but for the night that was in it, it would only undo her pretence at laid-back. Not for her the stop-start logistics of wives. She puked later that night and enough of her precious little pink pill must have come with it to give James the power over her life that she never intended him to have.

Did the manufacturers pick the shape deliberately? Those two intersecting lines, the safely married free to read them as 'X', the kiss of their wanted future. While the ones like her saw only the cross they invited onto their own backs.

'I don't want my parents to be worried,' Orla said.

Orla must have been thinking and worrying about her family all the while, Lucy realised. If she was struck down for her own selfishness, it would be no more than she deserved.

'My mother will tell them you're here with me and that we'll mind each other.'

A kind lie would rebalance the karmic scale, wouldn't it? Her mother would know full well that Lucy could hardly look after herself, not to mind somebody who's retarded. God, she wasn't supposed to use that word. What was it she should say? It was important not to label people, so she couldn't say 'a retarded person', wasn't that it? Instead she had to say it like it was only one aspect of Orla. Although did that mean that saying 'a person who's retarded' was all right? On television, she would skip over that part and just call Orla by her name, as if she was the kind of person who treated everyone the same, even the ones with special needs.

Special needs, that was it. She exhaled in relief. Orla had special needs.

'They're probably having a cup of tea and telling stories about us while they wait for the machines to take up all these stones.'

That wasn't so hard. It just took a bit of imagination and a few white lies. Maybe she wouldn't be such a bad mother. But, oh, Jesus, her mother would kill her. She was already mad at Lucy for not having a proper job. In the two weeks she had been home, her mother's friends – who seemed to be there every night, a conveyor belt of white wine and mascara – asked her repeatedly what she was 'up to', what her 'plans' were. She could hardly say she was still fannying around doing postgrad support work and considering yet another career change. Especially not with Pat hovering.

It was hard to blame her mother. With all the years of further education – Lucy had not one but two postgrad diplomas, for crying out loud! – her mother had assumed that a life on easy street would be theirs for the taking. But the fucking recession put paid to all of that and Pat still dragged herself to the job that a decade ago, high on the promise of Lucy's brains, she had boasted of leaving just as soon as she could. An unwanted baby would be the icing on the cake. Her mother would never forgive her. She could forget the flat, too. She could never pay for it herself and James wouldn't want anything to do with her. The move to her mother's house would be permanent. It would be like her freedom never existed.

'I'd like a cup of tea,' Orla said. 'With a scone.'

'Me too,' Lucy agreed. 'Two scones, even. I'm starving!'

'What did you have for your breakfast?'

'I didn't have any breakfast.' She didn't add that she had been too busy sneaking out the door of her creepy ex-boyfriend's flat before he woke up and barricaded her in, like last time.

'You should always have a breakfast,' Orla said. 'My mother says it's the most important meal of the day.'

'I forgot to set my alarm clock,' she lied. 'What did you have?'

'I had a bowl of cornflakes and a slice of toast. It's what I always have. Except on Saturday mornings when I have an extra slice of toast because I have my dance class and my mam says I need to have extra energy for it. Dancing is my favourite thing. I want to be a dancer. It's been my dream since I was a baby.'

Granted she couldn't see much of Orla from this angle, but she looked to be a bit on the chunky side. Surely she was too old to be a dancer? Even assuming she was any good.

Lovely, Lucy. Just lovely. She should be right proud

of herself, sniggering at the dreams of some poor special needs kid to make herself feel like less of a loser.

'What kind of dancing do you do?' she asked Orla, trying to make it up to her even though Orla couldn't know what she was thinking.

'All kinds. Modern dance. Tap-dancing. Ballroom dancing, sometimes.'

'Which one's your favourite?'

'I like tap best. I like the clicking noise my shoes make.'

'Those shoes are pretty cool.'

'I got them for my birthday from my sisters. They were teasing me about my dancing, but then it turned out the teasing was only so I didn't guess that they got me tap-dancing shoes for my present.'

Clearly the ruse had worked, the charm of the surprise was still plaited through Orla's voice.

'It must be nice to have sisters,' she said.

'I have two. Ailish and Emer. They're both lots older than me. Do you have sisters?'

Ailish and Emer. The names rang a distant bell. 'No. There's just me. You're lucky.'

'I know. Even though they don't live at home any more, they still come over every Sunday. We watch TV together. *So You Think You Can Dance* is my favourite. The shows are all on Saturday nights, so I record them and we watch them together on Sundays.'

This girl was in the heart of her family, their grown-up lives were still built around her. She would have liked that for herself. To have someone to sit on the couch with her and watch movies. Or to play with on Sunday afternoons when her mother was in bed with the curtains pulled against her headache. Lucy brought her cups of tea and sat with her back against the door, dealing hands of Patience until it was time to scramble eggs and toast bread. She had to be careful not to burn anything so that her mother would not shout down the stairs that it smelled too horrible to come down to. 'Disgusting,' she would screech, putting strong emphasis on the first part of the word so that it sounded like the noise of a bee landing on skin. Lucy still smelled eggs whenever she heard that word.

'Lucy?'

'Yes, Orla?'

'Will it be much longer?'

Sweet Jesus, give her enough patience not to answer. Not to say, 'I hope so, because I'm not sure how much air is left in here, or if that's only a problem on TV shows. I hope so, because I'm too young to die here. I've never done anything and I don't even know who I want to be when I grow up'.

Instead, she smiled so that the younger girl could hear it in her voice. 'Any minute now, Orla, I'd say. We just have to sit tight and be brave until someone comes and gets us out of this mess.'

* * *

She woke to the sound of someone coughing. James. No, not James. The other one. Kieran. But even before she opened her eyes, she remembered it was neither. It was Orla, which meant this wasn't just a bad dream.

'Are you all right, Orla?' she asked into the darkness.

'My throat hurts,' Orla said.

'Do you have any water or anything in your bag you can drink?'

Orla began to cry. 'I needed to go to the toilet, Lucy, but there was nowhere to go so I had to go in my pants.'

'That's all right, Orla. Don't worry about it. There *is* nowhere else to go.'

'People will think I'm a baby!'

'They'll have to think we're both babies so,' Lucy said, keeping her voice cheerful. 'I had to wee in my pants too.' She even managed to tack on a bit of a laugh. One little white lie wouldn't hurt. Or, rather, one more.

'Gross,' said Paul, his voice thick and low.

'Paul! You're awake. Do you feel all right?'

'Thirsty,' he said.

'There's nothing to drink. Unless you have something near you?'

'No,' he said, '… bag.'

'Don't worry about it. I'm sure someone will be in to get us out in a few minutes and then we'll have all the water we want. Toilets, too,' she added, for Orla's benefit.

'Paul, this is Orla,' she said, even though neither could see each other and, really, did it even fucking matter at this point? Funny to still be worrying about being rude. It was one of her mother's mantras, how she didn't rear Lucy so she could let her down. 'Orla wants to be a dancer,' she said.

Paul said nothing.

'Paul is still in school,' she told Orla.

Orla coughed again.

'The woman,' Paul said, with difficulty. 'Old. Teacher.'

'She wasn't old,' Lucy said. 'She was only in her forties or something.' She pulled it together. 'Do you remember her name? We could call her.'

'No.'

Orla started to cry. Not the gentle, pretty tears that Lucy herself employed in front of other people when she had to, but big noisy snorkles. She felt her own tears rise.

'How about I tell a story?' she said, trying to keep the edge of hysteria out of her voice. 'Orla? Would you like to hear a story? It'll be like when people are camping, the way they tell stories around the campfire.'

'Okay.' It took Orla a few minutes to calm down.

'I know a great adventure story,' Lucy said. 'Although it's not as exciting as our adventure. Maybe we'll be able to write our own story in a few days' time. What do you think?'

Silence.

'All right then. This is a very very famous story...' She started to tell them the story of the Princess Bride. Or as much of it as she could remember – she had the main parts right, but she wasn't one hundred per cent sure that there really was a wicked queen or a dwarf. Or whether she should use the word dwarf at all, but it was only a story, so surely it didn't matter? Orla and Paul didn't correct her, so she just ploughed on with it.

She always loved stories. Even as a little kid, it was one major bonus of spending so much time on her own. The highlight of her life back then was the fortnightly visit of the mobile library. She used to sit at the living-room window with the curtain pulled right back, waiting to see the bright yellow bus come around the corner before running out with her bag of read books, eager to swap them for new lives.

She was allowed seven books and she agonised over her choices, terrified of choosing poorly, afraid she would run out of things to read before the big bus rolled round again.

Most days, her mother came with her to pick out some books for herself. Mills & Boon, Barbara Cartland, Jilly Cooper. Big joyful bricks that Pat raced through in the early evening, paging through them more slowly as the wine level lowered in the bottle. She used to laugh at the idea of the mobile library. 'The national bid to civilise the culchies,' she called it. But she never missed her chance either, even when Lucy got older and faster and burned through her books so quickly that she begged her mother for her book allowance too.

It was always the same two people, Hugh the driver and Martha the librarian. Martha ruled over the library cards and the shelves, ensuring respect for the books from behind the card table set up behind the passenger seat. Lucy used to imagine them driving home in the evenings from a happy day of dream-giving. In her head, they parked the library behind their little cottage before each choosing a book to read aloud to the other that night. For a long time – a mortifyingly long time – Lucy had assumed they were married. There was a quiet understanding between them that suggested they were on the same team.

Her mother used to shake her head at Martha, particularly in sunny weather. Never Hugh, of course. Her mother's scorn was reserved for women.

'Poor Martha, carting that bulk around in this heat. No wonder she's hidden away in that bus.'

Lucy liked the comforting look of Martha in her mid-calf skirts, showing a slip-on shoe underneath or, in the summer, a man's wide backless slipper, cut up the inside seam to give her swollen foot room to breathe. From time to time, she imagined that Martha would confess she was her real mother and they would live happily ever after in their world of books. The guilt after such daydreams was enormous, she could hardly look at her own mother. She would potter around trying to make it up to her. Bringing her a glass of wine from the screw-top bottle in the fridge, rushing over with the bottle whenever the level dropped below halfway. It was too much and never enough, but it was all Lucy knew how to do.

Those days, there was no bigger world than the one inside that narrow little bus. Nothing since had come close to the sense of possibility she felt walked up the steps, the pleasure she took in imagining all of her futures, all the things she wanted to do. Yet what had she done in the end? Stumbled from course to course. Lurched from man to man. Every decision slightly worse than the last. Telling herself she was too young to settle down, even though that stopped being true a couple of years, and at least one postgrad course, ago.

Lately, she had browsed the postgrad catalogue again, trying on and discarding other possible futures. Well, all that was fucked now. She downloaded it the night she had the idea for the poker party, the first night James hadn't sent her a hurried text from his family dinner table. It thrilled him to text her with his wife sitting in front of him. She could picture him, handsome bastard that he was, hard against the vibration of his phone in his pocket. She thumbed through the catalogue and thought that epidemiology sounded interesting, the underlying causes of communicable diseases and syndromes. It was a pity there was no hope for the terminally stupid.

'You were already five when I was your age,' was

another of her mother's frequent observations. She didn't want the same for Lucy, she said, and yet she lorded it over her, the one small success she had that her daughter did not.

'They all rode off together on the four horses.' She finished the story, finally. There was only silence. 'Did you like the story? It's a famous film.'

Still nothing. Maybe they had fallen asleep. That might be a good thing, at least there would be no more tears for a while.

'Did you... pee again?' Paul asked, after some time had passed.

'No! I didn't the first time! I just said that to make Orla feel better,' Lucy said.

'Water around... my... ankles,' Paul said.

Lucy moved her legs back and forth as much as she could. He was right, there was water on the floor of the bus. She was almost certain it hadn't been there before.

'Something must be leaking.' Brilliant deduction, Lucy!

'Drink?'

'Groundwater would be dirty,' she said, firmly. That was one decision she could make for the three of them.

'Where—?' Paul began, but she cut him off.

'We should be quiet now and save our energy for the rescue.'

She couldn't bear any more questions to which she had no answers. Besides, she had read somewhere about the amount of calories that thinking used up. At the time, she was surprised, but couldn't remember now if that was because of how many it was or how few. How long since she had eaten? How long since the crash? She wished she wore a watch.

'Are you never afraid of being late for things? For work, even?' James had asked her, his fingers tracing the watchless span of her wrist.

'I'm worth waiting for,' she said, leaning so close she practically transferred the words from her mouth to his, no ears needed.

God, but he was an asshole. What was she playing at, making herself into something designed to attract him? Kieran was a weirdo, true, but at least she hadn't shared him with anyone else. Although he was the reason she didn't wear a watch any more. He gave her a pink Swatch once, far too girly for her taste. She felt like asking him if he ever actually looked at her.

'I worry about you when you're late,' he said, not letting go of her wrist even when he finished tying the strap.

That was before the properly claustrophobic stuff started: reading her emails and screaming the name of every man she mentioned, up to and including the professor in her department, a man who was eighty if he was a day. Before he started phoning her friends to ask where she was.

'Why are you waiting up for me?' she shouted at him. 'You're not my father.'

'You don't even know who is!' he shouted back.

He apologised, holding her close and explaining how much he loved her. How love made people worry.

James barely acted like a father to his existing child. How would he react to the news of a pregnancy? With money and a plane ticket, most likely. Hadn't her mother always told her that her father ran off before Lucy was born, that the reality of a heavily pregnant Pat was too much. There was something deeply unforgivable about a baby, it seemed.

231

She imagined herself being interviewed, one hand on her bump in a classic Madonna-and-child pose. 'I knew I had to survive the crash, for the baby's sake,' she was saying.

It was all well and good imagining herself being admired for her maternal strength, but what kind of mother would she make in real life? Her patience with Paul and Orla was stretched to the limit in the space of a few hours – assuming it was a few hours, it could well have been a few days for all she knew – and she was practically holding her breath in case they woke up again.

Oh, Christ. What if she had a baby like Orla? Stuck with a child with special needs, how would she cope?

Ailish and Emer. There had been an Ailish in her year, with a younger sister. She saw them once with their mother. The woman was beautifully made up and well turned out, in her leather jacket and heels. She held the hand of a small girl whose backpack was carefully strapped over her two shoulders. Look at Orla now. She seemed to be managing fine, able to get up and out and live her own life. Granted it was less of a life than most people would want, but she didn't seem bothered.

A normal baby would be the easiest thing and even that seemed impossible. How would she do it on her own? She couldn't, was the simple answer. Plenty of people were naturally caring and protective and that was what this baby should have. Someone who worried. Someone who waited up. Someone like Kieran. The maths could be made to work in her favour, couldn't it? The accident, after all, could surely cause all sorts of anomalies with the length of a pregnancy.

The march of dates through her head soothed her and

she fell asleep. She dreamed she was on a talk show. She sat on the sofa, naked, her hair too short to cover anything.

'I want my hair back!' she cried. A fairy godmother in a police uniform appeared and waved a machine gun at her. Then she was sitting on another couch with long, lustrous hair down to her feet, but when she leaned down to touch it, she felt a snap of pain and saw the ends of her curls caught in a mousetrap. She got up and ran to a window, where she could see out over the hills and mountains of her childhood. She flung her hair out of the window and the mousetrap fell, only to be caught in the beaks of passing birds and borne away to nests where baby birds would hatch into their deaths. 'I'm sorry,' she cried. To her surprise, someone shouted back, 'I'm coming!' She felt someone begin to climb up the length of her hair and she wished it gone again. She began to pull and tear it from her scalp, sobbing as the clumps fell on the floor by her feet. Outside the window, someone hammered on the wall as he climbed and she froze, waiting.

'Hello?' Hello?'

'Hello!' Lucy answered.

'Got one!' the voice said. 'I'm Leo. What's your name?'

'Lucy. I thought I was dreaming.'

'No dream, Lucy. We're really here. We'll be in there to you shortly.'

His voice was so warm and calm. Nobody would have time for that kind of warmth if there was any real danger.

'Who else is there with you, Lucy? Do you know?'

'Paul. Orla. Some woman, a teacher, I think, but she

hasn't said anything. An old man. Someone else. I can't remember.' Her voice broke and she stopped.

'Is anyone else talking?'

'Yes. Paul and Orla. But not for a while. They're asleep, I think. And the water, there's water…'

'How much water, Lucy? Where can you feel it?'

'I don't know. It started around my feet, but now my legs are cold. I can't tell where it stops.'

'Paul? Orla?' Leo called. Nobody answered.

'Orla… Orla is below us,' Lucy said. 'Orla is where the water is.'

'When did Paul and Orla stop talking, Lucy?' His voice was chatty. He might have been an old woman taking her time at the church door after Mass.

'I don't know. They both fell asleep a while ago. I don't know what time it is. I don't wear a watch.'

'Okay, Lucy. That's great. You're doing fine. Tell me about the water, did it come in all at once in a big gush or is it coming in slowly all the time?'

'Slowly, I think. We just sort of noticed it, Paul and me. Paul is hurt, I think. His breathing sounds funny. And I think Orla is caught in her seat belt.'

'Can you move at all?'

'My leg is trapped in the seat. It hurts when I try to pull it out.'

'How much does it hurt?'

'A lot. A screaming amount.' She laughed shakily. 'Is that bad?'

'You can still feel it so that's a good sign. The ambulances are all waiting outside and you'll be whisked off to hospital and fixed right up just as soon as we get you out of here, okay?'

'Okay.'

'Now, we're going to have to be really careful getting you all out so that we don't move the bus around too much. That means we'll be moving slowly and it'll be noisy, I'm afraid. You might feel some rocking and swaying but just a little bit, hopefully. We'll lift this guy—'

'Paul.'

'Okay. We'll lift Paul and get him out and then we can get a proper look at whatever it is that's trapping your leg, all right? Do you understand, Lucy?'

'Orla. Start with Orla. She's… that's where the water…'

'You let us worry about all of that, Lucy. Okay? We'll get to everyone. One last big effort, that's all. It's nearly over. I need you to hang in there just a little bit longer, all right? We want to keep you all as safe as we possibly can. Otherwise your mam will kill me, right?'

'My mother is there?'

'She certainly is. Pat has been keeping us all on our toes. She's waiting to see you safe and sound, so let's do our best to get you out to her, okay?'

'Yes.' Her voice cracked on the word.

'You ever been in one of those little turbo-prop planes, Lucy? The ones that… well, excuse my language, but there's no other way to say it, they shake like fuck, but they get you there in the end. This is going to be like that. Do you understand?'

'Shake like fuck. Then out.'

'Good girl.'

'Do you hear that, Orla? Just like a roller coaster.'

But there was no answer.

In the darkness above her, she heard Leo's voice. 'Three confirmed alive post-crash. One talking. No other confirmations yet.'

She imagined the words travelling up through the rock and out into daylight, racing through the air to her mother's ears. Her mother was waiting for her. She would see her soon.

Her mother was going to kill her, but it didn't matter. She would see her soon.

PART FOUR – UP

INCONTINENCE OF THE SOUL

If this were a film, the camera would show the bus emerging from the ground. A giant split-snake shaking off its old concrete skin. Spirited survivors waving from between the teeth of its windows. Wouldn't that just warm the heart?

Instead, everything happens with Marx Brothers speed. The lifting of people out of the ground, onto stretchers and into waiting ambulances. No cheers, just a frozen hush. Information relegated to the bottom of the list.

The vigil becomes elastic at the edges. The families a convoy of fear on the greasy road from here to the city. At the hospital, fear sets up a new kind of stall, powered by other kinds of machinery and fallibility. People stand in small groups, saying the wrong things. Endless questions crushing the mercy that might be found in silence.

In this place, this new quiet place, answers – unlike hope – can wait. They do not come in response to questions. They must be tempted forth by silence.

They must be heard.

ALINA

Alina stood at the kitchen door, watching Seán get ready.

'Are you sure it's okay for me to leave?'

The question wasn't really about her, he was simply asking for permission to leave. He needed to remain blameless in this abandonment.

Alina nodded. 'There's no one else to cover for you today.'

'Exactly!'

He was quick to write off possible misunderstandings as small, amusing quirks. Her parents' English coming through, he called them. He didn't hear his own 'amn't's and 'twasn't's stacked up beside her careful grammar.

'I'll be back at lunchtime, with your mother.'

He didn't know he did a little dance each time. Left hand pat left trouser pocket for wallet, then breast pocket for glasses. Right hand pat right trouser pocket for keys, then a tap on his rear end for phone. Kiss for Alina. Caress for the holy water font hanging by the door, two fingers into the wetness. Something almost obscene in the flick of his fingers towards his face, sprinkling himself.

She closed the door to her bedroom quietly, not wishing to alert Annie that she was awake.

Is this what it would be like if they had a child? Seán leaving for a life outside while she tiptoed around like a thief in her own home?

* * *

'Still resting, are you?' Annie knocked and entered in one fluid movement.

As if she herself was not still in her dressing gown, with sleep crusted in the corners of her eyes.

Alina closed her eyes and counted to ten. Without actually closing her eyes, of course. That would be rude. But it was possible to achieve the same effect with her eyes open. The trick was to glance at the floor and unfocus the eyes. She could have drawn from memory every line of the carpet in the cubicle she shared with Margo.

'I would have thought you'd be up watching the news,' Annie said. 'They got those poor people out. Dead, every last one of them.' She crossed herself. 'Merciful hour, but you're lucky to be alive, child. Wouldn't you get up and be thankful you can?'

She meant well.

Alina dressed slowly, her body stiff and sore. They died. All of them. The boy with the headphones and backpack. The young woman with Down's syndrome, who was so careful to close her seat belt. The man who had tipped his old-fashioned hat. The middle-aged woman with the smart handbag. The girl with the ragged hair, who Alina recognised from her university days. The man in the tracksuit who stared openly at her. All dead.

In three short days, they would be returned to the ground that had done such harm. Boxes made of wood, not metal. She shivered. Her father, when he died, had left instructions. His surprising wish that his death should follow the traditions of his homeland. Modesty, compassion, speed. Shrouded and buried within twenty-four hours. It disappointed her, somehow, that the integrated convictions of his life were undone by fear in his final weeks. 'What could be more integrated than eternity here?' her mother wondered when Alina voiced her concerns, but it did not satisfy her. She told herself that was why she visited so rarely. A choice rather than the practicality of the three-hour drive to the cemetery.

The TV in the kitchen showed pictures of them all, dressed up and smiling, tilted at awkward angles where others had been cropped out, stiffer versions of the people she remembered getting on the bus. The older woman was photographed alone, looking out to sea as if remembering, or deciding something. Her face, its foreboding or longing, made Alina shiver.

'They said two of them drowned, imagine. Lord have mercy on them.' Annie took butter from the fridge and began to layer it on thick white toast. 'Here you are, love. I've tea on.' Annie must have brought the bread with her. Chew for thirty seconds, swallow. It would still sit like a stone in her stomach.

'Turns out one was alive when they got her to the hospital,' Annie said, as if it wasn't the most important thing.

'One is alive? Which one?' It shouldn't matter. Someone to share the burden, that should itself be enough. Yet it did matter. Let it not be the old man, she thought, shocking herself.

'One of the women. They said her name, but I don't remember it. She'll probably never be right again.'

241

'Like me, I suppose,' Alina said. 'I will never be right either. Is that what you mean?'

'Not at all,' Annie was dismissive. 'Sure, you were barely there. Weren't you out nearly the minute it happened?'

'Which is it, Annie? I am lucky to be alive or it was nothing at all?'

Annie looked sharply at her. 'It can be both, you know. Don't be getting excited about it now.'

'I'm not excited. I'm asking what you mean. You tell me one thing and then you tell me the opposite. I should be giving thanks but not making a fuss. They are all dead, but, no, wait, one is alive. I am part of the family, but…' She placed the butter knife carefully on the table and watched the white fade from her knuckles.

'What has you so touchy?' Annie paused, then came over and patted her hand. 'Never mind, love. I used to be the same way when I got my monthlies. There's always next month. You and Seán will be lucky yet.'

Alina sighed. It was impossible. She was uncomprehending, immovable. More jelly than woman. What could a person do with that?

* * *

Lucy her name was, the survivor. The girl Alina had once watched across a crowded lecture theatre, surrounded by friends. It felt strange to know her name now, having never known it then. Alina showered and thought about her. Where she was, how she might feel. She dressed and wondered if Lucy was awake. If she, too, felt guilt. She looked in the mirror at her covered hair and wanted kinship.

'Where are you going?' Annie stood in the kitchen doorway, a rolling pin in one hand.

Pointless to ask her what she was making. It would be apple tart or sponge cake or trifle, something to withstand the sticky weight of cream.

'I need to fill a prescription,' Alina lied. 'They gave it to me yesterday and said to take the tablets if I felt stiff today.'

'Leave it until later and Seán can go for you after work. Or I can run out, if you can't manage the pain for an hour or so?'

Alina shook her head. 'It's fine, thank you. Perhaps a slow walk will help with the stiffness.'

She let the first bus go by before finding the courage to get on the next one. Once on, she ignored the free seats and stood in the space by the driver, holding the bar to stop her hands from shaking.

Approaching the city, the bus drove along the quays. Alina watched the harbour water sparkle in the sunlight. Her father was fond of saying that the city was like Beirut. That, as port cities, both had their arms open to the world. His persistent belief in his original impressions had come to seem wilful. Ireland's welcome no longer the great warmth he remembered, but a thin thing, with the air of having its patience tried by overuse.

The bus stopped at the direct provision centre and Alina was up and out of the bus before she quite knew what she was doing. She stood a little way inside, between the gate and the barrier, watching people enter. Women with buggies, mostly. The occasional young man. The women looked her up and down, looked past her face to her shoes, bag, coat, and knew she was not one of them. Yet on the street outside, passers-by glanced only at her face, her covered hair, and looked away. They assumed she belonged here, she knew. Such liminality was why her father feared this place.

When she got to the hospital gates, she could see the news vans parked near the Accident & Emergency entrance. She went the long way around, fearing questions, or – worse – a microphone in her face.

There were many corridors and she lost her way several times, the stiffness worsening with every wrong turn. It wasn't until she reached the half-empty waiting room that she realised her mistake. She had expected to find them all there together, as if waiting for her. Keeping a place that only she would fit. Instead, a tired woman bounced a toddler on her knee while an older child walked the perimeter of the room, kicking the leg of each chair as he passed. For a moment it seemed like he might kick her too as he crossed the doorway, but he settled for curling his lip at her until she took an obedient step backwards. If they had a child, she and Seán, who was to say he might not turn out like this? Sullen and destructive, despite the efforts, all the love and good intentions. This mother, after all, looked nothing worse than tired.

The arrival of a nurse asking if she had signed in at reception sent her back the opposite direction. She pushed through sets of double doors until she found herself in a quiet corridor, where a sign told her that the eye clinic was closed for the day. She sat on the chair furthest from the door and read the posters on the walls, urging her to contact her doctor if she had dizziness, blurred vision, black spots, as she might have glaucoma, cataracts, retinitis, dry eye. She could have all of these things. The longer she sat, the surer it seemed.

Were there such diseases back home, when she was

a child in Lebanon? Her memories were few, more stories than things remembered. The limits of what she could and could not ask as clearly prescribed as if they were written in their hallway. She didn't remember the fetishisation of doctors and hospitals. Blood, in certain volumes, meant the doctor. The hospital only if it became unfeasible to deal with it at home. Every woman could stitch a wound, in a pinch. 'It is not so different from a button,' her mother told her, while they waited for the freezing spray to kick in. 'Keep your hand higher than your heart, my love, that will slow the bleeding.' Alina, sitting on the kitchen worktop with a gash on the back of her hand, was less certain. Yet, looking at her hand in the harsh overhead strip lights of the hospital corridor, her mother was proved right. The scar was hardly noticeable, a child sitting on her lap might not even remark on it. Not too many years from now it would be covered by wrinkles as she shrank inside her own skin. Unbidden, the thought came: five of her fellow passengers would never have that chance.

'I never said you shouldn't be here.'

Alina stiffened before realising that the man's voice wasn't speaking to her but, instead, came from around the corner.

'You were always a terrible liar,' a woman's said.

Her voice was familiar, but Alina couldn't quite place it. Perhaps it was someone from work. It was difficult to know whether to stay where she was or risk the noise that leaving would make.

'I worry about you, that's all.'

'It's a little late for that, Tim, don't you think? You weren't long clearing out when I needed you.'

'That's hardly fair, Nina. I was grieving too.'

That was how Alina knew the voice. It was Nina, the woman who interviewed her yesterday. She really should leave. Even though they made no effort to keep their voices low, it was evident they believed themselves alone.

'It was hard to tell from the outside. That's where you kept me, you know. On the outside. I had my family on one side pretending nothing had happened, and you on the other side pretending we could just go on as if nothing had happened—'

'Just stop. You can't possibly actually believe this and I can't listen to it. I just can't.'

'That's right. Walk away. You're good at that.'

Alina froze where she was. Half-standing, half-sitting, poised in indecision, while the footsteps moved and a distant door swished first open, then closed. In the sudden silence, she heard the hitch and sniff of silent tears. The kind she used to cry in the school toilets at lunchtime. There was no lonelier feeling than trying to keep your tears to yourself.

She walked around the corner and saw Nina. 'Here.' She held out the tissue packet, one already neatly slid out, waiting.

'Thank you.' Nina took it and wiped her eyes. 'Alina, isn't it?'

Alina nodded and sat down beside her.

'I don't suppose there's any point in pretending I was just reading this?' Nina reached into her bag and pulled out a book.

Alina looked at the mournful dog on the cover. If refugees were dogs, they would all find homes.

'I was sitting in the corridor for the last few minutes,' Alina said apologetically.

'Shit.' Nina blew her nose again. 'Thank you for not asking if I'm all right.'

'It seemed to answer itself,' Alina said.

To her surprise, Nina laughed.

'True. That doesn't stop other people from asking though. There are days I swear if I hear it once more, I'll scream.'

'People are funny about things like that,' Alina said carefully. 'They ask questions they don't want the answer to. So much of politeness is lies.'

'Lies, damned lies and politeness. We're all brought up to believe that not upsetting the apple cart is the pinnacle of achievement in life. Leave the world as you found it, not a mark made nor a feather ruffled.' She began to cry again. 'I'm sorry. I don't usually cry like this over... things. I don't know what's wrong with me today.'

'When my father died,' Alina said, 'I didn't cry for a long time. My husband and his mother didn't understand. I could see them watching me, as if they were not satisfied until I wept.' She shrugged. 'Tears are a crude measurement of grief.'

'Everyone says it feels better to let it out,' Nina agreed. 'But, if anything, it just makes me feel heavier.'

'My father used to say that fighting difficult feelings was wasted effort. Like trying to raise a kite on a still day,' Alina said.

They laughed together, before Nina said, in a rush, 'I feel I should apologise. My... Someone said I manipulated you in that interview.'

Alina's laugh was bitter. 'That is the safer option. That my words had no meaning because I did not know what I was saying.'

'I'm sorry if—'

Alina shook her head. 'My husband said something similar. It's because people are frightened.'

'If the public reaction—'

'The public.' Alina waved her hand as if to shoo them away. 'Who are the public to say the shape my belief should take?'

'Just because other people have an issue with it doesn't mean you have to change who you are,' Nina said.

Alina sighed. People who persisted in their naïve idealism were somehow worse than the overtly hostile. 'When we first moved here, my mother was young and beautiful. Then she began to eat. I always assumed she ate for comfort, because she was homesick or lonely. Or because she liked to eat, I don't know. Now I can see that she eats to make herself invisible. People are happier to see her as simply one thing: fat. It makes their reality easier.'

'Reality can be untrustworthy,' Nina agreed.

'What do you do when you have done everything you can and still it is not enough?'

'I would say you should drink, but is that even...?' Nina gestured at Alina's veil.

They were still laughing when the door opened again. A heavily made-up woman looked at them with disapproval. 'I was looking for the toilets.'

'They're just through the double doors there,' Nina pointed, but the woman made no move to follow her directions.

'Isn't it well for you to have so little to worry about that you can sit around reading and giggling. And don't think I don't know who you are.' She pointed at Alina.

'What business have you back here, come to see your handiwork, is it? To see the wrecks of people you left after you?'

Alina felt rage surge in her throat. 'Actually, Madam,' she said, careful to keep her voice even, 'we were simply discussing this week's book-club choice.' She held up Nina's book, her hand steady and satisfying.

'Shame on you both,' the woman hissed and stalked away in a series of indignant clicks.

'Her daughter survived,' Nina told Alina, when the woman was out of earshot.

'Gratitude would serve her better than rudeness, in that case,' Alina said. She heard her own mother in her words.

'You said something before,' Nina said. 'That we invite the things that happen to us.'

'It was something my father used to say. *These things happen, Alina, because we make them so*. He meant good luck, friendships. He believed that positivity could overcome everything.'

'Is that what you believe too?'

'I believe...' Alina stopped. 'Nothing is as simple as my father wanted it to be. We can't assume that in the worlds of our actions only the good remains while the bad vanishes as if it never was. When I lose my way, I can only trust that Allah knows the way for us both.'

'Does it comfort you to believe that?' On seeing Alina's look, Nina continued, 'I'm interested, truly. My husband – ex-husband, the man that just left – he believes that God has a plan. That our daughter... That things happen for a reason. I don't know if I pity him or envy him.'

'My husband cannot understand why I don't yearn for "my homeland", as he calls it. Marriage is a strange thing. Nobody can understand what the world is like for another.'

Nina nodded. 'You know, when Plutarch's child died, he told his wife to be careful not to show too much grief. *You must fight against the incontinence of your soul*, he told her.'

'The deeper that sorrow carves into your being, the more joy you can contain,' Alina said, remembering. 'Khalil Gibran. My father used to tell me that whenever I struggled.' She sighed. 'And so all families fail each other.'

'That's a pretty lonely statement.'

Alina stood. 'It is a lonely world.'

Outside, she left the bus stop behind her and walked until she found a pharmacy.

* * *

When the front door opened and her mother stepped through, Alina rushed to her arms as if it had been years instead of weeks. Mai held her for a long time, her lips moving in prayer, warm on Alina's ears.

'Mrs Haddad,' Seán's mother came out of the kitchen, her hand extended.

'Mai,' Alina's mother said, as she always did. 'Call me Mai, please, Mrs O'Reilly.'

'Well,' Annie said, and gestured them into the front room.

'Was the traffic bad?' Annie asked Seán as they settled themselves into chairs and onto sofas.

'Not too bad,' he conceded. 'It's early yet though.'

'You're the right end of the city for coming out here, of course. Lovely area, but just that bit too built up for me, Mrs Haddad. How long would it take you to get into the city centre, now?' Annie demanded.

'Perhaps fifteen minutes,' Mai said. She did not add that she no longer went into the city.

'That would be on a good morning though, I'd say,' Annie said. 'But if you had a run of traffic lights against you?'

Alina's mother conceded that, under certain circumstances, it could take up to half an hour on the bus.

'No,' Annie shook her head. 'Give me a little town like ours any day. Everything within five or ten minutes. That's the only way to live.'

It used to amuse Alina, the Irish obsession with timing every activity. Entire conversations were based on how long everything took, how much time the business of living took from life itself. As if the cure for cancer might have been found had the commute been slightly shorter.

'Too far entirely,' Annie repeated.

It was an interminable afternoon, full of simmering politeness. One moment, Alina wanted to scream and hurl obscenities, the next, she found herself wanting to take the hand of each woman – each widowed woman – and say, *look how much you already share. Look! This, here, now, is family.*

Over it all was a longing for Annie and – guiltily – Seán to leave so that she could talk to her mother, really talk to her. Instead, they were solicitous, jumping in with details she had forgotten, telling her story for her. In the end, she sat back and left them to their imaginings of what might have happened. Annie's earlier dismissal of the danger had been overtaken, it seemed, by more interesting angles.

'You should get checked out, you know, Alina love,' Annie said, rounding on her as if she had spoken out of turn.

'The hospital was very thorough,' Alina said, confused. Surely Annie knew she had been there for many hours, many tests.

'I don't mean that. I mean... you know.' Annie jerked her head and winked, and it took Alina a moment to realise what she meant.

'Oh! No. No, there's no need. Everything's fine,' she said, flushing.

'Still. To be on the safe side. There's no one getting any younger.'

'Mother.' Seán shook his head and pantomimed zipping his lips closed.

'For heaven's sake, why tippy-toe around it? We're all family here. I'm sure your mother is as keen as myself to have a little one to dandle on her knee and spoil.' She winked at Mai. 'Am I right, Mrs... Mai?'

'All things in their own time,' Mai said.

Had they been alone, she would have said *Inshallah*, Alina knew. Her gentle mother, living her censored life.

'Lebanese grandparents don't view their grandchildren as something to spoil,' Alina said. 'Their role is more important than that.'

'Nothing could be more important than grandparents,' Annie agreed.

Had she deliberately misunderstood or was this more of the careful obtuseness that Seán cultivated, patting around the edges until she fit into a neat, subdued package? If they had children, she would ask her mother to speak to them in her own tongue. There would finally be honesty.

252

'I don't think—' she began.

'Alina, I have some things for you,' her mother cut across her. 'Is my bag—?'

'In the spare room, Mai,' Seán said.

'How long is she staying?' Alina heard Annie say in an undertone as she left the room with her mother.

'Alina needs her mother,' she heard Seán reply, and was torn between love and rage at his failure to anger on her behalf.

Alina followed the slow width of her mother's hips down the hallway. The smell of boiling cabbage and roasting lamb fat came from the kitchen. Annie would expect gratitude for this dinner that Mai would praise and yet be unable to eat. Every time, this same dance. She was so weary. If she sat, she might never again stand.

'I think I need some air,' she said to her mother. 'Do you want to come for a walk?'

As they walked, they talked about the small things of interest. A neighbour building an extension. The failed marriage of an unremembered cousin. The street was peaceful in the early evening and Alina felt the tension seep from her feet, to be left behind on the footpath. Would it be washed away by the rain or evaporate in the sun? Perhaps the next person to pass would pick it up and carry it for a while, unsure where their sudden anxiety had come from.

For now, though, the winter sun was angled low in the sky, winking brightly around the corners of buildings and through bare branches of the ash trees, bringing the sensation of air and freedom. Her father used to say that the Irish ash was like the cedars of Lebanon, their place carved in the stories of the land. That was his gift, to see a hybrid world where none existed.

'You've been walking more,' she said to her mother. The issue of her weight was not one they discussed. The shape of a woman's body was private business.

'Carol calls for me most mornings and we walk for half an hour,' her mother said.

'That's neighbourly of her. It only took fifteen years.'

'Should I reject her friendship because it was a little slow?'

'Fifteen years is not "a little slow", Mama. It's her expecting you to help her now that she has had her hip replaced and is afraid to walk alone. Why should you come running just because she calls?'

'So I should sit alone in my house and not go out?'

'You know that's not what I meant. You should go out.'

'Out where? With whom, if not my neighbours?'

'With your friends.'

'My friends are in Lebanon.'

Alina forced herself to breathe once, twice, before saying anything. For years, her mother had clung to this idea, her refusal to go back there to visit allowing her vision of the past to remain unspoiled. Alina's father asked her to stop trying to convince her mother to visit, afraid that if she went, she might never return. It was a half-life, Alina saw now, giving Mai the worst of both worlds.

'That's not true.'

'I cannot be friends with my neighbours, nor can I have friends back home. It seems you know my life better than I do.'

'How can you find it funny that you have lived here for this long and still say you have no friends?'

'I have friends here,' Mai corrected her. 'I simply

believe my true friends are in Beirut. My family is there. My blood.'

'Your blood is right here, Mama!'

'You remember how it was there: your aunts and cousins in and out all day long, so much talk and laughter. Here it is only the radio that makes noise in my kitchen.'

The truth was Alina didn't remember. When her mother mentioned childhood, she thought *snow* and *skipping* and schoolyard talk of Santa Claus and the tooth fairy. But it was true that every child and every parent remembered these things differently.

She looked at her mother. 'Why did you never go back? I know Baba never wanted to, but after he died you could have.'

Mai sighed. 'On my own, they might not have let me return here. Without your father, who would argue for me?'

'Mama! You are a citizen here. You have a passport, the same as anyone else.' She thought fleetingly of the direct provision centre, the women with the buggies, waiting for others to decide their right to stay.

'Yes, but I came originally on your father's visa and now he is gone…'

'That's not how it works,' Alina said impatiently. 'They gave it to you. They can't just take it back.'

Mai smiled at Alina with something like pity. 'Rules can change,' she said.

'We should go,' Alina said. 'Together.' The lightness with which the words came! She could have danced all the way there. 'We should go and spend some time with the family.'

'Your family is here now,' her mother chided gently.

'They will still be here when we get back. I'm not talking about forever, Mama, just a week or two. A month. We can book an open return. Don't you want to?'

'What about Seán? What would he say? Will he want to come with us?'

'He will understand that this is something we want to do, just us.' In the face of this plan, she could admit to herself that Seán's interest in her culture had long dwindled, the nuances fallen into a global category of 'different'. She could not blame him for never having known uncertainty about who he was. 'Let's do it.'

'What if too much has changed?'

'Even if the place has changed, the family has not,' Alina said. She couldn't have said where her certainty came from, yet there it was.

'For in the dew of the little things the heart finds its morning and is refreshed,' Mai said.

On hearing Gibran's words from her mother's mouth, Alina knew they were as good as packed. 'It will take a few weeks to organise everything. We can be there in the springtime.'

'We must walk faster, I cannot go home like this.' Her mother patted the great roll of her belly. 'As a girl, my figure was the envy of Beirut. Is a few weeks enough time to make a difference?'

'Yes, Mama.' Alina hugged her mother to her and watched their shadows stretching and growing taller on the footpath in front of them. 'It can make all the difference in the world.'

LUCY

'I know,' Lucy told the doctor. 'I hadn't taken a test or anything, but I was pretty sure.'

'For now the heartbeat is holding steady. But we'll keep monitoring things closely and if you start to feel any heaviness or cramping, then call one of the nurses straight away. In the meantime, I've arranged for one of the hospital social workers to come and talk to you in a little while.'

'Because of the baby?' her mother asked.

Pat was so composed, Lucy wondered if she had already told her and simply forgotten it. People kept talking about shock, after all.

'Sometimes people who go through things like this can benefit from talking it out with someone.'

Lucy couldn't imagine wanting to 'talk it out' with anyone. Talk what out? She didn't ever want to think about it again.

'Thank you,' she said, but the doctor had already left.

For a second she thought, stupidly, that the cracking noise was something to do with the door closing. Then her face filled with fingers of fire where her mother's hand had connected.

'You silly little bitch,' her mother hissed. Her face was so close that Lucy could see the anger dancing in her eyes, shaking its tiny multicoloured fists and swinging its hips. That's what started all the trouble in the first place. She had to work to keep the giggle from leaking out. 'Now look what you've done,' her mother said. 'All my sacrifices and here you are. Unmarried and pregnant, like a common tramp.'

'Like you were,' Lucy said. Was it the medication that made her feel so dreamy and fearless? Or did they refuse to give her anything because of the baby? It was hard to remember. Time seemed to move in short bursts then stop entirely.

'Don't you get smart with me, lady,' Pat said. 'Don't you dare. You can't ever get high and mighty with me again, let me tell you.'

She paced the room in a crackle of polyester, filling the air with static. Lucy could see her fingers flexing, itching for the peaceful action of a cigarette.

'At least I married your father,' Pat said. 'At least I had that much sense. No fear your fella will marry you, is there? He can't, can he?' Her mother's voice was triumphant. 'Did you really think I didn't know you were carrying on with a married man? Living the high life on his money like a… like a…' She couldn't say it.

Slut. Mistress. Bit on the side. Her mother read the *Daily Mail*.

Tart. Strumpet. Scarlet woman. She also read Mills & Boon.

'Did you think I didn't know that he dumped you and that was why you came running to my door, like you always do?'

How long had Lucy been breathing in and counting? One-two-three-four, but how many times? 'Not that it's any of your business, but that's all over. Kieran and I are thinking of getting back together.'

'The baby is Kieran's?' Her mother spun around to look at her.

Lucy closed her eyes. She thought about the baby. Her baby, stubborn enough – stupid enough – to have made it through the last couple of days.

'Yes,' she said. 'The baby is Kieran's.'

'So that's why he's here.' Pat's voice was triumphant.

'Kieran's here?'

'Who did you think drove me over from the accident site?'

Of course he was here. Where else would he be? It wasn't like he had a life of his own. Here he was, indispensable and pernicious. Like ivy.

'They said family only, but, sure, they'll have to make an exception for him under the circumstances. I'll go out and get him—'

'No, please. He doesn't know yet. We were only just starting to work through things and I—'

'You don't want to scare him off with baby talk until you know you won't miscarry,' her mother nodded. 'Sensible girl. You don't want to chance losing a good man over what might turn out to be a thing of nothing.'

Was this what she had invited in, with her impulsive decision? Months of unwelcome solidarity, of tips from a woman whose idea of accomplishment was to trap a man into looking after her? Dread churned her stomach.

'Where's Auntie Kit?'

'She went back to the house a couple of hours ago for a rest.'

'That's a bit rich, don't you think?'

'Laugh all you like, Miss,' Pat said. 'I'm glad to

have her support. It's a comfort to me to have her. You wouldn't understand what it's like between sisters.'

Whose fault was that? If there had been two of her, would things have been different? Would she have been half-normal? So many giggles to swallow, she would be hiccupping shortly.

When she opened her eyes, it was still dark outside her window. Her mother shook her arm.

'The social worker is on her way,' she said. 'You know I'll support you, with the baby and everything? We'll make it work. You came home for a reason, after all.' Pat's eyes were too bright, darting around the room. 'You'll be sure to tell her I'll stand by you, won't you? Here, let's get you looking presentable.'

Lucy let her mother apply some make-up, her touch light across Lucy's cooled cheek. She wondered if James had seen the news. If he was surprised to see her face on the television. He might not care. Even if he did, what was he going to do? Her phone was somewhere buried under a pile of rubble and he could hardly turn up at the hospital.

'That's more like it,' Pat said, finally satisfied. 'Stay still now, don't smudge it before she gets here.'

The door opened and a woman stepped into the room with a pile of folders in her arms. No white coat, but shiny slacks and an oversized cardigan. Only her plastic ID card marked her as staff.

'I'm Doreen, the hospital social worker,' she said. 'How are you feeling, Lucy?'

'I'm all right, thanks.'

'Hello again, Mrs Phelan. I'm glad to see you again under better circumstances. I met your mother at the site yesterday,' she told Lucy, as if there was some confusion. As if Lucy might have thought they met playing bridge, or at a swingers' club.

Breathe in. One-two-three-four. Exhale.

'You were very kind to all of us,' Pat said. 'It was a relief to have someone on our side when we were being told nothing.'

'Everyone had their own job to do,' Doreen said. 'Now, I'm sure you'd welcome a coffee break after the long night of it, so if you want to step out, I'll have a chat with Lucy.'

'I thought I'd stay, in case—'

'Don't worry, I'll keep a good eye on her,' Doreen said easily.

Pat's smile faded at the shift in solidarity. 'I suppose I could use a coffee.'

'She was dying to have a cigarette anyway,' Lucy said, when the door shut.

Doreen smiled. 'It was quite the wait for her.'

Her smile made Lucy feel bad for bitching out her mother behind her back. 'Don't be telling everyone your business,' hissed the well-reared part of her brain. The part her mother slapped into shape with the heel of her hand.

'How are you doing, Lucy?'

'I'm in one piece, so I'm feeling very lucky.' It was what people kept telling her.

'Often, when someone is the sole survivor—'

'No,' Lucy shook her head. 'The bus driver got out. And Alina, the...' Her mind went blank. She couldn't say Muslim, that was presumptuous. So was Eastern. A lot of her kind at university had Cork accents. Oh, God. She couldn't say *her kind*, whatever she did. Ethnic, maybe? No, that made her sound terrified. She

261

had glanced at the woman's picture in the newspaper, certain for a second that they had shared an undergrad class years earlier, before dismissing it as unlikely. It wasn't racism, she assured herself. It wasn't as if she thought all the brown girls looked alike. She cleared her throat. 'The other woman. It wasn't just me.'

'That's true.' Doreen made a little note on her file and Lucy wondered what it said. 'You told the emergency workers that you spoke to two of the others while you were all trapped. Is that right?'

'You mean did it really happen or did I imagine it?'

'No, no. I didn't mean that.'

'So you want me to tell you what we talked about. Did their families ask, is that it?'

'I don't want you to tell me anything you don't want to. This is about you, Lucy, not anyone else.'

That was what they all said, but it was never true. There was something about her, Lucy knew, that made second place perfectly acceptable.

'We wondered what had happened. When the rescue teams would get there. Like being in a waiting room, that kind of small talk. They fell asleep. That's all.'

'They all got out, Lucy.' Doreen leaned towards her. 'It's important that you know you didn't leave them in there.'

Jesus Christ. She hadn't felt that. Not until now.

'In fact, Paul was taken out first,' Doreen continued. 'Sadly, his injuries were too profound and he died on the way to hospital.'

Was it supposed to help her to know that? To imagine him going through the same painful pulling and dragging that she had, only for it to be worthless? Going over it all wouldn't change anything. Six of them were trapped. Five of them died. She didn't. Not her.

'Would you like to talk to the families? To Orla's family, or to Paul's?'

There it was. The so-called concern was only because they wanted something from her. 'Why would I do that?'

'It might help.'

'Help me or help them?'

'It might help all of you, Lucy. It's important not to bottle all of this up and it would be good for them to know what you talked about. Maybe get a sense of their last few hours.'

'No.' Lucy turned away from Doreen. They would want stories of solidarity. Not the selfishness of the truth. How she would have sacrificed their children in a second. How she was glad it was Paul whose insides couldn't withstand the trauma, Orla whose breath turned to water. Whatever lie she told would be inaudible against the constant beating of her heart. The living trump the dead. Simple as that.

'I'll tell them you're not ready.'

'I need to rest now,' Lucy said. She looked out the window while Doreen shuffled paper and snapped the lid back onto her biro.

They had fallen asleep on the bus, that much was true. When Leo's face disappeared, the water was already high around her knees. Paul didn't answer when she called him and she was afraid to look at Orla, whose side of the bus had been lower than hers all along. 'Orla?' Her own voice had sounded small in the dark and it scared her too much to try again. She didn't know which would be worse: if Orla answered or didn't. Underground in the city, the water might have been sewage. There might have been rats. She remembered Orla's lisp and shuddered.

'Doreen? Tell them... Orla's parents... tell them she asked me to tell her a story and I told her the story of the Princess Bride. She liked it.'

'Thank you, Lucy. I'll tell them that.'

Her mother was in the door the moment Doreen left. She must have been waiting in the corridor. 'What did you tell her?'

'Nothing, Mam. I didn't tell her anything. There was nothing to tell.'

'I went out for a cigarette,' Pat said. 'The place is still crawling with reporters. They're all mad to talk to you.'

'I don't want to talk to anyone.'

'That Nina Cassidy is out there cosying up to the foreign woman, the one with the question mark hanging over her. She'll have it all her own way if you're not careful.'

What way might that be? Lucy wondered. How could her mother imagine their versions would undercut one another? 'I don't want to talk to anyone,' she repeated.

As a teenager, she told her mother there was no need to come to parents' night at school. Over and over she would have to say it before it sank in, from when she woke her mother in the morning to when she pulled a blanket over her on the couch.

'Maybe you're right. Give it a couple of days, let the furore over the dead cool down, then one of the papers or the magazines will be bound to offer you something substantial to tell your story.'

'To sell my story.' The disdain in her voice surprised her, she with her fantasies of couches and jewel-coloured dresses and bright smiles.

'Or one of the television stations, that might be—'

'The families want to talk to me. That's why the social worker was here. To try and get me to do it.'

'That sneaky little… They can want to talk to you all they like, but you're not to do it. It's too stressful on top of everything else. Bad for the baby.'

'I told her I didn't want to talk to them.'

'Good girl. You're right to wait until you can make the announcement about the baby. Who doesn't love a little miracle?'

She hadn't even thought of that. How awful, when those people had lost their children, to stand in front of them and tell them she was lucky. That the baby inside her slid between the jaws of death, too small to be captured.

Like Sylvester and Tweety-Bird, she thought, and realised she was drifting away again.

In her dream, the colours were bright and false, like something out of *The Wizard of Oz*. She wore a blue dress, disturbing against the blood-red of the sofa she sat on. Her hair was long, past her shoulders and still growing as she looked at it, spilling down over her chest and onto her feet, princess-style. Her bump was enormous, resting cartoon-like on her knees. She put her hand to it and the baby's face appeared through the skin. Orla's face. 'How lucky! An immaculate conception!' the gameshow host shrieked with glee, while canned laughter rang in her ears. She caressed her stomach for comfort, but, when she looked down, her hand had rubbed away some of its features, the face disappearing as she moaned in horror.

'Lucy!' Her mother's voice. 'Stop that! You're giving me a headache.'

'I was dreaming about the baby,' Lucy said, trying to sit up.

'I'll go and get Kieran,' Pat said. 'He's been waiting outside all this time.'

'Are you deaf? I told you I'm not ready to see anyone,' Lucy snapped.

'I don't need any of your cheek, Miss.'

You're not too old for another slap, you know, Lucy said inside her head. She would be the last of the slapped generation, she vowed. Any redness on her baby's arm would only be from where she held on too tightly.

'You want to start being a bit grateful to Kieran,' her mother said. 'You need him more than he needs you. You'll have to make an extra effort to help him get past the weight gain, take it from me.'

'He loves me the way I am.'

Pat snorted. 'Just because he says it now doesn't mean it will last. You won't know he's going until the day you wake up and he's packed his bags, believe you me.'

Just because you're hungry doesn't mean you're losing weight. It was another of her mother's staples when Lucy was growing up. An expression that held back Lucy's hand in her flat as James opened box after box of takeaway, spooning out the huge portions that his fat wife would lap up.

'I tidied up,' she would say, when he came back from the loo, running the tip of the tea towel up her thigh, 'I thought it was time for dessert.'

What was his wife doing while she was straddling him on the floor of the kitchen, a can of whipped cream in one hand and a handful of herself in the other? How the hell could Lucy be a good mother if she had never been a good person?

I am not you, she might have told her mother the day before yesterday, last week, last year. Now, for all her smartness, for all her education, for all the pity and shame she felt for her mother, she had done nothing more than follow the same path to the same mistakes.

If she was to have this baby, she would need to work harder to inure them both against her mother's negative drip-feed. Time was something she still had. It could be a project, like getting her winter-soft feet used to the push of air through summer sandals. She would no longer give in to the shared pleasures of shallowness that bound them together in the past. She would do it for her baby.

What if it wasn't enough? Nothing in her life so far suggested that this was something she could do. Who was she to protect anything, knowing that the last person she minded had died in the back of an ambulance?

Kieran was good at protection; it was his one strength. His USP. He would love the idea of a baby binding them forever. Once the baby came, his obsession might shift enough to give her room to breathe. This baby could bring her both protection and freedom, if she played it right.

She would need to leave behind this version of herself. Become sombre, grow her hair out, dress in shapeless clothing, make some pretence at enthusiasm. She would have to look past everything about him that annoyed her. His clinginess. His pained expression. His habit of holding one nostril and blowing out through the other. The way his skinny jeans flapped around his legs. Those would have to become items of fondness. Her hand in his, her life, the life of her baby, folded into it.

She could do this, she could. Starting with one strong decision.

'Can you ask Doreen to come back in?' she told her mother. 'I've changed my mind about seeing Orla's family.'

* * *

'Orla was always a good girl,' the woman, Vera, said.

'Never met a rule she didn't like,' the father, Denis, said. 'But a dreamer too, in her own way.'

'We wanted that for her,' Vera added.

The room was too hot. It sucked Lucy's brain dry. When she was little, her mother cooked chops and showed her how to suck the marrow from the bone. Her head spun and she felt sick.

One strong decision, she reminded herself. A new Lucy. 'She seemed very independent,' she offered.

'She certainly was!' Vera said, pleased. 'She wanted everything just the same as the other girls. The ordinary things, you know. A job, a bit of privacy, nobody to watch how much ice cream she was eating.'

Was she supposed to laugh or cry? 'We never wanted her to be limited by her condition,' Vera said. 'What you have to understand… when she was born, times were so different then. Everyone sympathised with us instead of congratulating us.'

'When I was growing up, there was plenty of families had a Down's child,' Denis said. 'It was just how things were and people got on with it. But that all changed somehow and when Orla was born, everyone acted like it was a death sentence.'

Lucy closed her eyes and remembered seeing the woman walking with her small daughter. The leather jacket, the high heels. It was hard to square that woman, her glamour, with the dry-haired, brittle-skinned woman sitting beside her. Not a death sentence but a life sentence.

'She had so many health issues the first couple of years, we were in hospital a lot. That was tough on her sisters, they were practically reared without us,' Vera said, still with a trace of sadness.

'To their credit they never held it against us,' Denis added.

'She told me about her sisters,' Lucy said.

'Did she?' Vera leaned forward. 'What did she say?'

'I... just... That they were very close.'

'That's it, exactly!' Vera beamed. 'They get on great, the three of them, thick as thieves always. Did she tell you about the Great Wall of China? They told her they would take her for her twenty-first. She was so excited.'

'She's had a thing about that wall since she first learned about it,' Denis said.

Lucy looked away while Vera cried and Denis patted her shoulder. She had told her mother to come back in fifteen minutes, but without her phone there was no way of knowing how much longer that was.

'She didn't say anything about China,' Lucy said. 'She told me about her dance class though.'

'She never takes a bit of notice of her limits,' Vera replied. 'Not one bit.' She twisted the tissue in her hand. 'She taught us to take no notice of them either.'

'It's what you have that counts, not what you lost,' Denis said, more to Vera than to Lucy. 'That was what we always said. Your child is the one that comes to you.'

* * *

'Those poor people,' Pat said, closing the door behind them. 'I didn't realise she was retarded. Still, it might be a blessing to them in the long run; they're not getting any younger.'

'I don't think they see it like that.' Lucy's voice was icy.

'It all happens so gradually, you see. The life they should have had slipped away bit by bit. They don't even realise how blinkered they are, the creatures.'

There were times she couldn't tell if her mother was straight-talking or downright tactless. Hadn't she herself had a similar thought when they were... *in*? Had she internalised her mother's skewed cruelty or inherited her honesty? Was it as simple as Orla's parents said, that you took what you got and were grateful for it? Would the answer be determined in a single moment when her baby arrived? Or would she be the frog in the fucking saucepan, happy and clueless?

Kieran arrived, breezing in the door without knocking. Hoovering up what little air was left.

'You wouldn't believe what happened when I was on my way over.' He kissed Lucy, then Pat, draping his coat over the back of a chair. 'This asshole – excuse my language, Pat – cut into my space, just as I was about to reverse in.' He sat on the bed beside Lucy, pushing backwards until his narrow arse was against the pillows.

'Boots, Kieran,' Pat said, pointing.

'Sorry.'

The thud of one boot hitting the floor, then the other.

Lucy winced. 'You can't just leave them there, this isn't a hotel,' she said, poking him with her elbow.

Pat lined the boots up under the window and shot her a warning look for her bitchy tone. 'Are you sure you wouldn't like me to call the nurse, Lucy? You've been complaining about that headache for a couple of hours now.'

'You have a headache?' Kieran's hand was clammy on her forehead. 'Why won't you let them give you something for it?'

'It wasn't that bad until just now.' If her mother thought this was hers to control, then she could just fuck right off.

'She thought it was better not to, under the circumstances,' Pat said. 'You know, because of the—'

'Mam. Please.'

It felt like a long moment before Pat finished, 'Because of the risk of a head injury. After the crash, you know.'

'I thought they did all the scans?'

Kieran's concerned face was probably the least attractive of his unattractive faces. The way his eyes narrowed and his forehead crinkled, he looked like one of the less appealing *Wind in the Willows* creatures.

'They're just being cautious,' Lucy said.

'The family of that little Down's girl were in earlier, wanting to talk it all through. I think they overstayed their welcome, it wore her out,' Pat said.

'Rest assured that won't be happening again,' Kieran said. 'I'll make sure of it.'

Lucy watched her mother's eyelid twitch at the shift in pronoun.

'Maybe we should let her sleep,' she said.

'I could do with a kip myself,' Kieran agreed. 'It's been a long night.'

Lucy glanced at her mother, willing her to understand, trying to put all the years of shared history, of being a twosome against the world, into a single look.

'I could do with some food,' Pat declared. 'The food in the canteen is inedible. How they expect people to recover on white bread and potato croquettes, I don't

271

know. Let's pop over to the shopping centre for an hour, let Lucy have a rest.'

'I don't think we should leave her.'

'I'll be fine. I'll be sleeping and the nurses are right outside the door if I need anything.'

'You go and get the car, Kieran,' Pat said. 'I'll meet you at the front door.'

Lucy braced herself as the door closed behind him.

'You'd want to watch that tone,' Pat said. 'You won't be so smart when he up and leaves us on our own with the baby. You needn't think I'll be minding it while you're swanning around doing whatever you please.'

'I don't think I can do it. I look at him and I just...'

'Do you want me to make an appointment for you in London, so, is it?'

'No! That's not what I'm saying at all. Jesus. It's not either/or, Mam.'

'In a fantasy world, maybe not. But here in the real world, that's exactly what it is. A lot is riding on this. You have no money, no flat. You barely have a job. What you do have is a man who loves you and who wants to protect you. That's more than most.'

'At what price?'

'Don't be melodramatic, Lucy. Let him hold your hand and whatever else he likes every couple of days. It's hardly slavery.' She sprayed a cloud of perfume from a tiny travel bottle in her handbag, wiggling her body until the vapour settled.

Was it cynicism or realism? Did it matter what she called it if the decision was the same in the end?

'I have to go. He'll be waiting.' She leaned in as if to kiss Lucy on the cheek. Instead, she tapped her daughter's abdomen with one long fingernail.

'Remember, you've a lot to be grateful for. Don't fuck with the fairy tale.'

Lucy's head buzzed and the perfume clogged the air. After ringing the call bell three or four times, a nurse came, bustling in the door as if it was all her own idea. 'How are we doing in here? Everything all right?'

'Would I be able to go for a walk? I need some air.'

It took her five minutes to get out of bed and arrange herself on the crutches. She hopped around the room a few times to find her balance.

She kept her head down as she moved slowly out onto the ward, not wanting strangers to see her. Kieran and her mother would be huddled over a pizza, talking about her as if she were a child. Anger propelled her further than she intended to go. Half-turning to go back the way she had come, the swinging door caught the tip of her crutch and nearly knocked her over.

'Watch it!' she shouted, once she righted herself, but the man was long gone.

'Here, sit down.' An arm appeared out of nowhere and guided her to a chair. 'Those things take a bit of getting used to. I remember my first time on crutches, I was like a baby giraffe on one of those behind-the-scenes zoo videos.'

'Thank you.' She sat and stretched her cast out in front of her, still tingling from the slap of the door.

'You're very pale. Can I go and get someone to help?' the man asked.

Lucy shook her head. 'I just need a minute to catch my breath.'

'Okay. Mind if I sit, just to be sure?' He looked at her expression and laughed. 'Occupational hazard. I used to be a firefighter.' He held out his hand. 'Tim.'

'Lucy.'

'You've had a rough couple of days, Lucy. I worked the site,' he added. 'Or at least my team did. These days I'm more of a behind-the-scenes guy.'

'You were there?'

'I was.'

'Aren't you going to tell me how lucky I was?'

He sighed. 'Luck means different things to different people.'

'Nobody else seems to agree. They all want something. Gratitude, memories.'

Tim's voice was gentle. 'Try to remember that you didn't cause their pain and you can't take it away either. That's the best and the worst of surviving.'

Lucy picked at the edge of the seat where the fabric was worn soft. It was the shade of grey her imaginary grandmother used to wear when Lucy closed her eyes and pretended someone was reading her a bedtime story.

'I don't think I allowed myself to feel really scared until the rescue team came.' It was a relief to admit it, to stop pretending that gratitude took the fear away. 'The guy that came in to get us – Leo, I think? – his voice was so warm and calm. I wasn't expecting everything after that to be so... violent.'

Tim smiled. 'Leo's that calm all the time. Except when the Irish team is playing.'

If she had grown up with a father, would Sundays have been spent on sport rather than romcoms? Perhaps she would have been sporty, happier outdoors, more rooted in the local area. Or she might have been terrified of the dark, of a man's footsteps to her bedside in the darkness. Who the hell knew?

'Aren't you going to ask me about the others?' The

ones who didn't get to keep taking breath after breath, simply because they sat on the other side of the bus.

'Should I?'

'That's all anyone wants to know. What happened down there in the dark. The ghoulish story of Lucy and her dead people.'

'The dead aren't ghoulish,' Tim said.

She was about to tell him that was easy for him to say, when she saw his face. His eyes were somewhere else altogether.

'Since my daughter died, I enjoy remembering the time we had. To think of that time as creepy would be a terrible waste.'

'Orla's father told me they wouldn't change anything, that Orla was their child no matter what. I don't understand how he can be so accepting.'

Tim smiled and got up to leave. 'That's part of the deal with parenting. It seems unimaginable and then suddenly you get it.'

What if she didn't? What if the baby arrived and she felt nothing but regret at everything she had given up and everyone she had invited in? Take what you get and be grateful for it, that was what the advice amounted to. But she wanted more. She might not know what more looked like, but she knew where it started. She would apply for that epidemiology course. This could be it. The One. Her do-over. Look at Orla, with everything stacked against her yet doing exactly what she wanted to do. Kieran would love to mind the baby while she studied. Lucy trapped at a desk in the tiny spare room of his flat would be his idea of the perfect family set-up. He would save the child from Pat. From afternoons of dull chat shows and sharp criticism. Having a baby wouldn't rule her out of the course. In fact, it might help her chances of getting a place. Positive discrimination and all that. Hadn't she seen it work for others for years? The crash wouldn't hurt either. If she got an interview for the course, she could play it up a bit. Make it so that when the panel looked at her they saw a line of coffins.

* * *

She woke to find Kieran hugging her. 'Lucy! I can't believe it. A baby!'

'What...? How...?'

'Don't be cross with your mother for telling me. She explained that they could tell this early from the scans and blood tests and things. Isn't it amazing?'

'Where is Mam?' She kept her voice casual. As if she wasn't going to rip off her face and make her swallow it.

'One of the reporters wanted to ask her a couple of questions, I think.'

This time, Kieran lined his boots up under the windowsill without prompting.

He pulled Lucy into his shoulder. 'It'll be a girl,' he said confidently, resting his hand on the flat of her stomach.

It wouldn't help if he felt her tensing up every time he touched her. She forced her shoulders down from somewhere near her ears.

'Could you go and get a nurse for me?'

'Can't you use the call bell?' He frowned. 'I just took off my boots.'

'It's broken,' she said. 'Please, love.' She winced a little, pretending she couldn't see him looking at her.

'Anything for my baby mama.' At the door, he

turned. 'I opened a bank account for the baby, just now on my phone. I know it's early, but I want to do this right, you know?'

'Wonderful.' She managed a smile and when he blew her a kiss made a show of raising her hand to catch it.

She brought the kidney dish to her mouth just in time, retching the little she had eaten at lunchtime. Well, she thought grimly, that was one lesson she learned well at her mother's knee: do whatever it takes to survive.

* * *

By the time Pat returned, Kieran was back on the bed beside her and Lucy's face ached from smiling.

'Aren't you just the very picture of a happy little family-to-be?' Pat said.

Her eyes were bright. There must have been a bottle of wine with dinner. Two beers was Kieran's limit. Another point in his favour.

'I know, I know.' Pat pantomimed zipping her lips. 'It just slipped out. Are you very cross with me?'

'Of course not,' Lucy said. 'I'm just sorry I didn't get to tell him myself. I would have waited a while, of course. This isn't exactly the place for celebrating.'

'Lucy's right, Pat. We need to be sensitive to other people's suffering,' Kieran said, in a tone of great magnanimity. 'Not everyone got the happy ending.'

His hand weighed down on her belly. Six more months of this shit and the child would be born with a flat head.

He kissed her fingertips and pressed them to his cheek. She could no longer think of it as stealing.

It's what you have that counts, not what you lost, Denis had said. Well, she had a plan and that was a start.

TIM

The rain came in heavy horizontal slashes, as if all along it had been held back by the power of prayer or wanting. Tim told himself that it was the weather trapping him in his car and not the walk across the hospital car park that would send him into a past that could take the legs from under him.

On the radio, news stations were full of the rescue. Confirmation of the dead changed the tone, opened the door to outrage and less measured words. Politicians were eager to be seen to offer sincere condolences from their safe distances. God forbid any of them would sit their arse into their state car and stand eyeball to eyeball with the families. Who would have guessed Donnellan would turn out to be the best of them? The rest listened more to their media advisers and stuck to the script carefully written for them. The sentence or two of sympathy, then the straight shot to blame. Talk of compensation. Empty assurances that the families could never be truly compensated for their loss and yet the implication that money greased the wheel into silence.

He slammed the radio off. Useless fuckers, the lot of them. With their hollow statements and their unbroken lives.

At the start of every callout, there was a moment

when everything was still theoretical. When nobody had any idea how things were going to go. The adrenalin would hum under his skin and make his veins pop. His breaths, slow and deliberate, crackled inside his ears. The world went silent and time stood still. A lot of the lads wore miraculous medals pinned to vests and inside helmets, gifts from religious mothers and superstitious girlfriends. Some of them insisted on a prayer in the truck on the way out, or – sometimes – on the way back, if things had gone south. On good days, prayers of thanks were forgotten, or done privately, spinning through the air with the beer caps at the end of the shift. Back then, if he held perfectly still, Tim could picture Nina and Aisling, only a blink away if he needed them.

He no longer wore the helmet. They would never be replaced.

He grabbed an envelope from the glovebox and banged the door shut before he had time to change his mind.

* * *

Inside the hospital, he headed straight for the makeshift media centre.

'I'm not here to tread on your toes,' he told Loretta. 'I know you're on point from here on.'

'Right. What can I do for you?' she asked, in that tinkling tone that certain women used to conceal aggression.

There was an unspoken rule in hospitals that nothing was ever confronted directly. Wiggle room was always left for doubt. For a last-minute reprieve. God's head around the door.

'Loose ends for the board,' he told her. 'Nothing more. I just want to talk to the families.'

'The families…' She consulted her file. 'They were put in the waiting room of one of the day clinics after it shut.'

* * *

They had taken a side of the room each, as if by agreement. The unity of the crash site had been left behind at the traffic lights. While drama might be shared, grief never could be. Through the glass doors, he saw Denis and Vera, sitting with two young women who could only be Orla's sisters. Vera got to her feet, touching each of her daughters' heads as she passed by. That casual touch, the privilege of parents the world over. He saw it between Deb and the kids, her hand on the back of Brendan's neck while he sat at the table, or on Laura's shoulder as she waited at the front door for her lift to arrive.

Jason's wife was playing cards, with the mechanical motions of someone accustomed to passing the time. He said something to her and she put her hand on his arm.

'I am being patient,' he said, loudly enough for Tim to hear him. 'You're the one who has to be entertained. You're the one sitting there flipping cards. I'm just waiting.'

If she replied, it was too low to hear. She continued dealing her hand of Patience.

'Can't you put away the goddamn cards? You're not a child.'

This time, her voice carried. 'I taught Paul to play Clock Patience when he was a little boy. He played it for hours, all summer long. So I'm not entertaining myself, I'm remembering. I'm happy to remember.' She snapped the cards onto the table with increasing force.

'Elmarie—'

'No.' She shook her head and refused to look at him.

'He used to leave those damn cards everywhere,' he said and covered his eyes with his hand.

There was nothing Tim could say to them. Without answers, he was worse than useless.

* * *

The code for the paediatric ward hadn't changed. The walls were a different shade of cream, the old rainbows replaced with new. The fish swimming in the tank were new or old, it was hard to tell. He had no reason to remember them. He had never got to stand beside the tank with Aisling, pointing out first one, then another, each of them picking a favourite.

They brought Aisling here from the resuscitation room. He and Nina had joined the parents whose lives were reduced to shopping bags of microwaved meals and watching the clock until doctors' rounds. Even now, he heard the same murmured phrases, the bright low talk of being missed by siblings, of 'taking you home soon'.

In their driveway, the paramedics had loaded Aisling into the ambulance and assumed that Nina would be the one to accompany them. He raged all the way behind them, tailgating the ambulance as it screamed through wet streets and red lights. Outside the resuscitation room, Nina did the talking.

'O negative,' she said.

'8.25 kilos at her last check-up,' she said.

'Nothing since 10 p.m.,' she said. 'She finished with night feeds two months ago.'

Her memory of the minutiae of Aisling's life undid him. If asked, what would he have said? When she cries, she likes to have her belly rubbed. The sound of snapping fingers frightens her. Reggae music makes her laugh. She sleeps curled like a comma. Like a diver. Like a baby.

He said nothing while they stretched her out on her back, more tube than baby.

You know what's important now, was one of the things people said. *You're in our prayers*, was another. He wanted to shake them and tell them that sorrows did not have to be infinite in order to appreciate life's joys. He had already known how lucky he was.

It took seventy-one hours for the infection to take her. For the world to end.

Seventy-one hours until the doctors turned off the machines that breathed for her.

Two years on, he still couldn't bear silence.

* * *

'How are things now?' Deb answered on the first ring. 'Are they all out?' Her voice connected him to reality, to the sheer miraculous flesh-and-blood of her.

Deb and the kids. It was like coming back from the dead.

'When Aisling died, I could still hear people out on the corridor. Laughing. Making plans for lunch. Joking about football matches. I wanted to scream and rip the doors from their frames.'

'I can't imagine,' she said gently.

'I don't know where it went, that rage on her behalf.' Breathe into the little box in his chest, breathe deeper, push the walls of the box, make room, breathe out. Deb waited and he loved her for her patience, that most unsexy and desirable thing. 'The more time passes, the more it feels like Aisling's death has become about me surviving it. My life makes her death smaller. Does that make me crazy?'

He found Nina in the bathroom the night after the funeral. *Was she only a dream I had?* she cried. He lifted her T-shirt and traced her stretchmarks in the mirror. Counted her rings, like a tree.

'There must be things to cause you to lose your reason, or you must have none to lose,' Deb said.

'Is that a quote?'

'Would you believe me if I claimed it was my own?'

'I'd quit my job and start printing tea towels,' he said and they both laughed.

'I know you think about her all the time,' she said. 'I'm happy for you to talk about her as much as you like.'

'I don't want to upset Brendan and Laura.' He knew that was only a half-truth. Knew he tensed at the idea they would ask questions that underlined her strangeness to them. The distance that might open up between his life then and his life now.

'Sometimes life is upsetting,' Deb said. 'They know about Aisling, they just don't feel they have the right to ask about her.'

'Laura seems so fragile this past while,' he said. After weeks of wondering if he should say something, if it was his place, the words came surprisingly easily. He waited for her to tell him that it was not his business.

That he saw death everywhere. That just because he lost his daughter did not mean that everyone else was equally careless.

'I know.'

He wanted to ask her why they hadn't talked about it before now, but he already knew the answer.

'I think I've been holding out for the move to secondary school next year, hoping that getting away from some of those girls will help.' She sighed. 'That just boils down to ignoring it and hoping it'll go away, doesn't it?'

'You were trying to give her the chance to work it out for herself.'

'But?'

'No buts. It just might be time to step in.'

'That's a but masquerading as a just,' she said, and they laughed again.

'I'm going to talk to the school,' she said. 'Will you come?'

'If Laura is comfortable with me being there.'

'She'll need us both.'

'She'll have us both.'

* * *

The hospital chapel was as empty as ever. Perhaps the designated 'reflection room' now bore the brunt of the whispered wishes.

He came here on every one of those three days, while Aisling's life hung in the balance and there was nothing to do but wait and hope. In the third row from the front, he knelt and prayed for recovery. He asked for too much, he knew that. He should have been grateful for any version of her, instead of hoping for her old perfection.

Nina didn't understand the transformation of hope into prayer. Nor the reverse effect in the weeks and months after Aisling's death, when prayer became hope for the future.

'Off to buy the snake oil?' she asked one Sunday morning, as he folded his paper and reached for the car keys.

'I don't expect you to believe or to come with me,' he told her. 'But the snide comments need to stop.'

'I'm not the one fooling myself into thinking this was all part of some fucking plan.'

'As opposed to your grand plan to replace her with another baby?'

So went their weekends. Her fury grew, its coldness filling the space between them in the bed. What she never understood was that in order for her to win that battle, he had to be defeated.

'I thought I might find you here.'

Nina slid into the seat beside him, as if his memories had conjured her out of thin air.

'Faith expects a lot on days like today,' he said. 'I don't even know why I'm here.' He waited for the onslaught, the picking-apart of any little comfort.

Instead, she sighed. 'Science and technology didn't have such a shit-hot day either.'

They laughed, brief and guilty.

'How about you, are you okay?'

'You know what I keep wondering?' she said.

There was something in her voice, the kind of false brightness that used to signal that the day had been a bad one. That she saw a baby about the right age in the supermarket. Or met someone on the street who didn't know and asked how Aisling was doing in crèche. Or found some marketing whatnot in the postbox, Aisling's name on the envelope like a slap.

'Tell me.' Her voice was almost chatty. 'What do you call yourself? In your own head, I mean?'

'I don't understand the question.'

'I can get my head around the idea of a broken marriage, but I just can't hit on an expression for Aisling, you know? I read a lot of grief books,' she continued. 'One of them suggested "lost parent". What do you think?'

'I—'

'I'm kind of on the fence about it, to be honest. It's not the expression itself, it's what it implies. If I am a lost parent now, what happens when Aisling stops being the biggest thing in my life? What happens when I lose that too?'

Her breath was coming fast. He caught her hand and held it. Breathed in and out. In and out. It was something people fixated on. As if a collective noun for people like them, people whose memories were riddled with bullet holes, would make them easier to deal with.

'Maybe there isn't an expression because there doesn't need to be one,' he said, at last. 'I'm Aisling's father, whether she's here or not. You might look at… things and think that I'm forgetting her, but I'm not. Nor are you. Just because you hold a child's hand or take them to the movies doesn't mean you're leaving her behind. If life moves on, it moves with her, not without her.'

'What's it like?' she asked. 'Living in a house with children. Being around them.' She kept her eyes trained on the altar, as if there would be a quiz later on the number of thorns in Jesus' crown, the precise angle of his ribcage.

'It's complicated.' He owed her more than that. He took away her chance to have another child, for fuck's sake. 'I walk on eggshells a lot of the time. It's hard to know whether me being more involved would make them feel more secure or less. I'm flapping in the dark most of the time. I haven't grown into it.'

'I miss our girl. You, me, all of it,' Nina said, so softly he almost didn't hear her.

Tim gathered her into his arms, a wordless comfort. When they kissed, it felt like the most natural thing in the world, but when they stopped, that, too, felt natural.

Nina dried her eyes on her sleeve.

'Here,' he said. He handed her the envelope he had taken from the glovebox of his car.

'That's not a tissue,' she said.

'It's not. It's—'

'The letter,' she finished. 'Why?'

'I wrote it for you. You should have it.'

'You didn't—'

'No!' He wouldn't have added to it. Couldn't have, even if he had wanted to. 'That was ours. Ours and Aisling's.'

'Thank you,' she said.

They sat side by side, as easily as if it had never been otherwise.

'I should go,' she said finally.

'Are you okay?'

'No,' she said and they both laughed.

'That's a good place to start.'

'It's something,' she agreed.

He didn't turn to watch her walk away. They had

been here before, like many broken couples before them. Loving each other most at the moment of parting. A tempting hole to fall into, but a hole no less. If they were both in it, who would be there to pull them out? The job of a partner was to make the other better, not worse.

He looked at his watch. He needed to go and get ready for the final press conference. Leo and the Chief would appreciate the show of support. It wouldn't be easy for them to stand at the podium and follow the map for situations like this. 'It is regrettable', but never '*We regret*'. 'Everything that could be done was done', but never '*We did everything we could*'. The careful words that he himself had written earlier in the day. Three versions, one for each of the possible outcomes. None of which addressed either blame or responsibility. That passive voice. Oh, but if he could only give it form, he would belt it into pulp. His stomach growled with upset.

'Smile and smile and be a villain.' His voice was loud in the empty chapel.

At the site, before leaving, he had stood beside Leo while the last of the ambulances sped off into the black.

'Would you say you're happy, Leo?' he asked.

'In the job or in general?' Leo frowned.

'Either. Both. I don't know.'

'Happiness isn't something I can think about today,' he said.

At the time, he had nodded his agreement, unable to imagine it otherwise. Now, he thought of home. The kitchen warm with condensation and argument. Deb steadfast against Brendan's attempts to avoid his homework. Laura handing him a cup of coffee.

Leo had it all wrong. Days like today, happiness was the only thing to think about.

NINA

Nina left Tim in the chapel. Funny how it wasn't any easier to be the one who walked away. She felt unsteady, as if she were on solid ground after years at sea. If she drove like this, the car would judder along the road in a series of bunny hops, inviting swears and horn-blowing. On the corridor, a sign pointed to the reflection room. Inside, Nina lowered herself onto one of the cushions lining the walls.

In her hand, she still held the envelope. If there were any doubts about the importance of that kiss, they were swept away by the embarrassment with which he handed over the envelope and she accepted. The distance between people, it seemed, was not a function of time. It was not subject to the laws of physics. Funny how that happened. In the beginning, they had marvelled at the idea that they were ever strangers. Now, it was hard to believe in the intimacy they shared. As if all that shared welling up at TV talent shows and peeing with the door open and all the mess and muck of childbirth were imagined or invented.

There was a momentary flicker, useless to deny it, when his hand slid into the back of her hair and pulled her closer. She might have been twenty-eight again, touring Rome's tiny churches, as awed by themselves as by the architecture around them, kissing while old men tutted and muttered under their breath. His holidays now were zoos and skate parks, presumably, while hers were a few days of afternoon movies and driving past the office while pretending she was on her way somewhere else.

Was it better to be with the wrong person than to be alone? Nights, she lay in bed, the sheets pleasantly cool against her skin if it had been a good day. Before – for those were her twin time frames, Before and Since, the two halves of her life – two bodies had pressed the length of each other in the bed, legs curling around their overlap. But that pressure of skin to skin had reduced without a word spoken, leaving each of them on their own little cotton island. Blame filled the space between them, bringing an odd sort of comfort. Had he, too, indulged it in the belief that it was temporary?

Yet there is a different truth now. A relief in knowing that the space beside you is boundless. No stray leg to catch you off guard with its warmth, no gaping mouth stealing your oxygen. Occasionally, the expanse of it frightens you, sinks you into the bed, where the mattress might take and smother you entirely. Only the fear that nobody will find you pushes air into your lungs.

A yawn. Smother it. Ignore it. The room is warm. Tiredness is not something you admit to. What right have you to something so trivial, so fixable, when Aisling is dead? Not everything has to be compared, the social workers told you. Some things have to stand alone or we would never get past them.

Your half-life is still half more than Aisling got. What have you done, other than squander it in her name?

You are suddenly so sick of yourself that you want to

open a hatch in the top of your head, climb out and walk away, leaving your traitorous self behind.

* * *

The noise and busyness at the crash site were a shock. Already less memorial than building site.

'The bus has to be taken away to be examined by some sort of specialist high-tech team,' one of the remaining cameramen explained.

The new footage would please Noel. The short attention span of the public was even now finding the hospital car park a bit samey. Besides, that shot of the bus being pulled out might turn out to be the iconic image. Wouldn't want to get caught with your pants down on that one.

The bus protested its exhumation, metal grinding against the gash before it let go of the ground with a howl. Years before, in Amsterdam, she and Tim saw the bed that Rembrandt's wife had slept in. A wooden box, essentially, mounted high against a wall, two wooden doors on the fourth side, designed to be closed for privacy or warmth or to keep out the smoke from the fire. They had laughed and shivered, delighted at the horror of it. Later that day, as they drank frozen daiquiris in bright sunlight, they called it a living coffin.

By the end of next week, the road would return to normal. Only plastic-wrapped dead flowers and mildewed teddy bears would show that anything had happened here. The families would split into two branches: those who avoided the road and those who were drawn to it.

Nina turned towards the fire station, where the final

press conference would be held in the lobby. She rubbed her tired eyes and let the starry black ants on the edge of her vision lead her there.

* * *

It must have been tiredness that kept them all from screaming and banging their heads on the wall as they detailed the rescue step by step. A version of every other statement of the past two days, in redux. The investigation would be expedited, the results made public. Not because there was a danger of the same thing happening again, they were at pains to stress, but in order to be fair to the families. They had lost their loved ones, the logic went, the least they might expect was a report notable for speed rather than accuracy.

Tim stood with Leo and the Chief, nodding in all the right places. He looked calm and assured, the kind of man a person would choose if they were doing schoolyard picks for apocalypse teams. Had all the faking-fine in their personal lives equipped them better for their jobs? Keep that one away from the headhunters, the thought came bitterly, otherwise they would all be looking for the devastated.

You were very calm at the funeral. People commented on your strength when faced with the box, the lip of the grave. The moments that told other people the kind of person you were, whether resilient or self-indulgent.

'People keep telling me how brave I am,' you muttered to Irene in the funeral home.

'There's probably a pool going on what you're taking,' Irene whispered and squeezed your hand. You had to move away from the normality that might tip you,

at last, into tears. They were right in a way, you were taking something. You were taking a whole lot of things: taking one minute at a time, anything else too long to think about getting through. Taking each breath and trying not to hold onto it, that was a dangerous road of thought. Take, take, take. More than your share. Ticking items off a list you never wanted to make.

You were planning her birthday party, imagine, your mind skipping so far ahead you couldn't see what was right in front of you, looking at your lists when you should have been watching her breathing. Wanting to spoil her, to make a princess of her for the day. You had already bought her a dress and little funky trainers to go with it, with butterflies on the sides that would light up when she walked, holding your hands. They won't do much twinkling under the lid. They will remain as pristine as the day you put them on her. You would have done better to be a little more afraid of her. A little more afraid for her.

It snowed that day. That orphan day, with nothing before or behind it. Even the rain was frozen. The world a Tim Burton fairy tale. The church was beautiful, at least that. At the top, the priest simpered his way through the Mass, well-meaning fool that he was. What could he know, what could he offer you or anyone on the death of a child? Only empty words. No child of his own to flesh them out and give them meaning. 'To everything there is a season,' he said, and you couldn't help it, you hummed along. Your laughter bubbled out of you, spiralling like smoke above Aisling's coffin. If it had a colour, you thought wildly, it would be lime green and she would reach her hands out for it. They did their best, your broken families, and you hated them for it, for all of it. Tim was the only one you could bear to be near.

* * *

The press conference ended and people began to leave. As she watched, a woman approached Tim. Blonde and neatly dressed in the middle-aged-mother uniform of jeans tucked into boots, belted wool coat, oversize scarf. Deb. If Aisling were alive, this woman would be in her life.

No. If Aisling were alive, this woman would be in none of their lives.

She watched the two of them walk towards her, her feet frozen to the ground.

I kissed him, she could shout. But what was that one kiss, only the echo of all the years and all the kisses before it.

'Nina, this is Deb. Deb, Nina.'

'You must be worn out,' Deb said.

Was that an expression she used on her children, a way of letting them off the hook for bad behaviour? It would work, Nina could see that. It was one she might have chosen herself. She almost wanted to tell her it had been a bitch of a day, ask her for understanding.

'I was only on the sidelines,' she said, instead.

Deb nodded and waited for a polite moment longer before laying her hand on Tim's arm. 'Do you want to leave the car and come back with me?'

He shook his head. 'I'll follow you. There's something I need to do first.'

'Don't go there alone,' Nina said, when Deb had walked away.

'Sorry?'

'You're going to Aisling's grave. Don't go there alone. Ask her to go with you.'

'How did you know?'

294

She shrugged. Some things you just knew.

'Did you want to…?'

She shook her head and pushed him gently, watching as he caught up with Deb and took her hand.

* * *

The house was quiet when she let herself in. Everything was exactly where she left it that morning. Sometimes it was hard not to wish for just a little more mess.

Her baked potato was too soapy, the sofa too lumpy, the TV unworthy of attention. She was like the princess and the pea. There was nothing for it but to ring Irene.

'Thank God you distracted me,' Irene said. 'I'm fighting my conscience here. Trying to decide between home-made or shop-bought biscuits for this thing with the neighbours. It's an epic battle, I assure you. How are you?'

'I'm so tired of being miserable!' Nina burst out.

'I know,' Irene said. 'It's wearing. Did you try a bath?'

'That won't fix anything. Anyway, they're never worth the trouble.'

'Fair enough.'

'I met Tim's… I refuse to use the word "girlfriend" for any woman who must be well into her forties.'

'Lady friend?' Irene suggested.

'Too Victorian. Love interest?'

'Too… cutesy. Partner?'

'Too… something.' Permanent, Nina thought. It sounded too permanent. Even if it was clear that it was. 'She seemed nice. He needs someone nice.'

'He had someone nice,' Irene said.

'I admire your loyalty, but you were always a desperate liar. I was never nice.'

'True. Do you think she's in the market for a new sister?'

They laughed.

'Is that what made you miserable? Not that it has to be anything specific.'

'I don't know. It was just one of those days.' She couldn't face dissecting it, not after spending what felt like the whole day inside the whirl of her own head. 'How's Dónal Óg?' 'My boy', she used to call him, until the words took on unbearable weight.

'He's grand. Up to new mischief every day.'

Bless Irene for understanding what she needed to hear. For not being one of those thoughtless parents that declared they wanted to freeze their kids at that particular moment in time, whatever cute or sweet stage they were in. The kind of parents too stupid to know their own luck. Faced with them, she kept her smile tight, trapping the mean words behind her teeth.

'He spent twenty minutes this evening telling me about people being persecuted by the pixies,' Irene continued. 'I thought it was some fairy story they read in school. But it turned out he meant the Nazis.' When they finished laughing, she said, 'Come for dinner tomorrow, he'd love to see you.'

'I'm not sure yet what time I'll finish work. It might be another late one.'

The refusal was automatic. She stood in her bathroom, brushing her teeth and counting the number of excuses she kept to hand as a way of avoiding people. The few that didn't look at her as if she were the bogeyman made flesh. Work, of course. Dinner with a different group of friends. Chest infection. Tickets to something. Never the truth. Never a bottle of wine on her own, or home baby movies, or the desire to go to bed early and wake as the sole survivor of her little family.

She turned on the baby monitor and got into bed. If she were Rembrandt's wife, she would close the doors in around her, shutting the world outside. How carefree and cruel her laughter at the raw, hard horror of those times, the constant daily tangle of normality and mortality. How unaware she was that keeping death close reduced some of the fear.

How sometimes it was the only way to get through the day.

* * *

Nina waited a moment before knocking on Noel's door. He would listen to her idea, she knew, then ask if she was okay, if she was up to it.

Was she?

In the three months since the crash, she had covered the funding crisis for a donkey sanctuary, the proposed closure of a long-standing primary school due to lack of numbers, guerilla gardening and the return of crochet as a pastime. She enjoyed standing in the presence of solutions. Life, not death. If there were days when the voice in her head insisted that *one of these things is not like the others*, then she took a minute to listen to it before reminding herself that those feelings belonged to past events. To ask herself what her current feelings were. To pick one and focus on that. It was often sadness, but that was okay too. A lot of therapy was bollocks, granted, but this new woman seemed to understand how Nina worked.

'Aisling. A dream or vision.' It was something he used to say to her in the early days, a way of remembering, of checking in. She told him once that she worried it was a name that was only waiting to float away from her. That she lay awake at night wondering what might have happened if she called her daughter something else. Joan or Margaret or Bernadette. A name with the assumption of sensible middle-age built in.

'Why now?' Noel asked, when she finished talking. 'What's the angle?'

'The inter-agency report on the crash is due to be published shortly, so I thought we could do a follow-up with the families.' Nina paused. 'Here's the thing: I want to do it as a written piece.'

'That's not going to be much good to me and my television station, now is it?' He shook his head. 'I know someone who'll want it. I'll make a call. What am I selling them?'

Nina lifted her chin. '*The Lost Parents.*'

* * *

Nina looked at her list of names. With the report due, Tim would be the logical place to start. She wasn't brave enough for logic. She tapped her pen against the paper and picked up her phone.

It rang several times before Richie picked up.

'I didn't hear the phone,' he apologised. 'I'm trying to stuff a piece of pork and the fucker won't stay rolled. Excuse my language.'

Nina laughed. 'That sounds fancy.'

'Too fancy, do you think? It's just for a couple of friends—'

'Roast pork is always just fancy enough,' Nina assured him.

'Thanks, but I'm sure you didn't ring me for my cooking tips,' Richie said. 'What can I do for you?'

'I'm doing a follow-up. Talking to everyone that was involved in the crash to see where they are, how they are coping. I wanted to ask if you would be interested in being interviewed again. The public would love to hear how our hero bus driver is doing.'

He sighed. 'Hero or villain, it's only all what other people think of it. To let in one, I have to let in the other. I'm trying to look after myself a bit more, walking, eating right, you know. It's not much of a new start if I keep hanging onto all that old stuff.'

* * *

The rest of the morning brought no luck. The teenager, Paul's, parents had been advised by their solicitor not to give any interviews 'until the implications of the report had been absorbed and decisions made regarding next steps'.

Orla's parents refused an interview. Denis was kind and distracted on the phone.

'Vera isn't doing too well,' he said. 'It's hard for her to get used to the empty house.'

The sadness of a child's empty room was something that there were no words for. No cure for.

'We always worried about what would happen to Orla when we died, who would look after her. We didn't want the burden of the future to interfere with her relationship with her sisters.' His voice cracked. 'After all the years, we forgot what it was like to worry that we could lose her.'

The pain in his voice had been sharp and inviting. It took Nina sixty lengths of the swimming pool before she could breathe properly, before she could be sure she had resisted the instinct to dive into it with him.

She swam on, slow and steady, lowering her resting heart rate. Her therapist wanted her to spend time around other people and the gym counted. On good days, she let the water take her, weightless as Aisling in the days she was safely tucked inside her. On difficult days, she remembered an article she read that said the slower your heart rate, the faster your perception of time passing, so that while children and insects felt days stretch out for weeks, adults feel time speed up on them. Beating her arms against the water, she wondered if Aisling, with her racing pulse, had felt time move slowly, if her little lifetime might have felt expansive.

* * *

'I don't think I can do this interview,' Alina said. 'After the accident, I tried hard to make everything like it used to be. To go back to believing the best of my life here.'

Nina closed her eyes. She knew.

'It is my own past but none of it feels real to me.'

'Just because it doesn't feel real now doesn't mean it wasn't real then,' Nina said and wondered which of them she was trying to convince.

'My mother and I are preparing to take a trip. We are returning home.'

Nina wondered if Alina knew how she emphasised that final word.

'I hope your trip brings you peace,' Nina said.

'For in the dew of little things the heart finds its morning and is refreshed,' Alina said, and hung up.

* * *

Nina crossed the hotel lobby to where Lucy sat, flanked by her mother and boyfriend.

'You'll have to keep her in check, Kieran,' Pat was saying. 'Nothing kills sympathy like cynicism.'

'Hello,' Lucy said, standing to greet her.

Nina had a brief pang at the visible baby bump. *I acknowledge my feelings and I put them aside*, she told herself.

'Thank you for agreeing to be interviewed, Lucy. Take all the time you need,' she said, when everyone was settled.

Kieran sat close beside Lucy, his arm around her shoulder and trailing onto her stomach.

'On that morning, when did you first know something was wrong?' Nina asked.

'I didn't,' Lucy said and they were off, working their way down the nuts and bolts of the story: the fall, the first rescue, the further fall, the time passing, the panic.

'It was like waking from a nightmare, only to find it was real,' Lucy said.

'You must have feared for your own life,' Nina leaned forward. *Don't ask if part of her would have welcomed the oblivion.*

'I don't think I allowed myself to feel it until the rescue team came,' Lucy said. 'Up to then, I honestly thought that as long as I could picture my future outside the bus then nothing bad could happen. But that doesn't mean anything. Orla could picture her future too. She wanted to be a dancer.'

'She sounds like an inspiring person,' Nina said gently.

'She made me think about my own dreams, my grown-up dreams, not just the ones I had as a kid.'

'One of those dreams is about to come true,' Kieran cut across her. 'Lucy has always wanted to be a mother and in a few short months she will be. We couldn't be happier about it. We're going to get married after she's born.'

'A daughter, how lovely.' Nina smiled. *Be careful*, she wanted to say. There are none so short-sighted as the happy.

When they finished, Nina gathered her things together, then realised that Lucy was still there, standing alone by the door. 'My mother went out for a cigarette and Kieran went to pull the car around. He doesn't want me to have to walk too far in the rain.'

'How are you feeling?' The question surprised Nina as much as Lucy. It was a long time since she had felt anything other than jealous of a pregnant woman.

'Tired, mostly. I haven't been sleeping too well. I have these weird, vivid nightmares when I try to sleep. Dropping her, forgetting her. Things like that.'

The memory came suddenly. 'I remember telling my daughter when she was very small that as far as I was concerned she was only as cute as her next nappy,' Nina said. 'To be honest, I kind of meant it.'

'Really?' Lucy smiled.

'Babies are very forgiving, you know. They give you time to learn alongside them.'

She patted Lucy's arm and said goodbye, letting

herself get as far as the ladies' toilet before scratching her arm until it bled.

After they had signed the forms that would switch off the machines, she had stood beside the cot, holding on to her baby's hand and letting her go. Every day she made that choice again. Every day she got up and went out into the world was another day she let her daughter go.

* * *

'You know exactly what I'm going to say,' Tim said, amused.

'The timing of the report is a comfort for families and you're confident that anything that warrants further investigation will be looked into with all appropriate speed and resources?' Nina tried.

'See? You don't even need me. Just put on a deep voice.'

She laughed. 'Helpful, thanks. You forgot to add that the report might be enough to give them some kind of closure.' It had been a shock to her, how the black-and-white of Aisling's death certificate had comforted him.

'There was a homeless woman at the site. May, I think her name was. She said something about the crash – no right of reply, she called it. How the people on the bus had no chance of defence, to say *excuse me but I think this was meant for someone else*. That...' He cleared his throat. 'I can see now how that could undo a person.'

Nina closed her eyes and let silence fall between them. If someone had told her five years ago, three years, even, that there would come a day when they had to think of things to say to each other, she wouldn't have believed them. 'You're dreaming,' she would have said. 'Not us. We're too well-met.' It was their expression, their shorthand, their us-against-the-world. How well and truly the world had beaten them.

A month ago, she would have told him about going, at last, to close Aisling's bank account. On her second or third vodka, she would have recounted the grubby little suit behind the desk interrogating her about her reasons for closing the account. The vicious pleasure she took in telling him, the savage contempt she felt for his embarrassment. How his blush of shame made her feel strong. Now, though, she breathed through the impulse, let the silence steady her.

'How are you doing, with everything?' he asked.

Three weeks separated Aisling's anniversary and her birthday. Spring, for Nina, was the season of holding her breath at the sight of hearses and birthday cakes.

'She would have been four,' Tim said. 'Starting school, nearly.'

He understood, he always would, that it was her birthday that was the killer. Her anniversary was just about her death, just one fact to deal with. Anniversaries were public property. Her birthday, though, was another story. Birthdays had a long and terrible reach, the list of things missed growing by the year.

'I'm going to clear out her room,' Nina said. 'It's time. I thought you might like to come and help, see if there is anything you want to take… you know.'

'Of course I'll help,' Tim said. 'It's not something anyone should do on their own.'

He was gracious enough not to remind her that she had said this twice before only to lose her nerve.

'I might really do it this time,' she said. 'I started seeing someone again. A therapist, I mean.'

'I'm glad. Are you finding it…'

'It's helping.' She shrugged even though he couldn't see her. 'She says I have to stop holding onto the pain. I have to want to let it go.'

'Mine told me that people can become addicted to suffering,' Tim said. 'That letting go doesn't mean I love her any less. Nothing can take away from my time with her. Our time with her,' he added.

For the longest time, she confused the memory of love with love itself. It took courage for him to make the first move when it became apparent that their pain only magnified each other's. It would never be unimportant, the time they had together. Their little share of family life.

'It must help to have Deb,' she said, without planning it. Someone to dilute the suffering, not augment it.

'It does. But it's not without its guilt.' He paused. 'We took Brendan and Laura to Aisling's grave. They asked a lot about her. They want to make a cake for her birthday. A "just-because" cake, Laura called it.'

She could hear pride and guilt in his voice. That was his future now, worrying about those children. Someone else's babies feeling all the love and support he held within himself.

She pinched the flesh between her thumb and forefinger, concentrated on its sting. 'A "just-because" cake. I like it. I'm glad she will be remembered.' *I'm glad you're happy.*

'I've brought her with me though, Nina, you know that,' he said, his voice urgent. 'I haven't left her behind.'

'We were lucky, the three of us. Our luck just ran out,' she said.

* * *

Later, she flicked through the news channels, coming to rest on a report about a couple who killed their teething baby by rubbing heroin on its gums. She sat on her sofa and cried tears that were three years old. Older than her child would ever be. It was a big ask, to live peacefully in this unfair world. But it was possible to move on without forgetting. She heard it in Tim's voice, clear as a bell: Aisling was still with him, too deep within to be cast off.

She dried her eyes and dialled her sister's number.

LIKE YOU WERE MY OWN

'Are we there yet?' Dónal Óg demands from the back seat.

'Not yet.'

'Do we have my armbands?' he asks, leaning forward, a study in anxiety.

'Armbands, check,' Nina says. 'Your mam packed everything we need.'

If Irene's reaction on the phone had been low-key, the size of her small son's bag belied her casualness.

'Are you sure?' he asks, again.

'I'm sure.' In the mirror, he still looks dubious. His face so different from Aisling's, despite their shared blood. 'If there's anything missing, then I'm sure we can buy it in the shop at the water park, okay?'

'Okay. Can I get blue goggles? I don't like my red ones any more. Red is for girls.'

'All the colours are for all the people,' she says, as she has heard her sister do.

'I'm bored,' he announces a few minutes later.

'Do you want a snack?'

'No.' He kicks the back of the seat once, twice, then brightens. 'Tell me a story.'

'What kind of story?'

'I don't know. A good one. With monsters in it. And an astronaut. And a car that can go really fast.'

'And a princess?'

'NO!' he roars. 'No girls!'

'No girls,' she agrees. 'Let me think… Once upon a time…'

At the next set of traffic lights, she glances in the rear-view mirror and sees he has dozed off, his hands loose in his lap.

She turns the radio on low so as not to wake him and signals to turn for the coast.

ACKNOWLEDGEMENTS

Thanks to Lauren Parsons and the team at Legend Press for that first heart-stopping email and everything since. To Steven Marking for turning lots of words into one perfect image. Also to Elaine Hansen and the Luke Bitmead Bursary, and the Lucy Cavendish Fiction Prize for seeing something in the earlier version of this novel.

Thanks to Wendy Vaizey, Paul Bailey and the Kingston University distance learning Creative Writing team. Especially to Rachel and Sylvia, for virtual writing and real friendship.

Thanks to the organisers, sponsors and judges of very (very) many writing competitions for the crucial confidence boosts along the way. Among them, the Irish Writers' Centre and all connected with Novel Fair 2019, the Caledonia Novel Award, the Blue Pencil Agency First Novel Award, and the Zoetrope and Fish Publishing Short Story Prizes. Thanks also to Hannah Weatherill and the Northbank Talent Management team for ongoing support.

My good friends know I write – for fun, for figuring-out, for sanity. Thanks for asking how it was going – a brave question and one for which I am always grateful. A special thank you to Julia for the invaluable side-by-side writing mornings and early readings of this novel. *May the hot chocolate and macarons never run out.* Thanks, too, to all the cafes that make writers welcome by not hovering or clearing cups too hastily.

Particular thanks to my family: to my parents-in-law, Eleanor and John, for giving me time and space and celebrating every little success; to my parents, Joe and Teresa, the only people to have read (almost) everything I've ever written – thank you both for the gifts of reading and curiosity (and for destroying the evidence of my primary school rhyming poetry phase).

Special thanks to Dee – sister, friend, future Dolly Bantry. Again: no, none of the characters are you. Sorry.

Much love to Colm, Oisín and Cara, for leaving me alone and trusting that I would emerge eventually and in a better mood. And for everything else, too.

IF YOU ENJOYED WHAT YOU READ,
DON'T KEEP IT A SECRET.

REVIEW THE BOOK ONLINE AND
TELL ANYONE WHO WILL LISTEN.

THANKS FOR YOUR SUPPORT
SPREADING THE WORD ABOUT
LEGEND PRESS.

FOLLOW US ON TWITTER
@LEGEND_PRESS

FOLLOW US ON INSTAGRAM
@LEGENDPRESS